STARLITE

A Novel

by Mae East

Cover Photo by Shutterstock

"Only when we are no longer afraid do we begin to live."
Dorothy Thompson

"Fear is only as deep as the mind allows."
Japanese Proverb

"When people hurt you over and over, think of them like sandpaper. They may scratch and

hurt you a bit, but in the end, you end up polished and they end up useless."
Anonymous

"People will hate you, rate you, shake you, and break you. But how strong you stand is what makes you."
Unknown

Table of Contents

Chapter 1

"**Good afternoon**, Miss Lani. Didn't know if you were going to make it by this evening." The gentleman rested his weight against the cold, grey wall while holding a wet mop between his feet. He shifted his eyes from the shiny, white floor up to Lani Love as she entered the doubled glass doors to the nursing home. "But then again, I should know better by now." He titled his head and gave her a wink.

"Yes, you should, Al." Lani pointed her finger at him and gave it a good shaking, chastising him for such a comment. "But I'll forgive you this time," she teased, knowing he had been leaning up against that wall not because a hard day's work had gotten the better of him but rather to have an excuse to wait for her to walk in those doors. Just like always. Every Friday evening for the past two years, Lani Love has passed through that entrance and in the process, let in a world of freshness every time she came. Not that the smoldering Austin air outside was full of toxins, other than the heavy pollen count that never seemed to ride its way out of the city, but more because the mere presence of her smile was like an ocean breeze that carried away a heaviness of another kind. The kind that weighed down an old soul such as Al after working for years taking care of others who were slowly drifting away. Others who seemed to fade a little more with each passing day yet still dreamed of returning to a place where they were once loved by those called family.

Unlike now where they were stuffed away like an old pair of shoes that the owner couldn't bear to part with. No longer shiny or new. No longer worn or enjoyed. So instead, those old shoes were put away in a storage called a nursing home that no one opened unless they were searching for something. Something other than an old pair of shoes before remembering that those worn-out souls were still around, sitting quietly in the darkness of life.

"As always, you are a picture of pure sunshine, Miss Lani."

Lani smiled, glanced down, and tried to hold on to that soft flutter of approval for the few seconds it lasted. When she looked up, she let it go, knowing it was too dangerous to hold on to such a fleeting emotion. One that had never belonged to her in all her twenty-two years of life. After all, it was just the polite thing to say, she reminded herself. Al was sweet on everybody. He was a gentle old man pushing 70 along with a mop and a broom and Lani knew the danger of letting a nice thought make a nest in her head. The feeling of approval, acceptance, love. None of them were real to her. None of them had ever visited her long as a child, and therefore, she had grown up with a mistrusted approach anytime one of them came knocking now. So she wiped away that foreign feeling of approval just as quickly as Al had, no doubt, accidentally spilled it upon her.

She let it go, and it evaporated into the heat and asked, “Is he awake?”

Al nodded. “Yes, ma’am, but don’t expect much today.”

“I never do.” Lani patted Al’s arm as she passed, then continued down the hall until she came to the familiar room. She gave the door a light rap and a voice called from inside.

“Come in.” The nurse was tucking a light cotton sheet around the legs of an old man. The bed was raised halfway and Lani could see he had just finished eating. The empty tray was pushed off to the corner under the window. The curtains were already drawn, which meant it had not been a good day. Anytime the sun was rebuked meant the man in the bed had been fighting the demons inside his head, and the dark seemed to hide the injuries of his internal war the best.

“Hello, Lani.” The nurse kept her voice low and didn’t look up as Lani walked in. She knew who it was, no one else ever visited this man except on rare occasions, and it was never on a Friday. Fridays were meant for more important things. Things like ordering take out and watching a movie or going out for drinks with friends. Anything except for visiting your grandfather, who had forgotten who you were long ago.

“Not a good day, I take it.” Lani walked over to the side of the bed.

The nurse continued to tuck the blanket in tightly around the man's socked feet. "No." She shook her head. "Not a good day at all." She sounded exhausted and Lani knew the nurse was glad to see her. Now she could hopefully move on to some of the easier patients. Those that simply smiled, and wanted to talk, and asked when the bridge game would begin, and if they could have cherry Jell-O for dessert.

Those were the easy ones, for they were simply old and not exhaustively challenging like her grandfather was.

"Hi, grandpa." Lani turned on the bedside lamp then leaned over him gently. She tapped his nose. "I hear you've been a handful today," she teased and gave his chest a light rub. "You better watch it or one day Sue here, is going to put sleeping pills in your pudding."

Sue muffled a deep laugh.

Lani knew exactly what to say to ease the frustration of caring for an Alzheimer patient. It was similar to giving a great white whale a piggyback ride around the city for a day before the weight got the better of you and needed to be let off. And Lani knew how to take off the weight.

"I'll be back in a bit, dear. Call if he gets worse." Sue gave Lani a warm smile and quickly left, relieved that she could now stand up and breathe again.

"So," Lani pulled out a book from her bag and held it up for her grandfather to see. "Shall we?"

The man looked at her with a blank stare. "Who are you? What are you doing here?"

"It's me, grandpa. Lani. I come here every Friday and read to you, remember? We just finished chapter seven of *For Whom The Bell Tolls.* We read all seven just last week and you loved every bit of it. Do you remember?" Lani's voice was soft as she smiled down at the old man wrapped in white. She took his hand and gave it a light squeeze, but he just looked up at her as if staring at a wall. Lani swallowed, trying not to let her emotions get the better of her. She hated to see him like this. She hated to see him with that empty look in his eyes as if he were already gone and just waiting for his body to catch up with him in death.

She lifted her hand and stroked his forehead. "I'm here, grandpa. I'm right here, and I won't ever leave you." She watched him quietly, still rubbing small circles on his wrinkled forehead as she waited for him to come back to her. "I'm right here and ready when you are. We still have a lot to read. Just let me know when you're ready."

Lani turned and pulled up the brown chair by the sink as close as she could to the edge of the bed. She then took out the book, held it up for him, and watched as his hands slid over the cover. She knew he was trying to remember. This is what he did to feed himself information. Information that sometimes was able to slip inside his thoughts and connect the wires that didn't quite seem to make contact any longer. Sometimes, on the good days, a spark would ignite, and he would be a whole other man. A man full of stories. Stories from books that Lani had spent two years reading to him. Stories that made him laugh, smile, cry, but most of all, remember.

He opened the book and his eyes danced over the page. He said nothing, nor did Lani. After a few more pages of scanning words, he handed the book back and looked up. And there it was. A twinkle in his eyes as if the light had just flicked back on. "I'm ready. What took you so long to get here? I've been waiting years for you."

Lani felt her heart warm as it did every time he reached for her. It was good to be wanted. It was good to be missed. It was good to be welcomed, even if it was short-lived at times. She'd take whatever came with taking care of this man because when he smiled at her, it took her to a place she'd never been before: into the heart of another.

"No, grandpa. It's just been a week." Her eyes shined when she looked down at his folded face. His skin drunk with age and drooped from his bones, although she didn't notice. When she looked at him, all she saw was her grandfather. A man who needed her and she him. "Shall we begin?"

He nodded and his smile overcame the demons. "Open the curtains before you begin. Let the sun back in."

Lani pushed back the dark fabric, then went and sat beside the bed. As she opened the book, she heard the door squeak opened and as always, she could hear Al quietly bring his chair up close, careful to keep it out of sight while he listened from the hall to the story inside.

Chapter 2

By the time Lani got home, the sun had long left the sky, and she fumbled in the dark for her door key that had found its way to the bottom of her bag. It had slipped down between the two books she had been lugging around for the past week now. One she read to her grandfather and the other was what she had picked up at the bookstore on clearance. It was some love story set in Paris that she had found for 99 cents. So far, it had been worth every penny as it kept her busy on the city bus she rode anytime her destination was further than a ten-minute walk or the bus stopped running, which for now, was only the nursing home and to work one way. She always walked home after her late shifts ended. Other than that, everything else was close enough she could walk to.

This is why she had chosen Austin. She had learned about it from a Social Studies project in high school back home in Michigan and the place seemed to be a dream for a girl with little means. She couldn't afford a car and needed a city where walking was the norm and not a hazard as well as the fact that it wasn't the snow-packed city of Lansing where she had been born and raised, at least until she passed her nineteenth birthday. A memory in which she tried to forget along with all the years leading up to that day. She let the chill run its course down her back, then shook it off, or rather let it evaporate, which was another reason she chose this city to live: the heat. She wanted the exact opposite experience of her ice-filled days of her childhood in Michigan. Something that perhaps could melt her pain away other than just keep it frozen as she had always done. Although melt or burn didn't really matter now. For she had locked away those thoughts deep into that arctic place where one stores all painful memories. Down past the reach of either ice or heat and into a place she had prayed never needed to exist in the first place. And although the cold of Michigan burned just as much as the heat of Austin, at least her lips and fingers didn't turn blue when she walked home.

She slipped the key into the door and was soon on the other side, shutting and locking it back up tight. She flipped on a light and let her bag drop to the floor. She kicked off her shoes and looked around the place.

It wasn't a lot to look at by any means. It was only one room with a tiny hole in the wall as a bathroom off to the side by her bed. But she had done a decent job at fixing it up. *Design on a Dime* would be proud if the show were still around that was. One look at this place, and they probably would have offered her job.

She had her bed off in the far corner, resting long ways under the only window. At the foot of the bed sat a desk she had crafted from the wood of discarded crates. She had torn off the planks and painted them apple green then glued them to the top of two bar stools for the legs. She then painted the legs black. She gave it all a light sanding and a coat of glaze, and it had turned out to be one snazzy desk.

Around the bed, she had attached more of the creates side by side and on top of each other to make shelves that served as an opened closet where she kept her clothes as a room divider for her bedroom from the rest of the space.

Her kitchen consisted of an antique black standing stove, a sink, an avocado green refrigerator, and a few cabinets along the back wall.

To add counter space, she used more of the wide wooden planks, longer ones this time, and attached them side by side then mounted them on two more bar stools to form a long island. She had painted it black with orange diamonds across the top. From the ceiling, she hung an old twin sized box springs wrapped with small white Christmas lights. When she turned it on, it lit up the entire place with a warm glow that reminded her of the sun. It was bright and energizing and she loved to bake under it. The island separated her kitchen from the living room where a love seat, a chair, and a small glass coffee table stood.

All of these supplies she got while roaming the streets on her days off from waitressing. She had found the wood and box springs in the alley and she bought the paint and other supplies. All in all, it had taken her a little over a month to put it all together. Time well spent, she always thought. She didn't have a television or computer so it had been a great way to kill time. That was over two years ago, and she hadn't bought anything for her studio since.

That was her place and she loved it. Mostly because it wasn't Michigan but even more because no one else lived there. No one but her. Just the way she liked it.

She walked into the kitchen and turned on the chandelier, smiled to herself, then turned the thick, old knob of the oven to 350 degrees. She walked to her fridge and pulled out eggs, milk, and butter and set them on the island. Next came vanilla, cinnamon, flour, bowls and the mixer.

Lani spent the next two hours cooking cupcakes and decorating them. She dressed them in soft pink icing she had whipped together from frozen cherries, honey, and cream cheese. After she was done, she set each of them out on the island then took a step back to take them into view. They looked like they belonged on the cover of their own magazine, or on their own shelf in a bakery, or in their own store, or maybe even all three.

Lani smiled to herself, wondering what they tasted like, but she knew she'd never know. After a few long minutes of letting herself feel good about her hours of work, she walked over, picked up the best-looking one and held it in the palm of her hand. She touched the sweet peak just enough to feel the creamy icing beneath her finger. She gave one last smile, then walked over to the trash and watched as it fell to the bottom of the bin. She then went back and took another one and let it slip from her hand and fall next to the first one in the trash. One by one, she threw each of them away, and when she was finished, she simply walked away.

"I'll do better next time," she told herself, then slipped into her pajamas and went to bed, dreaming of cherry frosted cupcakes.

Chapter 3

The next morning was Saturday, which meant she would be working a double. Which really just meant working at both her jobs. Something she had done since shortly after her move to Austin. But the good thing about Saturdays was she could sleep in a bit before her day got crazy.

She showered, slipped on her khaki pants and white shirt with the word *TED's* embroidered in green stitching across the front right pocket. She pulled her thick, brown hair back into a loose ponytail and looked at her face in the mirror. She had a scar above her left eye where a tennis racket had flown through the air and knocked her in the head. The handle had been worn down to the point where a few slices of wood splintered off and sliced her forehead when it hit. She would have liked to say the flying racket had come from a poor sported competitor, but she'd be lying. But that is exactly what she had forced herself to believe because that lie hurt far less than the truth.

She touched the scar, forcing the man's face from her mind and focused on her eyes. She liked her eyes. They were dark and she liked to think that they hid her pain well. At least she hoped. And if that didn't work, there was always the fact that she refused to let anyone get too close to her. She figured between the two, she was on pretty good grounds for keeping the world out, and along with it, the pain it came with.

She sighed and tried to swallow the lump of rejection in her throat, which proved to be about as easy as swallowing the splintered racket that had scared her head. She tried not to look at the mark and applied a light dusting of blush and mascara and looked at herself again. “Just another day,” she mumbled into the mirror then grabbed a change of clothes that she needed for her second job. She decided on a white shirt, hoping no one would notice the frayed hems of the sleeves. She paired it with a purple skirt with lace trim and yellow flowers. She folded the clothes carefully and slipped them into her bag. She then made her way to the kitchen and pulled a vanilla yogurt from the fridge and ate it over the sink. She drank a glass of water, picked up her bag, and ran down three flights of stairs to the bus stop.

The bus schedule on Saturday mornings was unpredictable at best. Yes, there was a timed schedule that the drivers were supposed to adhere to and yes, there have been numerous complaints about the very erratic schedule of the bus routine, but it obviously fell on deaf ears because the woman who drove the city bus on Saturday mornings lived by her own set of rules. She showed up pretty much when she felt like it, which was usually twenty minutes off schedule either way. If the bus was set to arrive at 10:00 AM that could mean 9:39 or 10:27 and everything in between and Lani didn't feel like guessing this morning.

She made it down the stairs and to the stop by 9:42, just as the bus turned the corner and rolled to a stop in front of her. The bus let out a fog of exhaust as if it, too, were relieved it made it somewhat on time.

Lani got on and found her usual seat in the back. She pulled out her book and ignored the old man who would always sit and stare at her for the next fifteen minutes. Lani didn't know who he was, nor did she care, but he was the reason she held her book up in front of her face as she read. When her arms grew tired, she would pull her feet into the seat and prop her elbows on her knees to rest her arms. Fifteen minutes later and three chapters further, she slipped the book back into the bag and got off the bus. The old man was then forced to turn his stare to another female passenger.

Once on the street, Lani walked the rest of the way to work, which she liked doing. The morning sun was soothing and it gave her a chance to relax before everything got hectic with a full schedule ahead of her.

TED's was a restaurant opened for brunch and dinner. It was owned by Ted Neely, who had started the place when he was only eighteen. He inherited enough money to buy the failing pizzeria that was there first and converted it to what is now his gleaming pride and joy for the past thirty-eight years. The menu consisted of a smorgasbord of comfort foods. Most of the items Ted learned to cook from his father before he lost him to skin cancer twenty years ago and the rest he learned on his own and hasn't stopped since.

Lani walked in the back door and could see a line of people through the windows already forming out front. It was going to be a busy day, just like every Saturday in the restaurant business in Austin, Texas. If the food was good, that was, and Ted's was definitely good.

"Morning," Lani called out to no one in particular as she set her bag into a locker. Ted was already chopping and dicing, along with the other helpers in the kitchen.

"Yeah," a voice returned her greeting although she couldn't be sure who it belonged to through all the clanking of pans and the high-speed rush of being ready when the doors opened shortly.

"Hey, Grace." Lani smiled to another waitress.

"Hi, sweetie. How was your Friday night?" The woman gave Lani a large grin in anticipation of getting juicy details on Lani's night, even though the woman knew it was more of a faux hope than anything else. It was no secret that Lani was not a girl who partied or went to bars or even ordered take out for that matter. In fact, Grace often wondered if Lani ever did anything except work, eat, and sleep. A huge waste in Grace's opinion. Such a beautiful young girl should not be living a life of an eighty year old woman. Despite Grace's many attempts to take Lani out to enjoy the world, the girl never accepted and just kept herself locked away. Such a sad sight to see in someone who should be taking life by the horns, Grace thought.

"I don't know why you keep asking about my Friday nights. You know I don't go anywhere except to see my grandfather and then to my other job."

"Well, sweetie, I just keep thinking that one day you are going to waltz in here and have something to tell me that will make me feel alive again. Lord knows I'm too old for anything other than a hot bath after ten o'clock. Heck, I'm lucky if I make it through two episodes of *Seinfeld* reruns. I'm out when my body hits the bed. Not too exciting, so I might as well get something good out of you. Lord knows you're young enough to be staying out all night for the both of us."

Grace was a single woman of three girls, all grown, married, and scattered about the place. Two of them moved up North, and the other went West. Grace's husband had taken off five years ago with a woman he was having an affair with at church. Now the only family Grace has close by were those at work, and she had taken a particular interest in Lani over the past years, although Lani was still pretty good at keeping Grace at arm's length.

The subject was dropped as soon as two other girls walked in. The first was Mandy and the second was Calli. Both were college girls and both didn't really like Lani or even Grace for that matter, but they managed to show up and work without much incident.

They did, after all, need those tips in order to pay for all the partying they did every Saturday night, at least that's what Lani had suspected from the way they chattered all the time. The two never shut up about going out, getting drunk, and all the pounding-feel-like-shit headaches the morning after. As far as Lani was concerned, that was a big fat pass in her book. She was pretty good at feeling like shit without help at disguising it as a good time. If that was the life Lani was missing, then she was sure she wasn't missing much.

Maybe Grace should hang out with them, Lani thought, then quickly left before she felt their eyes drilling into her with their righteous higher-than-thou glares mixed with looks of pity that they always bathed on her. Not only could Lani not afford college, but she wasn't from a wealthy life-line either. Not that Mandy or Calli came from homes of billionaires, at least not Mandy, but she wasn't so sure about Calli. There was a certain air about Calli that made Lani wonder what she was doing in a place like this. She had a certain style that didn't fit a working girl very well. Nails highly manicured and always immaculate. No matter how many times Calli chipped or broke one of them, they always looked brand new the next day at work. Her hair looked as if it was spun by a workforce of silk spiders. Her shoes weren't worn and dull like Lani's from years of beating the floor, but just the opposite. She wore a new pair almost every week. *Why?* Lani would wonder. *Such a waste of money*.

All in all, they were both snobs who Lani had the most unfortunate *privilege* of working with - the unfortunate part was from Lani's perspective and the privilege part theirs. They both had parents who could afford to pay their full college expenses, which was just as good as billions to Lani, for she knew she would never go to college.

She had wanted to once upon a time. She had wanted to play tennis for any college that would take her. She dreamt of getting a scholarship somewhere. Anywhere that would carry her away to another land far from her home. But every time she tried, her father would be right there to "set her straight" as he put it.

"You think you're good? You really think you're that good! Are you stupid? Are you winning every match you play? Are you always in first place? Do you stop your opponent from scoring? Here, let me answer for you. NO. Not even close," he would say with the same disgust as if he was spitting out spoiled food. "You have a long way to go before you stop embarrassing me, and *you* think you're good enough for college. Don't make me laugh."

Lani stopped the memory from melting further from the icebox she kept frozen where she shoved her painful past and tied on her apron. She watched as Mandy and Calli laughed together, their voices already excited about the night ahead, and Lani knew today would fly by for them. Unlike hers, which would crawl ever so slowly only for her to leave at the end of her shift and to hit job number two.

That's ok, she thought as she took in a deep breath to prepare for her day. *He needs it more than me.*

****

By 9:30, she was changed and walking into the doors of her second job: a waitress at a bar called *The Turnip*. Why that name she had no idea but then again she really wasn't one for questions. She'd never met the owner, so even if she wanted to ask, which she didn't, she wouldn't know where to begin. The bartender had hired her and she had just taken it from there.

As soon as she walked in, she felt her body stiffen. Why? She didn't really know other than she was about to work another night in a place where people were all dressed up, and she looked as if she'd been wearing her mother's old clothes. *Barbie meets Raggedy Ann*, she thought, then took a deep breath and went straight to the restroom.

As she freshened up her makeup and re-did her hair, which had escaped the restraints of the ponytail, she heard the sound of muffled laughter coming from a stall behind her. Lani turned and looked down. She saw two pairs of feet and knew instantly who they belonged to. She could smell them.

The pungent scent of weed drifted up from behind the metal cube and billowed out from the top in a cloud of smoke as if puffing out from the top of a teepee.

The stall swung open and a black haired girl made her way out. "Well, hello, Lani," Nikki smirked then turned to her friend. "Look who it is, Sarah. It's Lamely Lani."

"Lani." Sarah stood over the toilet, inhaling one long, slow puff before flushing the tidbit down the commode. Sarah turned around, her eyes closed as her head rolled carelessly back before exhaling. She then walked out of the stall and stood right behind Lani.

Both the girls worked at the bar waitressing tables with Lani, and they were actually decent at their job despite being high most of the time, but then again, maybe that's what it took to get through the nights of ass grabbing drunks most of the time.

Lani could see Sarah in the mirror but didn't look at her. Instead, Lani pulled out her lip gloss and rolled it across her lips. *Maybe if I just ignored them, they will leave.*

"I don't know why you even bother, Lamely Lani. Your face isn't the problem." Sarah's words dragged as she flicked up the back of Lani's skirt. "It this thing here. I mean, where do you shop, off the set of *Happy Days*?"

Lani took out her mascara and freshened her long, black lashes, still trying to pretend Sarah wasn't standing right behind her playing with her skirt.

"Hey," Nikki called and reached into her purse. "I have a great idea." She pulled out another joint and handed it to Lani. "Maybe if you smoke this the next time you go shopping, it will have the opposite effect, and you will actually buy something from this decade."

Nikki and Sarah began laughing. In fact, they couldn't stop laughing. Soon the two of them were giggling so hard that Lani couldn't even tell if they were breathing or not. *Seriously*, Lani thought. *It wasn't even that funny, but then again, I'm not the one who's high.* Lani slipped the items back into her bag and used the distraction to make her getaway.

She headed straight to the bar where Jake the bartender handed her a large iced coke.

"How'd you know?" She took the drink and ignored the way he looked at her. Although he wasn't as harsh with his tongue as Nikki and Sarah were about her clothes, Lani figured he probably wanted to be. However, Jake was always decent to her. Not over the top nice, but decent. And Lani would take decent in a world where there was so much worse. Yes, decent would do.

"I'm a bartender. It's my job to know." Jake then turned and took the order of a couple who had just sat down, and Lani took her cue to get to work. She downed a large drink and set the coke under the counter for later. She then strapped on her apron and headed out to make her first round of orders.

The bar was just a dive nestled somewhere in the middle of the street beside a hundred other street clubs, which were all visited by a medley of customers. Some regulars, some tourists, some one-timers looking for a place to meet their soul mate or more likely a soul to mate with even if it was just for the night, which Lani had seen a lot of. People who meet over drinks and then disappear with each other only for one of them to return the next night. The other, never to be seen again in the bar. Lani figured either the missing companion was either murdered or scorned or just too embarrassed to show back up. Who knew? But it was so common that Lani eventually just stopped noticing. But for some lucky few, it was a place of hope to find someone to love, although she'd never seen this for herself, she liked that option the best.

Whichever it was, Lani wasn't one to judge. She didn't have a lot going on herself. She was twenty-two, alone, no college experience, a workaholic, and single. Not only was she single, but she hadn't even had a boyfriend since she'd moved to Austin. Not so much as one simple date, not that back home she was Miss Social. In fact, who was she kidding? She'd never even had a boyfriend. Ever. How could she, with an angry father always breathing down her back over tennis? Making her spend every second either doing homework or hitting balls.

Food and sleep were both considered luxuries in her house, and only if she performed good enough to earn them. After school each day, she had to practice until late at night, long after the rest of kids her age had gone out and enjoyed life some. And forget the weekends. If she wasn't at a match, she was practicing for one, even before school. She was woken every morning at 4 am and made to practice until 7, then driven back home where she had thirty minutes to shower, eat and get to school. And needless to say, thirty minutes was not even close to an adequate time for any girl to prepare herself the halls of high school hell.

She wore no makeup, her hair was usually pulled back into a wet ponytail and her clothes were whatever she could put together in a hurry. Usually jeans and a sweatshirt. They were easy, warm, and comfortable. What more was there? This made her very unnoticeable at school. Which was fine because she wouldn't of had time for boys or friends or even the tiniest bit of fun in her life anyway. At least that's what she made herself believe. And most of the time, she bought her own lies because the truth was that even the plainest of girls wearing jeans and a sweatshirt hoping to fade into the background still wanted friends, even if they never said as much.

She would have taken anyone. However, it just wasn't written in her stars. In fact, whenever she looked up to see the stars in her own life, she was met with a black hole looking back at her. Empty and plain as if God himself hated her. There was no light in her dark night, and she knew better than to hope for a star.

It wasn't until she moved to Austin that she began to wear skirts, although her shopping usually took place in a thrift store in order to save money. Money that needed to go other places. Places more important than a fine clothing store.

She rubbed her hands along her floral skirt, almost feeling the soft petals of the flowers in the palm of her hands. She didn't mind the way she looked. She told herself it didn't matter what others thought of her. "They don't have to look at me if they don't like it," she mumbled. And although there were all kinds of freaks and weirdos in Austin, Texas, some people still just had to say something whenever they saw someone a little different. And she was a little different.

Lani pulled her shoulders back, knocked away the thought of the hurtful comments and put on a great smile. She then pushed her way through the crowd to take orders, her first stop a hard proof that there were indeed no stars in her sky. In fact, there was only more hell falling from the heavens and painfully pelting smack down on top of her.

Chapter 4

Lani didn't flinch as she approached Calli and Mandy. At least not much. Not enough for them to notice, however, neither of them needed a reason to react. It just happened. Out loud, rude, and in your face happened.

"Oh, my god! Look who it is!" Mandy was the first to say.

"Holy hell, that's a hideous skirt." Calli stood up from her bar stool with her mouth hung opened. "That's horrible." Her voice was purposefully loud in order to call unwanted attention upon Lani. "Do you even know what you look like? I mean, do you even have any mirrors in your house? Oh, my god, are you heading to a four-square dance or do stupid girls just lack all fashion sense!" Calli gleamed at Mandy and the two of them burst out laughing. Obviously enjoying their little act of evil.

"I know, right. I mean, you truly look god-awful. It's so bad, I think I'm speechless." Mandy stared at Lani's skirt.

"If you were speechless, no one would be listening to your big trap hacking away. So shut the hell up, why don't you?" a guy's voice from a table next to theirs called out.

The girls looked over to find a table of guys perched close beside them. None of the girls knew who just spoke, so no one knew who to reply to and Calli damn sure wanted to reply. She was not used to anyone disputing anything she said, and she was fuming to go at it with whoever just called her out, even though the remark had been said more toward Mandy than her, Calli still wanted revenge.

"Just because I know you guys, doesn't mean you can talk to me like that. Which one of you said that?" Calli said as if she were expecting one of them to meet her outside, where the two of them would settle this over a few punches. She, of course, would be the only one punching because she knew no guy was going to punch her back, loudmouth or not. She had called out enough tough guys in her time to know that much. Or maybe she had just been lucky, but it was luck she was willing to push.

No one answered. Instead, the four of them started laughing at her.

"I'm serious!" Calli fumed, ready to slap one of them at any second. "Tell me now or...are you too chicken? Not man enough to speak up, only can say something when my back is turned." Her face changed from a summer tan to an angry apple red, causing the table of guys to laugh even harder. It started out as a few chuckles but then somehow erupted into full-blown, outright, hold your gut laughing.

"Stop it. Stop laughing, all of you." Calli raged on.

Lani couldn't help but smile, not just because it was nice to have the attention off her but because there was one guy at the table who kept looking at her. She tried not to notice, but each time she looked over, he was staring right back at her, still laughing, but also staring. But Lani didn't know if he was laughing at Calli and her both or just Calli or even just her, so she turned and left without taking anyone's order.

She went to another table and waited on them, then did the same for two more. As she turned to go back to the bar and drop off the orders, she glanced back, which she instantly regretted. Not only was the guy still looking at her, but so was Calli and by the look of it, she blamed Lani for the outburst. A blame she intended on seeking retribution for, Lani was sure.

"Great," Lani whispered under her breath. "It's going to be a long night." She exhaled, waited for the orders to be filled then headed back to deliver the drinks, which she did without incident. Although she could still feel eyes burning into the back of her, she tried not to think about it. She wasn't sure who they belonged to. Calli's or the stranger's. She didn't want either. Calli was an anorexic, bleached blond, loud-mouthed, super-bitch, and the stranger was...well, a stranger.

He had a nice face, she'd give him that, but all in all, he was still a strange guy sitting at a bar laughing at a bunch of girls, or maybe...just her. Maybe he was laughing at her just like Calli and Mandy had. Like Sarah and Nikki. Just like her years at high school until she learned how to fade into the shadows of the world's social scenes. I mean, whoever really notices the girl with the plain hair and a plain face hoping to be swallowed up into her baggy jeans and oversized tops. And right now, she terribly missed being able to hide herself away in those big, bulky clothes that kept her invisible for so long.

But now, she didn't have the luxury of disappearing into clothes anymore, the weather forbid it. The sun was an unforgiving catalyst of pure heat, which many people accepted with opened arms. Wearing tiny Tees or strapless halters and short shorts or cute miniskirts but not Lani. Not Lani Love, whose father would set out her clothes for her until she was in the eighth grade, and then it turned from picking out her outfits to a full-blown inspection at the front door before she exited the premises. She would have to take off her winter coat so he could see the full view of what she was wearing. This progressed to him checking around her collar and under the shirt by her shoulders to make sure she wasn't wearing anything underneath that she could change into at school.

Next was her bag. Every morning he checked her backpack along with her tennis bag. He was going to make damn sure she never wore something he had not approved. And if he didn't approve it, it went straight into the trash. But that hadn't happened since the eighth grade when Lani had found a pair of shorts in the lost and found and had tried to wear them out one summer day. When he saw them on her, he made her change, then brought out a pair of scissors and forced her to cut them into shreds of black cloth and throw them in the trash.

"What the hell do you think you're doing, Lani? You think I'm stupid enough to let you out of this house looking like that? Trying to get some poor guy in trouble, I won't have it. Damn girls always out trying to trap some hard-working man into being their meal ticket," he had yelled as he left to retrieve the scissors. "I'm not about to let another man end up like I did." He made Lani change then forced her to shred the shorts.

In fact, he had altered her tennis attire as well. She was allowed to wear the skirt but only with black, baggy sweats underneath. Even in the summer. Not that Michigan was a scorching place in the summer, but it did get hot and definitely too hot for leggings for any sport other than perhaps ice skating and even that was pushing it.

She remembered her first summer tournament. It was in an outside court, which was common for the summer games. She had got there early to warm up with her team and try to put some distance between her and her father, but that never seemed to work. He always had a way of darkening the ground with his shadow anytime they went somewhere.

As she hit balls against the practice wall, he stood at the edge, *encouraging* her as she warmed up.

"Harder, Lani. Harder. You expect to win a match with that weak arm? You can't show any mercy. You have to dominate. Dominate. Dominate. All the way. Beginning to end. Now hit the damn ball like you mean it."

After every hit, he would start up again, not caring who was around or who heard. He didn't care if he embarrassed her, humiliated her, or deflated her because in his eyes, if he did any of those things, then she was weak to begin with, and he couldn't stand weak.

"Goddamn it, Lani, what the hell was that?" He said after her backswing had gone a bit off target and missed the wall completely. "Are you that pathetic that you miss the *entire* wall? Jesus christ, my boss is going to be watching this game." He walked over to her. "Do you hear me? My boss is going to be up in those stands watching his own daughter play, and he's going to see you. I'll be damned if you are going to cost me my job because you can't hit a damn wall." His face was red as he towered over her, speaking quietly now through his steel jaw. "You embarrass me in front of my boss and you will be hitting balls until your arm breaks off. Do you hear me?"

Lani looked up into her father's eyes and screamed as loud as she could without making a single sound. When she was done, she calmly replied. "I hear you," and went back hitting balls until it was time for her first match. She walked out to the middle court wearing her blue skirt, white shirt, and black sweat pants. It was 87 degrees that day with bright blue skies, although she only noticed the heat.

In her mind, there was no such thing as a bright blue sky because that would mean it was a beautiful day and she had never had a beautiful day.

As she greeted her opponent, she noticed the girl muffling a laugh and looking to her friend on the court over. The friend looked at Lani, glancing her over from head to toe then shared in the same amusing giggle.

Lani took a deep breath and extended her hand to greet her opponent as they had been taught to do in tennis class. The other girl accepted slowly, not able to submerge her laughter.

"Oh my god, who plays in sweats under their skirt? But then again, I suppose that's good for me. You'll be dead from heat exhaustion, and I'll be declared the winner. So yeah, thanks for being such an idiot." The girl gave a snide look and turned away and Lani knew they were right. She did look ridiculous wearing a pair of sweats under her skirt. She swallowed the chunk of pain, forcing it deep into her box of ice and focused on the match. Trying not to hate her father as she played.

Lani won every game but when the tournament was over, her father made her walk home because every opponent was able to score on her at least once.

"I said no mercy. I guess I'll just have to let you see what that means. Follow behind me as I drive. You know the routine."

As sweat rolled from her face, she picked up her gear silently and began walking. It took her two hours before she reached the front door. It should have taken no more than thirty minutes but her father took a different route. A route that would engrain into his daughter's tiny, little head exactly what no mercy meant.

When she walked into the house, her mother was in the kitchen loading the dishwasher. She looked up at Lani as she entered to get a glass of water but did not speak a word. Not because she didn't want to, but because her husband stood behind Lani with a fire in his eyes and the mother knew all too well to simply turn around and fade into the dirty water.

Lani hated that day, just like all the others, and tried to force it out of her head as she focused back on today. Tonight. Her job and making money. She walked back to the bar and took another drink of her coke. She set it under the counter and took a few seconds to regain her mental composure. She didn't need any more thoughts of her father poisoning her life right now; she had other issues to worry about.

She exhaled then went straight back to work.

Calli and Mandy and the table of guys next to them were soon waited on by Sarah, so Lani was able to avoid that tiny corner of the bar for the next hour. After that Lani saw Calli and Mandy get up and leave. They had already downed at least four drinks provided by some drunken guy and his friend and were soon out the door on the way to a frat party, at least from what Lani had overheard as they yelled their plans for everyone to hear upon exiting.

"One table down, one to go." Lani glanced over to the table of guys still sitting in their same spot. The size of their party had grown by three - all females. All tall scarcely dressed giggling girls who were rubbing knees with whatever guy they were closest too. The guy that had been staring at Lani was now totally engrossed with a bubbly brunette to his right and a redhead to his left. "What a stud," Lani said under her breath as she rolled her eyes in disgust. "Two girls? I should have known you were the type."

She wiped down a vacated table, piled the empty shot glasses on her tray, and finished her shift, never once noticing that the stranger in the corner flanked by two girls was only pretending to be entertained by his recent companions, all so he could secretly keep an eye on her.

Chapter 5

On Wednesday, Lani decided it was time once again to go shopping. It had been at least six months since she had taken the time to see what new deliveries there were. She got up a bit after 7 AM, pushed back her curtains to her only window and let the morning sun break the dimness as she went to shower.

She dressed in a cream skirt and black graphic T-Shirt with a hole in one of the armpits. "Oh, well." She eyed the tear. "It's not like I'm going to be raising my hand for anything." She tugged the bottom of the shirt down further over her waist and pulled the towel from her head. She gave her long hair a quick drying with the blow dryer, dabbed on a bit of makeup and went to the kitchen. She took a yogurt from the fridge and stood over the sink as she spooned the vanilla honey-flavored cream into her mouth.

She then picked up her bag and opened the front door, trying to dismiss the deja vu feeling from her muted morning routine when a voice sounded in the hall.

"Good morning, dear." An elderly woman stood in the opened door frame directly across from Lani's. "Off early today?"

Lani turned while still locking the door. "Hi, Ms. Belsky. I see you're all dressed up as always. I don't know how you constantly manage to look so wonderful at this hour." Lani pulled the key from the lock and faced her neighbor. Ms. Belsky was a petit lady in her late sixties and had lived in the building since her husband died twelve years ago. She wore a flowered pleated skirt just above the knees topped with a silk cream blouse with ruffled short sleeves, black stiletto heels, and lots of jewelry. Her hair was just to her neck, dyed to a perfect shade of red and matched her perfect lipstick. Lani was often amazed at how well Ms. Belsky took care of herself. If there was a magazine that had breathtaking women in their late sixties in it, Ms. Belsky would surely be on the cover.

The door opened further and Ms. Belsky peered down the hall. First to her left then right then at Lani. "You should always be aware of your surroundings, dear. Single women can never be too careful. Even married women for that matter." She shook her finger as if making a point when she spoke. "Anyway, so where are you off too? I'm guessing it's not to work since you usually don't work Wednesday mornings."

"No, not work, just thought I would go browse the store. See if anything new has come in."

"You and that silly thrift store. It's such a shame you waste your beauty behind such items, not that you don't look beautiful, dear, but they just don't seem to fit you. Your personality, I mean. You are young and gorgeous and should be dressed as such, not hiding yourself away, hoping no one will notice you." Ms.

Belsky tilted her head toward Lani and smiled. "And I know you are hiding, dear. I just don't know what from."

"It's not that, Ms. Belsky." Although it was, at least in part. She didn't want to be noticed. To be noticed meant only that disappointment would follow, and she was not ready to be someone else's disappointment. Snide comments on dated clothes were different than mean comments about her. Insults on skirts kept the insults off of her. It was a distraction, a magician's trick. Get them to look somewhere else. And besides that, it did help her save money. "It's cheap and I'm on a tight budget." Lani shrugged. "It's not that bad. Sometimes there are some really cute clothes there. And if I'm lucky, I'll find some today."

"Well, you must come show me as soon as you get back. I'll be dying to see what you get."

"Will do. See you soon." As she turned to leave, Ms. Belsky called out to her.

"Why don't you take the bike, dear? It has the basket for you to put your bags in."

"That's okay. I was just going to take the bus."

"Nonsense. Take the bike. It's free and I insist. No sense in paying for transportation when you don't have to. You know where it's parked, and I won't take no for an answer. Now hurry along so you can get back and start that fashion show."

"Okay. I'll take the bike." Lani knew there was no point in arguing. Ms. Belsky was positively relentless when she wanted something done a particular way:

her way, so Lani nodded and simply waved before disappearing down the stairs.

The bike was locked up in the bike rack around the corner of the building. It was a combination lock and not a very secure one at that, for it was worn past its usage. But it wasn't the lock that kept the bike from being stolen, it was the bike itself. It was painted a light shade of faded pink, at least what paint was left behind from years of old age. But as Lani study the bike closer, she wasn't sure if what she saw was paint or more of a nice crusted coat of rust that had invaded the frame. She reached up and picked off a large paint chip that was scarcely holding on only to have numerous others follow. She refrained from repeating the act in fear that a pile of paint crumbs would soon fill the grass. Then there was the basket. A large metal basket attached to the oversized handlebars, which was large enough to carry a horse. The basket was rusted as well but appeared sturdy enough. Perhaps not for a large animal but certainly for a small bag of clothes.

The bike was seldom if ever used by Ms. Belsky. It had been a gift some fifty years back from her husband so the two of them could ride together in the open air out of the city. It had been his idea. A good way to stay fit as they aged, but as his health failed over the years, so did their plans. Now, if Ms. Belsky needed to get out, she simply phoned one of her friends. She would call and they would show.

Friends Lani thought. *Friends...*

Lani sighed, then bent over and gently tugged apart the lock that didn't work. She then pulled the bike out onto the sidewalk and hopped on. It was early but already heating up, as was normal for an Austin summer. One of the hottest places on earth she imagined. At least it felt as such at times, and judging by the sweat forming around her hairline at 8:00 in the morning, she knew this was sure to be one of those days. All the more reason she liked to get up early to do her running around. To beat the heat before it beat her.

Moments later, she pulled up to the thrift store, "locked" the bike and went in. A familiar scent of old, stale clothes rushed her as she opened the door, but it didn't bother her much. She always washed the clothes before she wore them, which did wonders for the way they not only smelled but felt as well. A nice fabric softener seemed to trick her mind enough to where she felt as if she had bought the clothes new and worn them out herself.

She walked down the first aisle, checking the tags for her size as she went along. She pulled out a black pair of slacks with frayed bottoms from where they had been dragged while walking. Obviously, the previous owner had been too short for the length. She held them up trying to decide if she wanted them or not, but then something inside her instantly repelled the item, and she replaced it quickly. She shook her head to get rid of the bad memory. They were slacks and not sweats but the image was similar. Too similar for comfort and she went for a light blue skirt instead. She held it up to her waist and it hit right at her knees.

"Nice," she said under her breath then checked the price. $1.50. "Perfect." Lani folded it over her arm then found a cream cotton top to pair with it. Something she had learned early on when shopping, if you are going to wear something old, always make sure you have something to match it when you buy it. It's easier than trying to remember the exact color of the item later when you're shopping again because the vintage blue skirt is sitting back home and you're out spending all afternoon trying to find a top that makes it look cute instead of horribly outdated.

The skirt had a slight flare at the bottom and the shirt she found had the same flare on the sleeves. She smiled to herself. It was if she was in a boutique and had just hit pay dirt. She liked the outfit. It was one of the prettier ones she had found since shopping at the store.

She then found a few more items then headed for the checkout.

On her way, however, she spotted a pair of pajama shorts. They were pink with white sheep on them. They looked cute enough that she couldn't resist picking them up and adding them to her pile.

"No more," she mumbled to herself and stood behind a woman in line with four kids. The kids, all girls, were giggling and dancing and making funny faces to each other as they waited for their mother to check out. Moments later, each girl was handed a small bag of old, worn clothes, but by their smiles, none of them would have ever guessed as much.

"$14.50," the checker said to Lani then stuffed the clothes into a small plastic bag and seconds later, Lani was walking out of the store with the same happy smile as the girls before her, truly grateful for the magic of a thrift store.

She hoped on the old, rusted bike, put her bag in the oversized metal basket and headed to the nursing home with an undeniable feeling that it was going to be a great day.

Chapter 6

She parked the bike, threw on the old lock, grabbed her bag, and went inside. The halls were as quiet as the tile on the floor that reflected the sunlight through the windows. Wednesday morning is when the residents gathered in the recreational room for social time, so Lani went there first.

She poked her head inside, looking for her grandfather. All the tables around the room were occupied with chess matches, card games, dominoes, and gossip. She let her eyes scan slowly but did not catch sight of her grandfather anywhere. She backed up and headed toward his room.

"Maybe he's still sleeping," she mumbled to herself.

"Good morning, Lani," a voice behind the counter sounded as she passed.

Lani turned to find Sue hanging up the phone and looking straight at her. "He's still sleeping this morning. We had to give him some pain pills earlier. You know, the strong ones that knock you out. He should be up in about an hour or two."

Lani walked closer, her voice soft. "Was his pain bad today?"

Sue nodded. "Yes, I'm afraid so." She looked at Lani, her eyes laden with sorrow for the child. They both knew what was coming. What was on a collision course for the old man. The pain was a sign that the darkness heading down that path had picked up speed. Sometimes her grandfather would have wonderful days. Days full of laughing and energy where Lani thought there was no reason for him to be locked up in such a place. That she could just pack his bags and bring him home with her where he could rest and they could go for walks, and visit the library, and go to the movies. But then days like today brought back the reality of what was truly coming. The cold, painful, dark entity of death that had marked her grandfather and today was making sure no one forgot it.

Lani sighed. "Okay. Well, I came to pay this month's payment and just thought we could spend some time together, but I guess that will have to wait." Lani tried to hide the disappointment from her voice but Sue knew. She had watched Lani and George together for the past two years, and she knew this girl loved that man dearly.

Sue motioned her back into the office. "Let's get that payment taken care of."

Lani sat in a chair opposite a cluttered desk and lifted her wallet. She opened it and started counting out stacks of bills. She then handed Sue the large lump of money.

"$2100. Paid in full for this month." It was a cheap nursing home, nothing like the luxury ones she had seen in brochures. Luxury ones that cost over a hundred thousand a year, nowhere near what she could afford. At $2100 a month, it took her two jobs and a tight budget to afford this one but was happy to do it.

The rooms were clean and air-conditioned, the staff was nice, food was good, and the meds cheap. But more importantly, her grandfather never complained about it. Something Lani always worried about. Not that she had known him to yell or throw things around or become difficult. Quite the contrary. He was extremely kind and gentle and appreciative, which made Lani love him even more. He was a good man. Someone Lani felt deeply connected to and wanted to keep him in her life as long as possible, and if need be, she would work three jobs to make that happened.

"Will we be seeing you later then?" Sue wrote out a receipt and handed it to Lani.

"Yes, I'll try to be back in a bit to see how he's doing."

"All right. We'll see you then."

Lani left, got on the bike and took off down the street. She pedaled hard, not only to increase the breeze on her face, but because her mind was on her grandfather. She didn't know how much longer she had with him and the thought of losing him made her feel like she was drowning in hot air. Hot, humid air flooding her lungs and suffocating the life out of her as she sped down the street, imagining life without him. Her legs pumped quicker and the bike flew along the curb fast enough that she passed several slow-moving cars along the way.

When she came to the intersection, she didn't see the red light shining toward her and instead kept pedaling straight through. As she made it halfway into the street, she collided with a motorcycle sending her and the bike crashing to the pavement.

There was instant burning mixed with pain throbbing through her knees and legs from where she landed on the ground. She sat up and tried to focus on what just happened. She was dazed, disorientated, and shaken. For a moment, she wasn't sure where she was or what was going on. The next thing she remembered where a pair of hands pulling her to her feet before picking her up and carrying her to the sidewalk. She tried to grasp her surroundings, but her head was still spinning.

The stranger set her down on a bench, then went back and pulled his motorcycle from the street where he had left it after the collision and brought it beside the curb to clear traffic.

Someone else carried Lani's bike over, and the next thing she heard were voices all around her.

"Are you okay, Miss? Do you need an ambulance?" A woman sounded over her shoulder.

Lani looked up and shook her head. She was still in shock, but she didn't remember hitting her head, and the last thing she wanted right now was any more attention or medical bills.

"I think I'm okay."

"I must say, you were very lucky," the woman said. "Your knees took the brunt of it."

Lani shook her head, not knowing what to say at the moment. She was still tiring to piece together what had happened. The crowd was looking her over for their own satisfaction that she was okay. *Funny thing...strangers,* Lani thought through the fuzz in her mind. *They can be so cold and uncaring when you smile at them yet go out of their way to check on someone with banged up knees. Strange.*

She looked up at them, still feeling uncomfortable with everyone watching at her. "I think I'll be fine. Really. I'm okay."

"All right then," someone else answered. "She's good." And slowly the crowd dissipated. All except for one.

"Ever hear of a helmet?" A guy knelt in front of her and took her leg gently into his hands.

Lani glanced over and instantly knew it was the driver of the motorcycle. "Ever hear of stopping?" Lani snapped back, feeling a surge of energy flood back through her only to bring her full attention to a throbbing pain shooting through her leg. She looked down at her knee in the stranger's hands. She didn't think twice about him touching her. Her mind was too focused on the feeling that her knee cap was just smashed by a sledgehammer. There was blood gushing out and pooling onto the sidewalk. "Well, that's doesn't look good." She tried to keep herself from overreacting to a small puddle of blood.

"Indeed not." He pushed around on the top of her knee and Lani all but screamed in pain.

"What are you doing? Are you sadistic or just mean?"

The guy chuckled to himself. "Just making sure it's not broken."

"It probably is now." Lani couldn't help herself. She was in pain and not too rational at the moment.

The guy slipped off his shirt and wrapped it tightly around her knee, then tied it in a knot to stop the bleeding. They both simultaneously looked at her other leg. There were several scrapes and a bit of light bleeding, but nothing requiring immediate attention.

He kept his hands around her knee. "I think this is the worst of it. You're going to need to get this cleaned up then ice it, keep it elevated, and take something for the pain. But I think it will be all right." He then looked up at her. "I had the green light, you know."

Lani's eyes shot to his face and then it hit her. She knew this guy. Well, not knew-knew him but she had seen him before.

"You did not. I had the right of way and you crashed right into me," Lani said defensively.

He looked at her more intensely, trying to push down the instant attraction he felt to her. She was even more beautiful up close than when he had seen her in the bar. "Really?" He tried to muffle his amusement. She was so adamantly wrong about being right. "You obviously have no clue, do you? It's just a good thing that I was barely moving or it might have been your pretty, little head wrapped up in my shirt right now."

Her eyes fell to his chest. His lean, sculpted and very well defined bare chest.

"Holy shit."

He smiled at her, liking the way she looked at him. It took her a second before she realized what she had said. Her pain instantly subsided due to her humiliation and embarrassment of being caught staring at this stranger's half-naked body right in front of her.

"Uh-uh." He smiled, causing her face to burn even more.

"I mean, holy shit my knee hurts like hell." Not her usual vocabulary but since her first unconscious comment had slipped out, she knew she had to cover it quickly or this guy just might get the wrong idea. However, judging by his eyes, it was too late. Not that Lani didn't find him attractive, because he was every bit as sexy as she had seen any man before - times a hundred. But she wasn't used to having male attention, other than her father's, which was far different from what was going on now.

"Right, your knee, is it?" The guy stood and reached for her hand to help her up. Reluctantly she accepted, not sure how well she was going to be able to stand on her own yet. "I'm Carr, by the way."

"Lani," she responded as she eased her weight onto her injured leg. "I've seen you before."

"Correct. In the bar. I was at the table beside those lovely girls with the obnoxious mouths."

Lani smiled to herself, grateful that she wasn't the only one who thought as much. It was almost as if she had just gained an instant ally, but she knew better than to let that thought run away with her. She had grown accustomed to her reclusive state through the years, for it had become her favorite hiding spot. A spot she was in no hurry to leave.

"Mmm." Lani tried to hide her pain, but she instantly retracted her weight, giving away exactly the opposite of her next words. "Well, looks like I'm good to go. Thanks for your help and maybe next time you can watch where you're going. If you swing by the bar sometime, I'll get your shirt back to you."

"It's yours." He ignored the fact that she still felt it was his fault, still finding her amusing that she was clueless on the matter, and instead simply smiled as she turned away and wobbled to the bike.

The front wheel was bent to hell and back and was impossible to ride, but she picked it up anyway and headed toward home, using the bike as a cane to ease her limping, although it wobbled almost as much as she did.

Carr waited until she was a few steps in front of him and out of earshot. "Instead of watching where I'm going, how about I just watch where you're going," he said under his breath and took off right behind her.

There was no way he was about to let her walk alone down the street, injured or not. Not to mention letting her brush him off that easily. There was something different about this girl and her bad knee gave him the perfect opportunity to find out what.

Chapter 7

Lani limped, holding on to the bike for half a block before she had to stop and give her knee a rest. She hoped she had walked far enough for Carr to have disappeared in the other direction, or where ever he was heading to on his motorcycle, which almost flattened her in the middle of the street.

"Oh, no," Lani thought out loud. "I don't remember hearing his bike start back up." As she stood there, she debated with herself over turning around or not to see if he had driven off. "Maybe I just wasn't paying attention. I mean, come on, why would I care what he was doing anyway?" She continued to chat to herself until she conjured up enough courage to glance behind her. She put both hands on the handlebars to steady her weight and turned around, having no idea what she would do if he was still at the corner watching her. "He's not there, he's not there, he's not there," she chanted softly, hoping her words to be true as she turned back cautiously.

"Boo!" Carr said once she turned around, standing close enough that he could reach out and grab her if he wanted to, and he certainly wanted to. However, he had his hands tucked into his front pockets and cocked his head to the side and simply smiled.

"Son of a bitch!" Lani spat out, once again shocked by her own language. For some reason, talking with this guy was spurring out all sorts of surprises. She quickly turned back around and started walking, or at least limping full speed ahead.

He caught up and joined in beside her. "You know there's a better way, don't you?"

"Son of a bitch," she repeated, too embarrassed to look at him. "How long were you standing there?"

"Long enough to know you talk to yourself in the middle of public. You're not a little cuckoo, are you? Spend any time in a mental facility lately? A big white van isn't going to swerve over at any second with a group of men ambushing you to the ground as they jab a long needle into your pretty little neck, wrap you up in one of those Houdini jackets, and carry you away are they?"

Lani couldn't help but look at him this time. "You have quite the imagination, don't you?" she said, exasperated. "Unbelievable."

"Thanks. I do my part."

"And what part is that? Annoying the crap out of people?"

"Well, if you want to be one of those kinds of people..." He let his voice trail off as he baited her further, enjoying the way she got flustered as he purposely antagonized her.

"One of what kind of people? What are you talking about?"

"You know the negative kind. Always looking on the dark side of things."

Lani shook her head with a complete loss of words for a response. She couldn't figure out exactly what he was still doing hanging around. "I guess you really feel guilty about running me over, uh? But do you think following me around is going to make everything better?"

A deep laugh sounded in his throat, making Lani only want to ignore him more. The last thing she wanted was someone else in the world standing around laughing at her.

She didn't know when she started walking again, but it couldn't have been long because the pain in her knee began screaming at her. A throbbing deep enough that if she looked down, she was sure to see her entire leg ballooning in and out with each pulse of pain. She took a deep breath and tried to push away the ache and stared hard ahead, still wishing this guy would turn around and walk away.

"Back to my original question." He smiled at her although she didn't look at him. "You do know that there is an easier way, right?"

"Easier way for what?" Her voice was a bit harsher than intended, but she was okay with that. *Maybe he'll get the hint.*

"Easier way to get you where you're heading."

Lani stopped and looked at him. "Well, I obviously can't ride the thing. I can barely push it."

"No, silly girl. I can take you."

"No, silly boy, you can't."

"Well, technically, I can. I mean, I have the technology."

His comment totally caught her off guard. Lani couldn't help but laugh and she hated herself for that.

"If you mean that motorcycle thing of yours, then forget it. There's no way I'm getting on that thing. And besides, there's nowhere for my bike. I mean, it's not even mine, but I can't just leave it behind. I feel bad enough as it is." She looked at the front tire, wondering how in the world she was going to explain this to Ms. Belsky, let alone fix it for her. Lani knew how much she loved this bike and she really didn't want to go home and tell that sweet lady that she had crashed it.

"Silly girl-"

"My name is Lani, remember? Lani." she retorted.

"Silly girl," Carr continued without hesitation. "I know of a shop not far from here. We can stash the bike there. I can take you to my place, fix up that knee of yours and figure out a plan from there."

"Oh, really?" Lani's voice dripped with sarcasm. "You think I'm going back to your place? Then you are not only a *silly* boy but a crazy boy that that white van is looking for as we speak. You're out of your mind if you think I'm going to some strange guy's place so he can tend to my aches and pains." She turned around and began pushing the bike again. "Absolutely unbelievable. Completely crazy, you are."

"Well, if I'm already crazy and unbelievable, then this won't come as a shock to you."

She looked at him sideways, leery over what he was about to do. But before she could figure it out, he slid over in front of her and swooped the bike out of her hands. He dashed around her, carrying the bike as if it were nothing more than a pillow, and started jogging back the other way, looking over his shoulder to see her face.

"Come on, silly girl. Chase me. Oh," he gave a sad face. "That's right, you can't, you have a great big owie. I guess you'll just have to hobble behind me then. But don't worry, your pretty little head, I'll go slow so you can keep up." His tone sounded as if he was talking to a little kid, and Lani instantly felt heat flood her cheeks because of it.

"Bring that back right now! I told you that's not even my bike and I have to get it back." She stood there at first but then realized he wasn't going to stop. She began to limp down the block after him yelling as she went. "I'm serious. Bring it back. Stop right there. Do you even hear me? Wait till I catch you. You're going to be sorry you ever ran me over. You're going to wish you left me in the middle of that street."

The more she yelled, the more he smiled, and the more he smiled, the harder she chased him, and the harder she chased him, the more he liked her.

After what felt like an hour to Lani but was really only shy of ten minutes, Carr stopped in front of a small dive. He glanced at her to make sure she saw where he was going before he opened the door and went in.

By the time Lani made it inside, he had disappeared. She scanned the place over, noticing a few people sitting around before heading to the long bar against the far wall. As she drew closer, Carr appeared from the back. Without asking, he made her a coke with ice and set it down for her. She slowly sat on the barstool, careful to lift her knee as she situated herself, finally letting her leg rest on the upper rung of her stool, still full of pain.

Carr smiled and made himself a tall water as a voice sounded from the side.

"Stripping so soon, Carr? The sun's not even down and you're already shirtless."

"Hey, buddy." Carr and the guy exchanged handshakes. "Just making a quick stop." He nodded toward Lani then walked around the bar to where she was sitting.

"Greg, this is Lani, Lani, Greg." Greg raised his eyebrows and looked at her. "Got him out of his shirt kind of fast, don't you think?" He smiled but Lani only shook her head.

"Nice." She nodded. "It's barely lunchtime, and I'm sitting in a bar with two smart asses."

"Ahh, I see you fished in a spicy one," Greg said to Carr, although he winked at Lani. "You know, you do look kind of familiar." He narrowed his eyes toward her as if trying to place where he'd seen her, but Lani didn't bother to help. She was already watching Carr like a hawk as he reached for her injured leg.

Carr carefully propped it up on the stool close by and gently unwrapped the shirt. "I need the first aid kit and some ibuprofen. And grab me one of those muffins, will you?"

"Will do." Greg left and returned with a plate, a black case, and a bottle of pills. He slid them over on the bar toward Carr. "Don't worry," he said to Lani. "He's a doctor."

"Funny," Lani retorted and Greg smiled as he was motioned away to take care of something upfront.

"Here," Carr handed her the muffin and three pills. "Eat a couple of bites, then take these. You don't want to take pain medicine on an empty stomach."

Lani didn't fuss. Her leg hurt like hell, so she did exactly as ordered then watched as Carr gently cleaned her large gash. It burned as he did, but she was not about to make a sound. The last thing she wanted was anyone's pity, let alone a shirtless guy tending to her 'owie'. But by the meticulous way he was disinfecting and now wrapping her knee in bandages and tape, she wondered if Greg hadn't been kidding about Carr. "You're not really a doctor, are you?"

"No," he said dryly. "Definitely not a doctor."

His tone made Lani wonder if something had happened. It was almost full of disgust as if being a doctor was the worst thing someone could accuse him of.

"Okay." Lani didn't take it further. She didn't want to get involved and it was none of her business anyway. "Where'd you put my bike then?"

"I thought it wasn't your bike." He looked at her and gave a light grin.

"You know what I mean."

"It's in the back. It's safe for now. No one will touch it there."

"Well, I need to get it so I can take it back home."

"Nope. I'll take you home, but the bike stays."

"I believe that's called robbery."

"Nope. Robbery is with a weapon. I believe burglary is the word you're looking for."

"Burglary is when you enter a building with the intent to steal. Did you enter a building when you took my bike?" Lani said with wide eyes while giving her head a little bob as she spoke. Carr smiled but didn't answer. "I believe that's a *nope*," Lani continued. "In fact, I believe the closest word might be 'mugging'. You mugged me for my bike.

"Nope. I'm not an attorney, but I do believe that mugging involves violence. Was there any violence?" He matched her sassy tone.

"Uh, yes. As a matter of fact, I do recall terrible, terrible violence. Every time you opened your mouth, I've been under attack."

"I see you've gone back to the crazy side."

"Shut up and help me down. And take me to my bike."

"Yes," he answered and reached for her hand happily. "I will definitely take you to my bike."

"Oh no!" Lani's voice rose, not hearing his comment. "Where's my bag?"

"The bag you left in the middle of the street when you tried to kill me earlier?"

"No, the bag I left in the middle of the street when *you* tried to run me over earlier."

"Yeah, I don't know anything about that bag, but the bag I was referring to is tucked away safely *back on my bike*. You know, at the scene of the assault."

"You're relentless." Lani shook her head, knowing she was not going to win. If she wanted her bag, she would have to do things his way. "Fine. Let's go back to your bike, so I can get my stuff." She jerked her hand away, not wanting him to have the satisfaction of getting to help her any more than he already had.

He pulled a shirt down from the ones hanging above the bar to advertise the place and slipped it on. As she turned away from him, all he could think of was how to get in contact with her again, but then again, he already knew. He had the bike.

Chapter 8

They both walked slowly back to where Carr had parked his motorcycle, agreeing to leave the bike with Carr for now. The pain had let up some, which made walking a little easier allowing Lani to focus on their conversation, which was mostly about the heat or places that served up great hamburgers, in which Lani was adamant about *TED*'s.

"If you want a juicy burger with lots of flavor, it's the best in the city, at least the best I've had. Not to mention the oversized plate of hand-cut fries you get. Truly a mouth-pleaser."

"A mouth-pleaser?" Carr chuckled. "What the hell is that?"

"I think it's quite obviously what that is. Or then again, maybe not. At least not to you."

"Okay." Carr nodded and looked over to her. "I see. You want to play, do you? Maybe I'll just hold your goods until you're a little nicer."

"What?" Lani's voice rose in exasperation. "I think you've tortured me enough for one day, and I also think I've been more than nice to someone who *should* be in jail for a serious traffic violation against a pedestrian."

"Well, you weren't' really a pedestrian if you were on a bike, now were you?"

"Oh, just shut up. We're not going there again."

Carr smiled and let his eyes linger on her for a few seconds before looking away, his gaze settling on his bike in the distance. As they approached, he glanced down at her legs.

"Looks like we might have a small problem."

"What?" Lani said without looking up.

"Getting you on the bike in your skirt."

"I don't see that as a problem at all."

"Oh, really? You're a pro at riding motorcycles in skirts, are you?"

"I'm not getting on your motorcycle, so I don't see my skirt as a problem."

"How far away do you live?"

"Not far," Lani lied. "Just a block or so."

"Liar."

"No."

"Yes."

"No," she repeated. "And how would you know anyway."

"If you just lived a block away, you wouldn't have been riding a bike, now would you?"

"I'm beginning to hate you."

"Hate me or the fact that I hardly know you and can already read you so well."

"Shut up again."

"You're getting meaner and meaner the longer we spend time together." He teased then looked at the bike. "Now, I think you'll be okay if you sit with both of your legs over to one side. I'll go nice and easy, so you don't fall off and end up in the middle of the street again, kissing the pavement."

Lani knew her knee was in no shape for the walk home, it still hurt even with the pain medicine and the sooner she could get off it, the better.

"Oh, all right. Let's just do this. Tell me what to do."

Carr tried to hide the pleased look on his face, half expecting her to retrieve her bag and insist on walking back home, although he would have still followed her just the same. Making sure she made it safely home was something he had taken a keen interest in.

"I'll get on first, then you will use this lever here by my foot to push yourself up and sit behind me." He patted the seat where she would sit. "When you're situated, let both your legs rest on this side, but be careful to make sure they stay right here." He pointed to a spot on the bike that didn't get hot. The last thing he wanted was for her to burn herself and be in even more pain. "Got it?" He made intense eye contact and waited for her to answer.

Lani tried to ignore the butterflies in her stomach as his dark eyes bore into hers, telling herself she was just nervous about riding a motorcycle, but she knew better. She liked Carr, a little more than expected, and that was causing her to become over-anxious about what she was fixing to do.

"I got it." She nodded and looked at the bike to get her eyes onto something other than his face.

"And, Lani?" he said softly. "When you're on, you'll need to hold on to me when we take off. I really don't want you falling off."

"Yep," she said a little too quickly, but that was all she could say without melting right there. She knew if he continued to talk to her in that sexy tone, she would be a pool of mush in no time.

Carr smiled to himself, knowing the effect he just had on her and climbed on. He thrust his foot down, and within seconds, a thunderous roar sounded from the bike.

"Climb on." Carr nodded to her and Lani did exactly as she had been told. And right before he took off, she leaned in and wrapped her arms around him, careful to keep at least some distance between them. She didn't think she could handle too much of him so soon.

Seconds later, Carr merged into traffic driving slowly just as promised and listened to Lani give directions to her home over his shoulder, and before either of them were ready, the ride was over.

Carr pulled the bike up to the curb of her apartment and killed the engine. He let her slip off then did the same behind her. Without a word, he flipped open the small side compartment and retrieved her bag.

"As promised." He handed it to her.

"Thanks." She took it and let it dangle by her side. "So when should I come by for the bike."

"No hurry. It's safe. Just let that knee of yours get better, and we'll go from there."

"Yep," Lani said again, then turned and walked away, knowing he was quickly getting to her, and the longer she faced him, the more of a risk she ran of saying something she might regret, like inviting him in for a cold drink. And with the way she was drawn to him, that would be a bad idea. She didn't really want him in her life, and by the strange way she felt around him, doubted she would be strong enough to keep him out if this continued.

Carr watched her disappear as she went inside but didn't turn to leave. Instead, he sat on his bike trying to get Lani, the beautiful girl with the awkward wardrobe, out of his mind before he went in and tried to find her.

As Lani unlocked her door, Ms. Belsky opened hers.

"There you are. I was beginning to wonder what thrift store you ended up at. Come on in, dear. I've made us some lunch and fresh lemonade, one of my finest batches yet." Lani locked her door back, turned and hobble her way across the hall. "Oh, dear. What has happened to you?" Ms. Belsky's voice filled with concern, something that had a strange effect on Lani. Her father was never one to be concerned over her and her mother was nothing more than a shadow that moved about in the dark corners of Lani's life. Seldom talking to her and definitely never nursing any of her bumps and bruises. Perhaps there were just too many in that house for anyone to tend to.

Ms. Belsky's tone was warm and sweet and Lani felt her eyes burn with tears. She quickly blinked them away and thought of the gentle, beautiful woman in front of her. Ms. Belsky had her own children. Grown and too busy for her obviously, but Lani knew how much the woman missed them. Perhaps Lani made her a little less lonely and vice versa, and the lady needed someone to take care of so Lani knew Ms. Belsky was about to nurse her back to health, but little did she know, a sexy stranger had already done just that.

"Come on in and let's take a look. You will have to tell me everything, dear. And don't leave out that handsome young man who brought you home either. Don't think I didn't look out my window when I heard that loud bike of his. You know I've been on one or two of those things in my day as well. Oh, yes indeed. Walter used to take me on long rides when we were right about your age." Ms. Belsky shut her door and stood for a second, completely still as her eyes glazed over. "Oh, do I have stories about my handsome Walter." She took off toward the kitchen as Lani wobbled in behind her, listening to a beautiful old woman talk about the love of her life as if he was about to join them for lunch.

Lani couldn't help but wonder if she would ever love someone as much as Ms. Belsky loves her Walter. A love that breaks the boundaries of life and death and lives forever in the heart it captured so long ago.

Chapter 9

The week skated by without any sign of Carr, not that Lani expected to see him just pop up on her doorstep unannounced, but she might not minded it if he had. By the time Friday evening rolled in, she was ready to lose herself in Hemingway's words of Spain and love and war, not to mention how these words also affected her grandfather. She couldn't speak wholeheartedly about everything that had happened in his life, but she had no doubt that the look he gave her as she read to him was a story all in its own. And she would dare to guess, at least to her, it was one of the greatest love ever told.

"There's my girl," Al greeted her as soon as those double glass doors swung open and Lani walked in, no longer hobbling from her knee injury although it still hurt. She had changed the bandages and readdressed it with an extra-large band-aid that made bending her knee a lot easier. At least enough that she could get around without limping too much. "Right on time." He was leaning in his usual spot along the wall holding his mop. "You never disappoint." Al gave a large grin as if Lani was coming to read to him every Friday, and in a way, she was.

Lani was the sweetest girl he'd ever seen in a place like this. Not that other relatives never came to visit, but it was usually short and awkward. Not knowing what to say to someone once so full of life and now so old and tired and...well, different. No longer someone who could toss a ball without throwing out an arm, or dance with a grandchild without throwing out a hip, or someone who could paint a room on a whim, or flip a mattress because they had burrowed a permanent creator from years of sleeping in the exact same spot, or even someone who could sit through a movie without falling asleep. All lost to years gone by, which can make for uncomfortable visits for the young.

No. Visitors came here because they felt obligated and stayed out of guilt, and that stay was as short as they could possibly make it after looking at a person who barely recognized them any longer. In fact, most relatives and friends stopped coming after a few weeks. Some made it as long as a few months until that day when they just stopped altogether. No longer interested in that old, worn-out pair of shoes.

But not Lani. For the past two years since she had brought her grandfather here, she had shown up at least every Friday, if not more. And every Friday, Al would be shining that same spot on the hallway floor until he saw those doors swing open and the brightest sunlight he'd ever seen waltz in and smile.

You never disappoint, the words echoed in her head before making their way directly to her heart, but instead of warming her, they stabbed her like an ice pick. *If only that were true*. Lani tried to force her father out of her head. She hated the way her past wouldn't let her go, but when one molds a child with such ugliness, chains of doubt become permanent voices in the place of beauty.

She tried to push away the cold spots of her heart and smiled back. "The floor has never looked so good." Lani winked and chuckled as she saw Al blush. He was such a sweet man and she loved him for that. "How's he doing today? Better than Wednesday, I hope."

"Yes, ma'am. He's up and awake and waiting on you." Al watched as Lani passed. "And if you need anything, you just call, and I'll come a running."

"Will do." Lani gave him one last smile then finished her walk down the hall to her grandfather's room. The door was ajar but she gave it a light rap before pushing it all the way open and walked in. "Look who's up." She greeted him with stars in her eyes. "I hope you're feeling better. We have a lot of reading to catch up on."

"There's my girl." He smiled and every part of his aged face seemed to smile with him. He reached for her hand and she instantly took it. "My sweet Lani. What have I done to ever deserve someone as loyal as you?" His voice was quiet and Lani knew his mind was searching for an answer. His eyes turned from happy to sad in an instant and the pain on his face tore through her.

"Stop it." She looked at him. "You stop it. You know I don't judge you. I never will no matter what it is you have done or think you have done that was so terrible. I will never stop coming to see you. Ever."

He squeezed her hand and looked away, hating himself for not being strong enough to hold back tears. He felt weak in her presence as if she was the only one in the world who truly loved him, and he wanted so desperately for that to last. He never wanted her to know who he was deep down under all those years of skin and scars. He loved this girl and was moved every time she came. He didn't deserve her, and yet there she was, time after time.

Lani wiped away his tears with her hands and sat on the edge of the bed. "Have you been ornery today?"

He chuckled and patted the top of her hand.

"Not as much as I'd like too." He smiled, feeling his pain slide away into the darkness where he tried to keep it.

"Well, we'll just have to work on that. Maybe I'll throw in a book on practical jokes to pull in a nursing home. You could always leave your teeth in Sue's cereal box. That'll sure get her up and going."

He laughed. "Except I still have all my teeth. That may be a problem."

"True." Lani nodded. "But Ms. Carla next door doesn't. I'm sure we could borrow them. I bet she'd never know they were missing."

"Now that would be a sight. She's always losing those things. Never remembering where she put them. I don't know why she doesn't just leave them in her mouth. Seems like a good idea to me."

"Well, she wouldn't be so exciting if she was rational."

"Maybe I'll switch out her hand lotion with hemorrhoid cream."

Lani chuckled. "Now there's the spirit."

He looked at her for a long second, his eyes gently searching her face. So young and genuine and honest and pure, but he could also see something else trapped behind those innocent eyes of hers. Something so familiar. Something that reminded him of his own pain. Something he knew not to ask about but simply accept. He squeezed her hand again. "Who needs rational?" He smiled. "Now, tell me exactly where we left off."

Lani pulled up her large brown chair close to the edge of the bed and plopped down with the book in her hands. She opened it as she spoke.

"We are just starting chapter 14. Winter has fallen and Maria and Robert Jordan have never been more in love. War is soaring all around them, but they find peace embraced with each other." She gazed up at him from her chair. His eyes stared off and latched onto an invisible object in the distance and she knew he was ready. "Let's begin."

Lani opened the book and began reading and as she heard the light scraping of chair legs come closer to the door, she smiled and read louder for her friend with the mop.

She read well past visiting hours but no one minded. No one ever minded when Lani came to visit. It was almost if the world just stopped and circled around her. At least part of it.

When the heavy sounds of sleep sounded from the bed, Lani quietly stood and gathered her things to leave. She gently pushed the chair back into the corner, tucked the blanket in around her grandfather then kissed him on the forehead. She smiled down at him, staring at him through the soft light of the lamp. "You are a great man," she whispered, then turned to leave, never seeing the small smile slip across his face upon hearing those words.

As she passed, she found Al in the chair as always, his head propped up on his hand resting on the arm rail, eyes closed in sleep. She tiptoed out the door and down the hall as quietly as possible. As she opened the doors to leave, Al's voice came from behind her.

"Until next time," he called out after her and she turned and waved before leaving.

Once outside, the humid air snuggled in around her as she began walking. A few steps was all it took for her stomach to wake and remind her that she hadn't eaten in hours. It was late and she was due to go in to her second job to help waitress, so she knew that her stomach would just have to wait a tad longer.

She entered work and went to the back to put her bag up. She tied on her apron then headed to the bar. Jake made her up a coke and slid it to her.

"Thanks." Lani emptied the glass, hoping it would put off the grumbling of her stomach long enough to make it through her shift.

"We're packed tonight. Everyone was called in." Jake yelled over to her. "Sarah and Nikki are drowning out there."

"Got it." Lani quickly grabbed a tray and headed out into the crowd. She hit the table closest to the bar first. It was packed, most already bordering on inebriated judging by their loud behavior and excessive laughing. Perfect table for good tips, as Lani had learned early on. People who were happy and well hydrated with fun-feeling drinks had a way of sharing the happiness in the form of money. And the happier they were, the less they noticed her for anyone expect the drink-girl. And she was definitely happy with that. People who were sober when she walked in didn't treat her the same as they did after they were drunk. Soon, Lani was the one that made them smile when they saw her with a tray full of shots, and those smiles paid off.

Too bad it wasn't permanent, Lani thought as she plastered on an oversized grin and served up twelve shots of tequila for the third time to the same table.

As the night moved on, she couldn't help but wonder if Carr would show. She had never noticed him in there before last week and wondered if this was a place he had just tried on a whim. After all, his buddy did have a bar of his own, so she guessed, and he probably hung out there most nights.

She shrugged and finished the night out, carefully stashing away her tips and trying not to be too obvious as she continued to scan tables for a face that was sure to make her smile genuine.

Around three thirty, she unlocked her door, dropped her bag, and changed into her new PJ's then went to bed. As her head crashed into the pillow, she wondered how long she would have to wait before seeing him again. But just before her eyes closed, she had a thought that made her heart skip a beat.

Maybe it's time to go check on that bike.

And that's all it took for sleep to find her quickly.

Chapter 10

Lani woke around 7:45 to a soft knocking on her door. She peered out the peephole to find Ms. Belsky rapping lightly while calling her name.

"Lani, dear, open up. It's me, Ms. Belsky."

She unlocked the deadbolt and opened the door. There stood her neighbor, already dressed in an eye-catching blue sundress topped off with a stylish hat.

Lani was surprised to see her so early but not at all surprised that she already look fabulous before most people had finished their Saturday morning coffee.

"Good morning, Ms. Belsky. What brings you over this morning?"

"Lani, dear, it's that boy." The woman's tone was mixed between a soft whisper and full-on excitement. "That young gentleman you were with Wednesday. He's here."

Lani's eyes opened, suddenly feeling very much awake. "What do you mean here?" Her voice matched the same tone as her neighbors. "Here? Where here?"

Ms. Belsky pointed down to the bottom floor. "Outside in the front. I heard his bike and looked out my window and voila, there he was."

"He's outside?" Lani's voice rose, filled with sudden panic. She dashed across the hall and into

Ms. Belsky's apartment. "Where is he?" She pulled the edge of the curtain ever so slightly, not knowing if he could see her or not and peered out the window. "Oh, my god. He's here." She let the curtain swoosh close and looked at her neighbor. "What does he want?"

"If I had to guess, I'd say he's here for you, dear." Ms. Belsky nodded more to herself than to Lani. "Any boy that comes around before the sun's fully up, has reasons he's not sleeping. Especially early on a Saturday morning. My Walter was the same way..." She drifted off briefly before suddenly looking at Lani. "Oh, dear. You can't go down there looking like that. Run along now, go fix yourself up. He's just been sitting there against that bike of his waiting for you. Now, no more time to waste. Or-" she stopped abruptly, "Or I could just go down and invite him up. Now that would be nice, wouldn't it?"

"No!" Lani almost screamed then ran back across the hall. "Just give me a few minutes. I'll go down. Don't let him come up."

Ms. Belsky smiled to herself and shut her door back. She then walked into her kitchen, made herself a cup of hot tea and walked over to the window. She pushed the curtains all the way open and looked down to the street. When Carr looked up, she waved and smiled. Without hesitation, he did the same. She then pulled up a chair and nestled into a good spot to watch the show. "It should be starting any moment now," she mumbled and waited patiently as she enjoyed the warm cup in her hand.

As promised, Lani was out the door and heading down the stairs within minutes. She had brushed her teeth, brushed her hair, put on a tad of makeup and slipped on her flip flops. By the time she got to the door leading outside, she was out of breath and forced herself to stop for a second.

"Deep breath, Lani. You don't want to go out there acting like a fool. Just settle down," she consoled herself, grateful no one else was around. A few long, soothing breaths later, she pushed opened the door, took a couple steps toward him and froze. He had turned at the sound of the door and was now staring right at her, which made her next move impossible. The move where she quietly turns around before he sees her wearing her PJ short bottoms and a white tank top with no bra. She had completely forgotten to change. And worse yet, what if he wasn't even here for her? What if he knew someone else that lived here and was waiting on them? What if that them was a her? "Dear, god, why me?" she mumbled as he made his way over to her.

God, he looked good. His jeans were faded and worn and fit his body perfectly. His warm, brown hair had a light wave and hit right at his jaw. Then there was his chest with his sturdy shoulders and muscles that seemed to sing out from his shirt that unsuccessfully kept them hidden. She had failed to notice the full extent of all this before and was not entirely sure why it was crashing in on her now. Maybe it was because she felt very exposed at the moment. Feeling half naked made her suddenly aware of what others were wearing, or maybe it was the way he was jogging up to her from the street and that the breeze was pushing against his clothes and accentuating his amazing physic. Like saran-wrap clinging to a naked Ken doll. Not that he was naked. *Dear, lord. Why am I thinking of him naked!*

She pushed the thought away and slowly brought her arms up to cover her chest, careful not to move too fast, tipping him off as to her no-bra-top she was sporting in the middle of the sidewalk.

"Hey." He stopped a few feet in front of her. "I was about to think you were going to sleep the day away." He smiled and quickly scanned her. "Just got out of bed, did you?"

"I had no intention of staying in bed all day; I have to go to work. And since when is 7:45 in the morning classified as sleeping the day away."

Carr tried not letting his eyes fall to her body again, but he was finding it a challenge at the least. A challenge he wouldn't mind losing by the sight of what he saw the first time. Slender legs, curvy hips, flat stomach and then her chest. He swallowed hard in an attempt to prevent anything else from waking up and kept his eyes on hers.

"I need your assistance on something."

"You need *my* assistance on something? What? Are the police fixing to arrest you for plowing over a pedestrian and you need me to bail you out of jail?"

"You weren't a pedestrian, remember, and no, that's not it." He smiled. He liked it that she didn't lose her sense of humor so early in the morning. Most of the girls he had dated would have been furious at him for showing up at this time, not to mention unannounced and on a Saturday. But then again, most girls he had dated were still hungover at this time as well.

Lani began to unknowingly tap her foot on the sidewalk, her arms still folded across her chest, hoping to hide anything that might be showing and waited for him to give her more information. But he only raised his eyebrows and matched her own curious look then began to mimic her foot tapping.

"What are you doing?" she snapped, fighting the urge to laugh at his ridiculous behavior.

"Waiting for you to run your cute little tail upstairs and change. I said I need your help, remember? I mean," he glanced over her with a look of satisfaction, "You can go like that. It definitely won't bother me a bit."

"Oh, stop it." She stiffened her arms by her side and instantly regretted it.

Carr's lips gently parted as he brought his hand up to his mouth. "Oh, holy hell," he mumbled softly as his eyes drank in the soft outline of her breast. He didn't mean to react, but being so close and unexpectedly seeing what he just saw caught him off guard. As her arms shot back up, he quickly recovered. "Go on. Go change. I'll be right here."

"I have to work, remember?"

"Really? You have to be at work at 8 o'clock in the morning, on a Saturday?" He tilted his head in disbelief."

"I never said at 8, but I do have to go in."

"I'll have you back by ten. That should be plenty of time to get ready since I know for a fact that *TED*'s doesn't open until 11." He nudged his head up toward her apartment. "Now go."

For a second, she just stood there trying to wrap her thoughts around a guy she still hardly knew showing up early in the morning and barking orders at her.

"Who do you think you are?" she said without realizing what she was doing. "You can't just show up and tell me what to do."

Carr took a step closer and grinned down to her. "Oh, yes I can. I'm the guy who's fixing your bike remember, and if you want it back, you'll do exactly as I say," he teased, enjoying her defiance. "Or," he started but then tilted his head down further to look her straight in the eyes, "I could just sweep you off your feet and throw you on my bike as is. It's your choice."

"Fine," she snapped, hating the way he always seems to get his way, then whisked around and disappeared upstairs.

Carr went to his bike and leaned against the seat as he waited. After a few seconds, he felt eyes on him and instantly looked up to find the same woman as before looking down. She smiled and gave a big wave again. He waved backed expecting her to step out of view, but she only kept smiling and waving. Carr chuckled to himself and couldn't help but indulge the woman with another wave.

A few minutes passed until Lani appeared wearing an avocado green blouse with a cream poodle skirt. Carr turned his head and laughed. This girl was like no one he'd ever met before and that's exactly what he liked about her.

"I had to wear something that I could ride that thing in." She motioned to the bike as she approached.

"Nice choice," he said sincerely and Lani felt a small tingle in her stomach. No one had ever said anything nice about her clothes. She felt a surge of embarrassment and looked away from him. A cute guy giving her genuine compliments was something she didn't know how to handle and looking away seemed like a good option.

She climbed on behind him and loosely wrapped her arms around his waist as before. He started the bike and the sound of thunder vibrated through Lani as he slowly merged into traffic and down the street with no idea of where he was taking her. She was normally not this brave, but there was something about this guy she hardly knew that made her feel as if all was good.

A short ride later and they were pulling up in the alley of what Lani presumed was the same bar where the bike was at. Carr parked and held his motorcycle steady as Lani climbed off, then flipped down the kickstand and joined her.

The alley was narrow and the surrounding buildings cast cooling shadows from the sun's morning heat as a musty scent of damp dirt circled in around them.

"This way." Carr headed through a back door next to several large garage doors of a building. Lani followed. Once inside, she was taken aback, not expecting to see what's was in front of her. It was a large three car garage lined with tools, old vehicles, two broken-down motorcycles, and a hodgepodge of old furniture.

"This place is deceiving."

"What do you mean?" Carr walked over to one of the garage doors and lifted it opened, letting a cross-breeze linger in and lightening the scent of gas and oil in the place.

"I mean from the front, no one would guess this place was back here."

"Yep." He turned and smiled. "One of my best-kept secrets."

"Well, you're not really good at keeping secrets now, are you?"

"Why do you say that?" He titled his head, already anticipating her response. "Wait. Let me guess. Because I just met you, and I'm already showing you my secret hideout?"

"Something like that." Lani looked around, feeling uncomfortable with his eyes still on her.

"No worries," he said as he turned and walked toward the far corner to pick something up. He then walked back to her carrying the bike, except it didn't look like the same bike she had left with him. "I don't really think you're the stalker type."

Her eyes fell to the bike, ignoring his comment. "It looks so different." Carr set the bike up in the middle of the floor and Lani slowly walked around it. The front wheel looked completely new, the frame had zero dents, the basket had been removed and all the old paint had been scraped off.

"Don't worry; this isn't the final product." Carr watched Lani carefully, trying to gauge her reaction. The last thing he wanted was to upset her and he only prayed he hadn't done so already. He had taken things with the bike a little overboard, especially since it wasn't even his nor did he seek permission to strip it down as he had already done. But something inside him just couldn't help it. He had an eye and a passion for inner beauty when it came to old and broken down things. Some had called it an obsession, but whatever it was, it made him want to take those objects and restore them until that lost beauty shined once again. And this bike was perfect for that. It was a classic.

He'd known it the second he saw it come barreling toward him in the middle of the street. The bike and the rider. Although he had already been drawn to Lani the first time he saw her in the bar. A true classic beauty herself that he hadn't been able to get out of his mind since his eyes had found hers that night.

"No, it can't be," Lani said softly, letting her fingers trace the handlebars, "I like it already. What you've done makes it look so different yet still the same."

Carr nodded and silently let out a deep sigh of relief. "And don't worry. I'll put the basket back on after I paint it."

Lani looked up. "Paint?"

"Yes. That's why I needed your help. I remember you said the bike wasn't yours."

"That's right. It belongs to the lady who lives across the hall from me."

Carr gave a half-grin. "It wouldn't be that sweet red-haired one who likes to smile and wave all the time, would it?"

Lani chuckled. "Yeah, that's the one. Ms. Belsky. Her husband bought her this bike for her birthday when she was very young. He passed away awhile back and this bike still reminds her of him. Something she wants to keep forever, I suppose." Lani let her eyes fall back to the steel gray frame, picturing the old chipped paint that was once there.

"Okay, that helps me some."

"What do you mean?"

"I wasn't sure what color to repaint it. I could do the same as before, but I was leaning toward something a little different but wasn't sure. That's why I came to get you. I needed some input and you just did it."

"How so?"

"You gave me the story I needed. The story of the bike. Everything has a story and knowing the story helps me move forward with a project. I want to be true to the item I'm refinishing. I may strip the outside, but the soul must remain intact. You know, when someone refinishes an old house but keeps the small details the same, so they don't lose the character of it." Carr shrugged. "It's the same. I wanted to fix the bike but didn't want to lose the connection to its owner. I didn't want to deliver back something that felt strange, and you just helped."

"Okay...what exactly did I do?"

"You told me the paint color."

Lani shook her head, having no idea how she did that when she said no such thing. "Hum, I'm not sure I did."

"Yep, you did, and now I owe you coffee. It's the least I can do for dragging you out of bed so early."

He pulled the garage door closed then headed back to the front of the garage to a door that lead into the bar.

"Whoa, wait a minute," Lani called behind him. "What color did I tell you because I don't remember telling you anything about a paint color?" Carr didn't stop to answer; instead he walked into the empty bar, flipped on a few lights and headed to the cappuccino machine.

Lani followed briskly behind, still waiting for him to turn and answer her.

"Sit," he commanded and pointed to a bar stool.

"I really don't like it when you feel so at liberty to boss me around," she said without looking at him then purposely sat three stools down from the one he pointed to.

Carr saw what she did and turned and laughed as he prepared the coffee. "Stubborn," he muttered under his breath.

"Excuse me?" Lani called. "What did you just say?"

"Nothing," he called back. "Not a thing."

Lani shook her head then looked around the place as Carr finished the drinks.

It was dim inside with an eclectic feel to it. There were old hub caps and vintage signs scattered on the walls. A few of the signs were barely readable as the decor on them had all but faded. Other signs blinked brightly with neon dancing letters while others just hung there with the words *Coke-a-Cola* still quite visible in red and white vintage letters. The tables were wood with engravings on the tops. From a distance, Lani could make out a heart or two with something scribbling inside, no doubt the carver's initials along with whatever person had tagged along at the time. All in all, the tabletop inscriptions only added more character to the place, which is why she guessed they hadn't been switched out for something more modern. Five large TV's were scattered about, all titled down and facing different directions for maximum viewing pleasure, however Lani guessed anything that was showing in a bar was probably sports related and of no interest to her.

The bar top itself was a different beast entirely. It was a sleek red cedar wood with a high gloss polish. Against it were tall black barstools that twirled. There was nothing old or defaced about that section of the place. In fact, it was one of the best looking bars she had ever seen, not that that was saying much. Her bar visits could be counted to only the places she'd worked in, so including the one she was in now, the total came to two.

Over the bar hung a variety to shirts for customers to purchase if they found the urge and Lani found herself wishing she could do so herself. They looked soft with a heather finish to them - her favorite, and the writing wasn't obnoxiously big across the front. The letters were modest and had a worn look to them, just her style, and she found herself staring at them longer than intended.

Carr set down a small cup in front of her then reached up and snagged one down. He handed it to her.

"Size small, I'm guessing."

"Uh," Lani hesitated. "No. I'm good."

"That's not what I asked. You are a size small, are you not?"

"Yeah..."

"Then, here you go. Greg likes it when a pretty girl wears a shirt from the bar. He says it a gold mine for advertisement."

"Well, how much is it?" Lani said uncomfortably, knowing that unless it was a buck fifty or less, she couldn't afford it, and she knew it wasn't.

Carr tore off the tag. "Nothing." He threw it at her. "Stop protesting and put it on. I want to see what it looks like."

Lani caught the shirt but set it down. She picked up her coffee and took a sip to get her thoughts under control. She liked Carr. She liked him more than she ever remembered liking anyone, ever. However, there was a reason for that. And that was because deep down she knew better than to let anyone in. Because once they came in, once they got close enough to see inside her soul, inside that tiny, little ice box of who she really was, a girl who is an utter and complete failure at everything she tries, they would know the truth.

It was fine to visit at a distance. It was fine to even tease here and there, but that is where it needed to end. If it ended there, he would never know. He could still walk away thinking she really was someone that perhaps he could actually be friends with. Someone he could hang out with, drink coffee and paint old bikes with. But that was it. It couldn't go past that. She could never let him see her the way her father did, which meant he could come no closer.

"It's not really my color." She took another drink, stood and walked out the front door, leaving the shirt beside the cup on the bar. As she walked out, she felt a chunk of her heart break off, turn to ice, and slip down into that cursed box of pain. A piece that belonged to a boy whom she had once again, all too quickly lost.

Chapter 11

Carr stood there for a second, wondering what just happened. One moment they were conversing and teasing and having a comfortable time and the next they weren't. Like she instantly remembered her house was on fire and had to dash away like a bat out of hell to put out the flames.

He shook his head then went out the front door after her. He stopped once he was on the sidewalk and wondered if he should follow her or not, catch up with her and ask what the hell just happened. But he decided to let her go. He liked her, that was for sure, but he didn't know her well enough to go demanding answers. So he stood and watched her walk away. And even from the back she was beautiful. Her slender build and vintage skirt made for an eye-catching scene and that sadden him, for she didn't even know how beautiful she really was. He watched her until she slipped through the cracks of the crowd and disappeared.

He then went back inside and walked over to the bar. He cleared off their cups and picked up the shirt that seemed to have changed everything. He held it up, imagining what it would look like on her. The soft baby blue against her angel face was sure a sight he would love to see. He then gripped the shirt in his fist and went to the garage.

He found the basket that he'd removed from the bike and plopped the shirt inside.

"You're getting that damn shirt, Lani, whether you like it or not." He gave a light huff, still trying to make out what just happened. Never had a girl turned and walked away from him like that. Usually, it was just the opposite. He couldn't peel them off. Especially once they found out who he was. Who his parents were. But not Lani. She had no clue, and by the look of what just happened, didn't want one either.

He shook his head again, staring down at the bike. He let his fingers linger over the scrapped frame as if it was injured and he was avoiding hurting it further. It was as good as a living thing to him, and he could feel its pulse through the metal tubes. His eyes became distant as he brought his hand up along the handlebars, wondering just how beautiful he could make this old bike when he was finished.

Carr smiled and carefully stepped back to get a full view. "Oh, yeah. I know just the right color, indeed." His voice was soft, still thinking of Lani although he was trying not to. "Let's get started." He clapped his hands, feeling invigorated, and walked over to the counter. He grabbed a fresh can of paint and a brush then flipped on the radio, cranking the volume up until he could no longer hear his own thoughts. Up so loud that the entire block could no longer hear themselves think either, but that's what it took. That's the only way he had ever been successful in shutting out the world around him, including his dad, and now Lani. That and fixing up broken things.

****

Lani walked back up the stairs, careful not to make a sound as she slipped the key into her door. She wasn't in the mood for chit chat and wanted to avoid Ms. Belsky if possible, and it was. She was soon inside and able to lock the door without a sound.

She then went to the couch, sat and let out a long, slow sigh.

"Well, that seriously sucked, Lani," she berated herself. "No wonder people don't like you. You run away at the first sign of friendship." She shook her head and stared at a spot on the floor for no particular reason other than it was a dark stain that gave her something to focus on. "Why," she whispered in the quiet room. "Why do I have to be so different? Why can't I just be loud and fun and easy-going?" She flopped her hands into her lap, her thumbnail lightly scratching the palm of the other. It dug in and traced the long creases, and her mind traveled back to a boy. A boy who, for some odd reason, used to follow her around in school. He'd walk quietly behind her in the halls, stop when she stopped, walked when she walked. At lunch, he'd sit at a table diagonally from her where she'd been in his direct line of sight. After school, he'd walk a half a block behind her until she came close to her home before he'd turn down a different path. He'd always show up at her tennis matches in the stands somewhere. Just sitting there watching from a distance. Never speaking. Never waving. Always watching.

Until one day. It was spring and Lani had just finished a game. Her father had taken off by the car, where he revved up the motor and waited for her in disgust. She had won every game but only by a few points, and one was tied all the way up until the end where Lani had lofted the ball over the net, dropping it only inches inside the opponent's court. The girl had sprinted but wasn't fast enough. The ball bounced out of bounds without a return hit giving the final point, and win, to Lani. The crowd gave a polite applause, all except for the stranger who had become a familiar face for the past six months of her life.

He stood, clapped vigorously and smiled at her. She had put her head down so her father couldn't see her reaction: a forbidden smile.

After the game, she was standing under a willow tree gathering her things and stuffing her racket into her bag as her father waited in the car. She knew what was to come. Another long and winding walk home where she'd be lucky if there was food waiting for her, and even more lucky if her father let her eat.

As she zipped up her bag, a voice sounded close by.

"That was amazing." It was soft and warm and something about it made her almost cry. It was something no one had ever said to her. Not her coach, not her teammates, and certainly not her father.

Lani turned and there he was. The guy who was always there but had never said a word to her until this very moment. She looked at him. He was thin and his hair hung down almost hiding his eyes, but she could see them just the same. They were friendly and without even knowing this kid, all she could think about was running away with him and never coming back. Disappearing forever with a complete stranger. A stranger that had told her the sweetest words she had ever heard.

Instead, she stared for a second, letting his words wrap around her like a warm blanket on an icy day, or the sun glistening off the frozen branches of hibernating trees trying to get them to wake up. That's the way she felt with this guy. Like he had just reached out and shook her, telling her to wake up. It's time to pack your things and run away with me. I'll take care of you. I'll wrap you up in my long arms and cover you in warmth, just come with me.

Lani forced herself to step toward him, hoping she would say the right thing. Hoping this was the start of something that would never end. She was so starved for warmth that she almost shivered as she stood there in the warm sun, facing a stranger that had actually talked to her.

"Thanks." She took another step, feeling the edges of the iceberg that kept her captive begin to drip. She could almost see the water easing off her skin and rolling to the ground beneath her feet. She let her eyes dance over his shy face, hoping he wasn't a mere mirage of desperation.

He had his hands tucked deep into his pockets and Lani picked up on his nervousness. All she wanted to do was make him feel the way he just made her fell. She wanted to be his friend, and maybe one day, something more.

"I'm Lani." Her voice was sweet and that made the boy smile.

"I know. I'm Philip." He instantly stepped closer. "You're the best tennis player I've ever seen. I love watching you play."

"Who the hell are you?" a voice boomed from the side. Lani turned to see her father close enough to have heard everything, and she instantly felt the melting edges of her life become solid and hard again. If she hadn't been frozen inside, she was sure her blood would have drained and stained the ground by her feet. "The best tennis player, my ass. She couldn't beat a goddamn dog holding a stick."

"Daddy, please," Lani pleaded, knowing it was useless. Her father did whatever he wanted when he wanted and the world just stood by and let him.

"Daddy please what?" He gritted his teeth as he spoke. "You're never going to amount to a goddamn thing. You make me sick the way you let people take advantage of you. If you were any good, you would have annihilated those players. But you didn't, did you? You almost lost and almost means you don't deserve to call yourself good." He turned and glared at the stranger. "Like I said, she's no good, boy. She's doomed for failure and she'll never amount to a goddamn thing, so why don't you run along and go find yourself a nice girl who has the guts to become a winner."

"I think she's an amazing player." His voice sounded weak and scared and Lani shut her eyes. Her father could spot weakness, and when he did, he struck hard and fast.

Her father's body swelled as if someone had just plugged him into an air compressor and flipped on the switch. He took a step toward the kid and narrowed his eyes. His voice was a death whisper when he spoke. "Get your ass out of here before I beat if off and don't you ever show your face around here again. If I even see so much as a shadow of you, I'll rip your head off and beat it with a hammer until it's the size of a tennis ball and then force Lani to practice with it." He titled his head and gave a large grin that made Lani's skin want to run and hide. She hated him. Everything inside her hated this man. He had just murdered the only attempt anyone had ever made to talk to her, to be her friend, to like her.

The guy backed up, turned around, hung his head and walked off.

Lani's father smirked as he relished his victory. He then slowly turned his gaze to his daughter. He stepped in close to her and lowered his voice even more. "Do you really think you're good enough to keep a guy around? He may like you at first, but the second he sees who you really are, he'll be hightailing his way on the nearest path that takes him farthest from you. No guy is going to like what you have to offer once all the pleasantries are done. You have nothing to offer, Lani. I even have to force myself to tolerate you, and I'm your own family. What do you think a guy like that is going to think once he gets to know you?" He tilted his head and his eyes all but filled with pity. "You know the one who can't seem to do a half-way decent job at a goddamn thing. You see, Lani. I just did you a favor." He pointed his finger at her. "And one day you'll be glad I did. Now get to the car. It's a long walk home."

His words weighed down on her as blankets of heavy sand. She fought to breathe, but every time he opened his mouth, all she inhaled was a blast of sand that suffocated her lungs and cut like tiny knives to her face.

After that day, she never saw that warm face in her shadow again. He was the first guy she had lost all too quickly. He disappeared completely. And all Lani could think about was the hole his absence ripped into her heart. She'd barely knew him and yet she missed him every day, clinging to his words to keep her entire existence from freezing to death.

Lani stood, dropping the memory to the floor as she rose and went to the kitchen. She flipped on the bright lights above her makeshift island and started pulling out muffin pans and glass bowls. The only thing that helped her at a moment like this was baking. And she loved to bake. She loved to create something delicious and beautiful from something as ordinary as a bag of powder and a stick of butter. She enjoyed transforming them into small cups of perfection, bright and full of joy. Something to look upon with an irresistible smile, no matter what heavy chain wrapped around her at the moment.

Lani didn't know where she learned to bake. She had barely stepped foot into the kitchen when she lived at home, and when she did, it was only to sit at the table for the few short minutes she was allowed to eat. It wasn't until one day after she had moved to her own place that she began to bake. It was late and she was bored and one thing led to another and before she knew it, her counter was filled with dozens of cupcakes. She had found the process relaxing, methodical, mesmerizing. An escape that let her create something beautiful. Something so beautiful that it almost made her feel good.

Almost.

She didn't have much time before she had to go into *TED's*, so she opted for one small batch of six. She was good at adjusting the recipe to fit whatever number she wanted. It hadn't started off that way. In the beginning, anytime she had wanted to alter the mixture, the batter was either too runny and ended up like mini pancakes or so thick that it looked like a bowl of peanut butter. But she had improved quickly. Never measuring the exact amounts of any ingredient but rather adding what just felt right and that had been the golden key for her. Tuning in to her intuition and adding what felt like the perfect amount of flour or vanilla or cinnamon or whatever else she was mixing at the time. She had learned to listen to herself when it came to baking and it had made all the difference.

Sometime later, she was icing six fluffy vanilla oatmeal cupcakes with a strawberry cream filling. When she was done, she set them on a plate and scooted them into the middle of the counter. She stepped back and tilted her head.

"Absolute perfection." Her voice was distant as her eyes traced over the mounds of sweet beauty. She wanted to reach out and take one. She could see herself slowly peeling back the white paper and bringing it to her mouth, sticking her tongue out ever so slightly to lick the frosting. She imagined the taste of the vanilla and cream cheese sweetness blended so perfectly that it was light enough to float off the top and raise right toward the ceiling. She could feel her teeth sink into the moist center as she tasted the strawberries and oatmeal swirl in her mouth. "Absolute perfection," she repeated softly, knowing that once she tasted them, her father's voice would come crashing in swinging a pickax until his disappointment and anger destroyed the wonderful taste of those small cups of joy sitting on her counter. They would either be too tart, or too sweet, too fat, too skinny, too sticky, too everything wrong that could possibly be wrong.

Her eyes turned empty as she reached for the plate, then walked over to the trash and watched as each cup slid off and down into the bottom. The place where things belonged that were no longer needed or wanted, right where her father had kept her.

"I'll do better next time." She lifted her head and went to shower for work.

Chapter 12

By the time she got work, her shirt was stained with sweat. She had decided to walk instead of mess with the bus schedule. Work was a ways away, but walking down the street was therapeutic for her. So many things to look at that it helped settle the misery bouncy around inside her. The air was thick and muggy from the heat and Lani was glad about her choice of clothes. She decided on a red linen skirt and yellow sleeveless top. Ted didn't mind if they didn't wear their uniform every day, it was optional and Lani was glad because hers was covered in ketchup and barbecue sauce, which she hadn't had a chance to clean, so she opted for her own clothes today. The skirt wasn't much of an improvement, though. Lani had had to wash the skirt four times after she bought it before the musty smell lightened enough not to be noticed. But the skirt had a faded stain on the lower edge toward the back that refused to go away no matter how hard she had scrubbed. If she'd known what it was, perhaps it might have helped, but since the skirt was probably older than she was, there was no telling. And it was in the back, so she hoped it wasn't *that* noticeable, and for her, that was good enough.

"Hello, sweetie. How are you doing?" Grace greeted Lani as she opened her locker to put her bag in.

"Hey, Grace. I'm good. You?"

"Well, I can't brag, yet but I'm working on it."

Lani nodded. "You'll be there in no time." She smiled at Grace with confirmation that something good was going to happen for her any day now. "I can just feel it."

"You and me both, sweetie. And it might just hit before we know it." Grace gave Lani a look of intrigue followed with a quick wink.

"Okay." Lani looked sternly at the woman. "What's up? I know something happened, so come on, spill."

"Speaking of spills," a voice sounded from behind them. "Some kid just dropped his coke on the floor and made a huge mess. Ted said to get one of you chatterboxes up there to help." Calli glared at Lani, then spun around and went back out front. The place had only been opened thirty minutes and already packed.

"I'll go." Lani tied her apron on then turned to Grace before leaving. "But come break, it's you and me out there." Lani pointed to the alley, where the two would go and talk to get away from Calli and Mandy. And not only that, the fresh air was a welcomed escape after hours of smoked ribs and cheeseburgers. Two smells that others would have never guessed could get old after a while.

"I'll be there." Grace smiled and Lani could tell something wonderful had happened and she couldn't wait to hear about it.

Lani grabbed the mop and bucket and rolled it to the mess out front. By the time she got there, the kid's mom was already on the floor, scooping the ice back into the large plastic cup.

"I'm so sorry," she said when Lani appeared next to her.

"It's okay. I can get this." Lani put her hand on the woman's shoulder to stop her. but the woman, who looked sick with embarrassment, frantically kept cleaning the fizzy liquid from the floor. "Here, sit down. You don't want your lunch to get cold."

"No, I need to help. I'm so sorry. He didn't mean to. He was reaching for the ketchup and-"

Lani cut her off, then gently tugged the woman to her feet. "You didn't go out for lunch so you could clean. I have this. It's my job. Your job is to sit right down and relax. I'll have this taken care of in no time."

"You're very kind." The woman looked at Lani and smiled. "Thank you."

"You're welcome." Lani's voice was upbeat and light. After two years of waiting tables, Lani could spot a good-hearted person the second they sat down and the last thing she ever wanted to do, was to make someone feel worse than they already did over a simple accident. After the mess was cleaned, Lani returned to the table with another drink for the kid. It was in a large to-go cup with a lid and straw. "There you go." Lani looked at the mother and was met with genuine gratitude. Something Lani never took for granted.

She smiled again at the woman then got back to work. The place was busy, as usual. So busy in fact, that as Lani hurried from table to table, she looked right past the guy sitting alone in the corner. He wore a baseball hat, pulled down a bit too far, and a pair of sunglasses. He had purposely sat in a different section than hers so she wouldn't see him. All he wanted to do was watch her. He knew there was something beautiful about her and it was only confirmed after he watched how she was with the spilt drink and woman. She was a good girl. A good girl with a sassy mouth, eccentric style, and obvious roadblocks around her to limit a guy's approach. And the more he watched her, the more he knew those roadblocks needed to be blown off the road. He barely knew her, but couldn't stop watching. When she smiled, her eyes sparkled and lit the whole room. And she smiled often. And the more she did, the more he wanted to walk right up to her, take her by the hand, and get her out of there. Take her to a place where he could wait on her. She would smile and he would give her the world in return.

Right before her break, the guy slipped out the door without Lani ever knowing he had been there, but not before he dropped off a large tip on one of her tables who had just left. He didn't know why he had done it. He just had an urge to give this girl everything and at the moment, that was all he could think of.

When Lani entered the alley, Grace was already there. She was leaning against the side of the building with a distant stare in her eyes and a soft smile on her lips. Lani almost felt bad interrupting whatever magical thought she was having.

As she approached, Grace turned. "It's crazy busy in there."

"Yeah, typical for a Saturday. And look." Lani reached in and pulled out two hundred dollars. "Look at this tip. Talk about crazy. I've never seen anything like it."

"Wow, that is crazy. Someone must have recognized how amazing you are. I knew it was only a matter of time."

"I think it must have been a mistake. I'll hold on to it and see if anyone comes back for it."

"You do that, but I'm telling you it was no mistake. You are worth every penny and more."

Lani shook her head then changed the subject. She was uncomfortable talking about her own self-worth. What she was more interested in was what was going on with Grace. Lani looked back at her for a second and they both smiled and Lani knew. "You met someone, didn't you?"

"Yeah. I did." Grace nodded lightly. "Well, actually, I've known him for a long time, but two weeks ago something happened. And now he's all I think about. I just didn't know if I should say anything yet. I didn't want to jinx it."

"Well, who is he? Do I know him?"

They were interrupted when the back screen door opened and a kitchen worker carried out two bundles of trash. He glanced over at the girls, his face and hair wet with sweat. "Hey, Ted said if you two were out here to tell you to cut your breaks short. We're drowning in there."

"Yeah, okay," Grace said then turned to Lani.

"Only for Ted would I let someone violate Texas labor laws," Lani said.

Grace laughed and they headed right back in. "You and me both. Hey," she grabbed Lani's arm. "I'll just tell you later," she whispered and the two of them went back to the front where the rest of the day passed in a flash of loud voices, messy tables, and good food. By the time Lani was done, Grace had already left, and Lani wondered who the man was that had finally swept Grace off her feet. Whoever he was, she hoped he was good to her. She deserved at least that much.

Lani went to the back of the restaurant and sat on the bench. She gave a heavy sigh at the thought of her night ahead. She smelled like grease and smoke and knew she would have to take a shower before heading to the bar.

As she sat there, Calli came in and sat next to her. She looked at Lani, first at her clothes, then to her face. "Whatever," she mumbled but then said something else. "You going to the bar tonight?"

The question caught Lani by surprise. Calli wasn't one to make small talk with Lani and she instantly wondered what she was up to.

"If you mean to work, then yes. I'm going to the bar tonight."

"Yeah, me too. Mandy and me are going back to pick up some new hotties."

Mandy and I, Lani mentally corrected her. "Well, good luck." Lani stood, not really knowing what Calli was doing but didn't feel like finding out.

"Okay, we'll see you there," Calli called as Lani picked up her bag and headed out the door.

Lani didn't respond but wondered all the way home what was going to happen tonight. If she knew Calli, it wouldn't be anything good, and the very thought of it almost made Lani want to call in, but she couldn't. She needed the money and the tips were best on Saturday.

Lani walked into the bar wearing her black, felt skirt with white polka dots. It was trimmed with red lace, which Lani thought looked beyond perfect with the red tank top she threw on with it, considering the skirt was at least forty years old judging by the style. But it was always nice to walk out of a thrift store with a gem, which was exactly how she had felt when she had found that outfit. She only wore it on occasion, not wanting to wear it out even more than the faded black material had been through the years but the bar was dim, and the old and frayed skirt would not be noticed much, if at all, and that made Lani feel a tiny bit less apprehensive about seeing Calli tonight. At least it was something and she took it gladly.

Her hair was back in a loose ponytail that was looped over in a bun at the nape of her neck. It helped to keep her cool as she worked. It was her usual style since she always cut her hair herself. She had no real hairstyle other than this. It's all she had known, and even if she wanted a different style, she'd have no idea what to ask for or even where to begin.

It looked normal enough and more than anything, it was cheap and easy. However, one thing she had been oblivious to, was how good she actually looked in that red tank. It was snug but not overly tight and it shaped her figure nicely. The shade contrasted with her fair skin enough not to make her look pale but beautiful. Even sexy. But that is the last thing she would ever see herself as, so she was completely clueless as to why Jake kept staring at her when she went for her coke as usual.

"Hey," he said as he dried a set of shot glasses, not taking his eyes off her. He slung a damp towel over his shoulder and made her drink then slid it to her.

"Hey." Lani took a gulp, still unaware of the way Jake was eyeing her. "Thanks." She put it down in her usual spot, then turned and headed out to start her rounds.

"Yep." Jake watched her walked away, his head cocked to the side as she left. "Not bad, Lani," he said, then turned and twisted open a couple of beers.

"Hey, Happy Days." Nikki looked at Lani as she passed.

"Hey." Lani could smell a strong odor of pot coming from Nikki and wondered how no one else ever seemed to notice. But then again, the people around here were usually too drunk to notice how anyone smelled.

The music was louder than normal tonight due to the live band playing up on the stage. Every couple of nights, the bar would host some up and coming group to help them get noticed. It packed the place more than usual. The people and the crowd soon made it almost impossible to hear, causing Lani to have to lean in close to the customers when they ordered. No one minded, not even the girls because at this point, alcohol and sex were the main thing on everyone's mind.

Two and half hours flew by and Lani was raking in the tips, but the piling money didn't keep her mind off Calli. She kept her eyes peeled, waiting for when she'd show, but so far nothing. Not even Carr, who she half expected to pop in at any moment, although she didn't know why. It wasn't like she left him on terms of endearment.

And then in a flash, everything changed. Lani finished piling empty shot glasses onto her tray, and when she looked up, everything inside her hurt all at once. She couldn't believe it. Suddenly, her own soft breathing was like drums pounding in her ears as her eyes took in the sight before her. Calli did show all right, just as promised, but what Lani didn't expect was for her to be arm and arm with Carr.

Chapter 13

Lani froze. Everything went numb except the pain. A pain caused by something so cold it burned off layer after layer of life and you only wish you were numb. Just like when she had to walk home after practice in the dead of winter because she was everything horrible and absolutely nothing good and walking home in freezing weather was sure to teach her that. Her time to think about everything she had failed on. Everything she had done wrong and how to fix it next time, except no matter how much she improved, it always fell short and punished by a walk in the cold.

She would never reach the mark of acceptance with her father. She knew that, although it didn't stop her from wanting it. Just one smile from him. One, *I'm proud of you*, or *good job, kid*, or just a simple hug would suffice. Just one. One time and she'd never ask for anything more and she would try harder and harder for him. She wanted him to be happy. She wanted him to be proud of her. She wanted him to love her. Until one day she didn't.

Calli was looking right at Lani with a look of triumphant plastered across her face. Lani forced herself to move. She walked straight to the bar, set the tray down, then headed to the bathroom. The second she walked in, the scent of weed instantly hit her in the face, causing her eyes to water and she knew she wasn't alone. Without looking around, Lani walked to the nearest stall, went in and locked the door. She leaned against the metal wall and fought the rising pain to stay somewhere down deep, not wanting it to rise up and pop.

Too late.

Up came the pain as her heart sank.

Why do I even care? This is ridiculous. I don't care what Carr does. He can date whomever he wants. He's not my boyfriend. She tried to reason but the pain kept surfacing. She felt her throat shrink as if something had managed to rise high enough and was now stuck, making it hard for her to breathe.

Stop it, Lani. Stop it. You don't even like him. She lied, hoping to trick herself enough to deflate the floating ache. *You don't even like him. You barely know him.* That part was true. She did barely know him. But that didn't matter. Just like the boy under the tree. She didn't even know his name but had liked him the second he had cheered for her. And she had known the very second he spoke to her that she would have run away with him to a place where hurt and rejection didn't consume every inch of her sanity.

But it wasn't just that Carr had walked in with someone else. It was who he walked in with. Calli. Calli was one of the most snide, rude, condescending girls Lani had ever known and Carr was with her. Why her? Of all the girls in Austin, Texas, why did it have to be Calli?

Why did he choose her? She didn't even seem remotely his type. Not that she knew anything about what his type was, but she definitely didn't peg it to be a girl as vain Calli.

Now it made sense. That's why Calli wanted to know if Lani was going to be at the bar. That's why she was all of a sudden interested in her schedule. But how did Calli even know Lani liked Carr...unless it was something about the other night when the table of guys that he was sitting at stood up to her and Calli saw how Carr was looking at Lani. That had to be it. There was absolutely nothing else that would explain why Calli would try to hurt her with him.

Lani shut her eyes and swallowed a hard gulp of air, forcing down whatever hurt was still pushing its way out. She did it again and again. "I don't care about Carr. I don't care about Calli," she repeated several times until she felt strong enough to finish her night, no matter who was out there.

When she opened the stall, there was Nikki pressed up against the door, almost falling into Lani's arms.

Nikki caught herself then exhaled a puff of smoke into the air. She tilted her head to the side and stared at Lani. "Boy problems?"

"No." Lani looked at her suspiciously, wondering why she had been standing so close when there were others stalls unoccupied.

"Girl problems?"

"No." Lani looked down as she passed, then headed to the sink. She turned the water on, leaned over, and wet her neck with the cool liquid. When she looked back up, there was Nikki, leaning on the sink beside her.

"So, what is it then?" She took a long hit off her joint then offered it to Lani.

"No, thank you."

"It helps you know. Whatever you were beating yourself up over back there in solitary confinement, this can help." Nikki lifted the joint up again.

"Not my thing." Lani dabbed some paper towels on her neck.

"Sure. I can respect that. Just like I respect the fact that I don't think you judge me for smoking it." She narrowed her eyes to Lani as if she were testing her. Like she needed Lani to confirm that she, in fact, did not judge Nikki for getting high from time to time at work.

Lani glanced at herself in the mirror. "I'm no one to judge anyone." She then turned and walked out of the bathroom.

Nikki inhaled the last of her joint, ran it under the water then trashed it. After she exhaled, she called out, "What did I tell you? It wasn't her."

Sarah emerged from a stall and walked over beside her friend. They both turned to the mirror and touched up their makeup. "No surprise there. I'm the one that told you it wasn't her. If you'd quit that shit, you'd remember things."

"Maybe." Nikki reapplied her eyeliner. "And you're one to talk."

"I told you I quit, but there you go again. You can't remember. Just like I said. Before long you, won't' even know your own name."

Nikki shrugged. "I bet it was Jake. He looks the type to hijack someone's weed."

"Maybe he just did you a favor." Sarah puckered her lips and rolled on a heavy layer of lip gloss.

"Eh. Maybe. What do you think of Lani, anyway?" Nikki eyed Sarah.

"Are you kidding me? We talk about her all the time. She's weird as hell."

"Yeah, she is. I just heard her talking to herself back in the stall."

Sarah gave a light huff. "You sure about that, or was it just the voices in your head crying out for help?"

"Shut up." Nikki rolled her eyes. "I know what I heard. That girl has a lot more going on than a wardrobe malfunction. I think she has guy problems."

"It's probably Jake. If he took your weed, then he'd be high enough to date anyone."

"You're mean. I like you better high."

"Shut up." Sarah gave her lips a nice pucker then put her makeup away. "We need to get back to work. If we're lucky, no one will notice that you're high as a kite."

"They never do."

Lani went back to the bar to grab her tray and face the rest of her night, whatever that might entail. The band had only gotten louder, which she welcomed. The noise helped her drown out her thoughts and focus on getting people drinks and cleaning up after them. She was thankful that the place was shoulder-to-shoulder packed; it was all the better to hide unwanted faces in. She hit four tables quickly and refilled glasses and carried over beers. She was sweating now from all the body heat trapped inside the small bar and could feel her hair slipping from its ponytail. She took a few more orders, and while she waited for Jake to fill her tray, she reached back to fix her hair but felt someone else's hand on her instead.

She whirled around to find Carr standing so close that her face bumped his chin. Lani instantly stepped back. "What are you doing?" She wasn't sure if he had heard her, but the angry look in her eyes made it obvious she didn't like it whatever it was.

"Just thought I'd help." He looked down at her, his eyes intense and his jaw clenched. He was staring at her in a way that made her feel like she was his prey, and he was about to reach out and devour her at any second.

"Are you drunk or just crazy?" Lani stepped away further while fixing her hair. "Don't touch me like that."

"I'm sorry. I didn't mean to scare you."

"Please, you didn't scare me." Lani huffed. "You don't have that much power."

"Really?" Carr tried to hide his smile. "Because you sure looked scared to me."

"Startled maybe. Scared no. What are you doing here?" Lani demanded, harsher than she realized. She was angry, but she didn't want him to have the satisfaction of thinking she was jealous over him.

He held up an empty bottle. "Getting a drink. This is a bar, right?"

"Well, there you go." She gestured to the bar then picked up her tray and left without another word.

She was bumped and pushed and even rubbed against by drunken men taking cheap shots as she passed, but she ignored them all and stuck to her job. The job that helped her bring the only joy into her life that she'd ever known. Her grandfather.

By the time she went back for more drinks, Carr was gone and she didn't see him or Calli again the rest of the night.

"Thank god that's over," Lani said as she walked out the door around 2:45 in the morning. She didn't get far down the sidewalk when she heard someone calling her.

"Hey, Happy Days." Well, not exactly her name, but she knew it meant her. Lani turned to find Nikki and Sarah a few feet behind her. "Come get a drink with us." Nikki waved her back to them.

"Uh," Lani hesitated, this was a first. Not just a first to be invited somewhere by a couple of girls, but a first to be invited anywhere. "I think I'm just going to head home. I'm pretty tired."

"Bullshit," Sarah called. "Come on, we need your help."

Lani raised her eyebrows. That sounded suspicious. These girls needing her help? Not likely. "I really don't think I'm the one to help you with anything."

"Are you kidding me?" Nikki walked toward her. "You're perfect. Strange, weird, and pretty."

"Wow, is that supposed to make me a willing companion or just offended?"

Sarah and Nikki came closer. "Okay, Happy Days, here's the scoop. Someone stole a stash of weed from Nikki here and she's pretty damn adamant about finding out who it was. We need some help investigating and figured, well, why the hell not you?"

"Again. Compliment or insult? Wow. You two are something else." Lani turned to leave but Nikki grabbed her arm.

"You're right. We are a bit harsh. Drugs will do that do you, or so I hear." She looked at Sarah and shook her head. "But we think Jake took the weed and thought you could help us find out if it was him or not."

"Why me?"

"Because you're pretty damn innocent and no one will get suspicious if you start asking a few questions. Us two, however," Sarah waved her hand back and forth between herself and Nikki, "guilty as sin. And besides, we didn't find any decent guys tonight, so it's a perfect time to get this case a cracking. So what do you say, will you help us?"

Lani looked off down the street and wondered if she could trust these two. They weren't the nicest of girls, but then who'd she have to compare them to? And perhaps having something going on in her life would stop her from dwelling on Carr so much. She needed a distraction. She shook her head, feeling like she was on the verge of a horrible mistake. “Fine,” she replied in exasperation and heaved her hands in the air. “Why not.”

“Yes,” Sarah and Nikki said in unison and grabbed Lani then nestled her in between them. The three of them then took off with Lani and walked down the street for a night of scheming, plotting, and maybe even a little fun.

Chapter 14

Over the next few days at *TED*'s, Grace didn't show. Lani found it odd enough to ask Ted if he knew anything about her absence but he only said, "She's fine. No worries. Said she'd be back at the end of the week."

"Well, where'd she go? It's not like her to disappear and not say anything." Lani pressed further. "She'd tell me if something was up. So, where is she?"

Ted wiped the sweat from his forehead with a rag he kept tucked away in his back pocket for such an event, flipped over a few T-bone steaks before getting Lani her answer. "Went to visit her sister for a few days. Like I said, she'll be back Friday, now get to work." His voice was serious yet gentle at the same time. He was a good boss. One who knew the value of hard work and who had a deep appreciation of his employees who gave him as much.

"Right on that," Lani said with a twirl out the door. "I wonder if she went to tell her sister about that mysterious guy she met?" Lani nodded to herself with a faint smile. *Good for you, Grace. I hope you found love.*

Calli had also been a no-show Monday and Tuesday and for a second, Lani had hoped she had quit until checking the schedule. Calli had just been off but was scheduled to come in today, Thursday, at 2:00 to relieve Lani for lunch. With any luck, Lani hoped the two of them would miss each other, but even if they did, Lani knew she couldn't avoid her forever. *I'll have to face her some time,* she thought. *Might as well get it over with.* But she did have a plan in the works. She had been thinking about it off and on for the past few days.

At first, Lani thought she'd just come right out and ask Calli about her and Carr. It would be the last thing Calli would expect and therefore, could give Lani the upper hand. But the more Lani had thought about that approach, the more she knew it just wasn't for her. She wasn't good at hiding her emotions, in fact, she was more of a wear-your-heart-on-your-sleeve kinda girl and, therefore, dumped that option quickly. She knew Calli would be able to see right through her. Lani then thought she'd just start talking about a guy she'd met and how the two of them were now dating, but then that was also a flop. *I'm not a good liar.* Which then left her with her final option. *I'll just ignore it. I'll pretend that nothing is wrong and that I really couldn't care less about Carr. Easy enough,* she hoped.

Mandy, on the other hand, had been at work and had done nothing except give evil stares at Lani for the past few days. These weren't the normal looks of derision that Lani received from the two of them, but these were looks of pure hatred. The kind one gets after running over a puppy in the middle of the street.

It didn't matter if it was an accident or not, the dog was dead and the person responsible was the devil.

That's pretty much how Mandy had been looking at Lani. Even going as far to "accidentally" bump into her from time to time when their paths crossed. Actually, it was more like a full-on tackle knocking Lani off balance a few times to where she had to hop and wobble to regain her balance while praying she didn't lose her tray of food in the process. Then to add insult to injury, Mandy had just kept on walking. No apology, no turn back, no anything except for a tiny sound of satisfaction Lani thought she'd heard after the assault. No telling what would happen when it was Mandy and Calli there to team up on her together.

Lani wondered what she had done that had escalated the tension between her and them.

Again, her plan was to ignore it. That seemed to always be her default line of action. When the world got ugly, just look the other way and wait for it to pass. *What else am I going to do? It's not like a fight is going to solve anything.* She sighed, "This too shall pass," she said then went to take her last order before lunch. A single man at a table for two. *This won't take long.* She approached, wondering why someone alone would sit with their back toward everyone, but thought he probably preferred the view out the window.

She approached by his side while reaching down into her apron to pull out her pad.

"Hello," a warm voice greeted her, causing her head to snap up.

"Son of a bitch!" she responded before even realizing what she'd said. Everyone looked up at her, but she didn't notice. Her eyes were glued to Carr. "You have some nerve!" She spun around, walked to the back, whipped off her apron, and headed out the back door but not before Calli had seen it all, which of course, only made it a hundred times worse.

"Why am I mad?" Lani yelled at herself in the empty alley. "It's not like we've even dated, for christ's sake." She hated that this guy had gotten so far under her skin faster than anyone she'd ever known. What was it about him that got her so riled up over nothing?

She knew he was there for Calli. It wasn't a coincidence that he showed up right when Calli's shift started. He probably thought that was her section and Lani was the last person he wanted to see.

That only caused Lani to hate him more, and her only consoling thought at the moment was that at least he'd be gone by the time her lunch was over. Otherwise, she might just have to do something she'd never done before: go home sick from work.

She decided not to eat during her lunch. She already felt queasy and the thought of food only made it worse. So instead, she opted for a bus bench up the street to sit and watch the world pass. She had plenty of shade from the buildings around her, but even so, she was still wet with sweat but didn't really care. *Who do I have to impress*? she thought while watching a few ants scurry by in the cracks of the sidewalk.

She sat there watching those ants, watching people, watching cars, traffic lights, bikers, and tourists all moving about and wondered what it would be like to trade lives with them. Anyone would do. She just wanted to see what it would be like to actually have someplace to go - other than work, of course. What it would be like to go shopping with friends, or lunch with your mother, or a pedi with coworkers. What it would be like to have plans of any sort.

But then she felt ashamed because she did know what it was like. Every Friday she did have plans. She had someone who loved her and wanted her and was actually happy when she walked in, at least mostly. Most of that was true, on some level.

Before she knew it, she was back at work, dodging more collisions with Mandy and Calli. When Lani saw that their paths were about to meet, she would step back and wait for them to clear before she continued. She didn't like giving in to them so much, but it was that or spend her evening cleaning up messes and going home with bruised shoulders. Not to mention wasting all of Ted's food each time it hit the floor. It was a small price to pay to make it through the rest of her shift.

When eight o'clock finally came, she left feeling more empty and alone than ever.

****

Lani hadn't been home for more than twenty minutes before she heard knocking on her door. She peeked out, expecting to find Ms. Belsky standing on the other side as usual, but instead found someone else, rather two someones.

She opened the door but wasn't quite sure what to say. She narrowed her eyes at Sarah and Nikki. "What are you doing here? How did you even know where I lived?"

"Seriously, like it's hard to find out where someone lives these days." Sarah pushed past Lani and let herself in.

"Yeah, seriously, Lani." Nikki followed, carrying two paper sacks.

"Won't you come in?" Lani said with a tinge of sarcasm then shut the door behind them.

"Not bad," Sarah looked around the place. "Small but cute. Not what I expected."

"Thank you?" Lani shrugged with disbelief that she had just been ambushed by these two, but then again, that had been their style last time so she shouldn't be all that surprised. And after all, their night out together hadn't been all that bad. They went to a small 24-hour pizzeria and had planned out a rough draft of their covert operation for finding out who had stolen Nikki's weed. They talked, ate, planned, and even laughed some. Probably one of Lani's best nights in her life, although she still felt awkward around them.

Nikki walked into the kitchen and set the bags on the counter. She reached in and pulled out a six-pack of cokes, a bottle of rum, and some snacks. "Glasses and ice. Where are they?" she called out but didn't wait for an answer. Instead, she made herself at home and began to rummage around the kitchen until she found what she needed.

"So, what's up?" Lani tried to keep her tone normal, although it was somewhat of a challenge based on what she saw as she approached the counter. Sarah was now filling up three glasses with coke. *Dear, god, please don't say we're having a party. Ms. Belsky would flip.*

"We just thought our plan needed some fine-tuning." Sarah was now topping off the drinks with a rather hefty pour of rum in each.

Nikki was opening the snacks and setting them out on the counter. "Music. We need music," she busted out, and Lani jumped from her sudden outburst. Nikki and Sarah started laughing and Sarah handed her a glass.

"Here. I think you need this."

"Why not?" Lani took a drink. Sarah and Nikki picked up their own glasses and held them up then waited for Lani to do the same. She instantly followed suit.

"Here's to Operation *Kick-Ass*," Nikki said and Sarah looked at Lani.

"I guess it's better than Operation *Who Stole My Weed.*"

Lani laughed, and for the first time, she started to feel something. Something that stirred deep in her chest. Something that made her hope. A tiny shred of belief that maybe these two girls actually liked her enough to get past her oddities and want to hang out, even if it was for an ulterior motive. They needed someone no one would suspect to help them, and she was secretly glad to be included. But truth be told, Lani needed them as well. She had needed them her whole life but never thought she would be cool enough, or pretty enough, or have anything to offer someone else in a friendship. After all, she had had a father who had drilled that so deeply in her head that now she was always afraid she would only disappoint others.

"Or operation *Jake you stealing bastard*," Nikki threw in.

"You don't even know if he's the one who took it." Sarah looked at her. "Maybe you just lost it, ever think of that?"

"No." Nikki looked at Sarah like that was the most absurd accusation she had ever heard. "Hello...I don't lose stuff. Especially valuable stuff. Don't you know me at all?"

"Exactly why I said it," Sarah said out of the corner of her mouth to Lani then raised her class. "Let's do this. Here's to Operation *Kick-Ass!*"

"Operation Kick-Ass," Nikki and Lani repeated and the three of them drank.

When they set their glasses down, Nikki turned on some music from her phone, then reached for one of the bags and pulled something out. “Here’s what’s called *The Dress.*” Nikki held up a scarlet red dress that looked like it was made from spandex. It had spaghetti straps and was very short, not to mention extremely low cut. Lani guessed that a girl could neither sneeze nor lean over without something popping out while wearing that thing. “This dazzling, little beauty has never let me down. Not once. Anytime I set my eye on a guy while wearing this, I never went home alone. It’s magical, I tell you.”

“Whoa.” Lani nodded. “I bet you look amazing in that.”

“Well, of course.” Nikki shrugged as if she was told that every day of her life.

“Except she never wears it anymore because all she can think about is getting high.”

“Not true, Sarah.” Nikki paused for a second, lost in thought. “Okay. It’s a little true. Fine, it’s completely true, but you don’t know how amazing the stuff is. It’s just like......amazing.”

Sarah nodded. “Yep, and the more I listen to you talk, the more reassured I am that quitting was the best thing for me. Your vocabulary is like...*amazing.*”

“Shut up.” Nikki rolled her eyes at Sarah, then playfully threw the dress at Lani. “Here, go try it on.”

“Oh, I don’t think that’s a good idea.” Lani tried to hand the dress back but both Nikki and Sarah put their hands up.

"Nope. We need you looking irresistible and no offense, but your Happy Day clothes aren't going to cut it." Sarah took a drink. "Go try it on, let's just see what it looks like. There's no harm in just looking."

Lani looked the dress over. It seriously looked like it was made for a two-year-old, except for the plunging neckline that was. There was very little to the dress and she was nervous about wearing it. This dress would most definitely show her body and she just didn't know if she was ready for those particular comments yet. Whatever comments that might be. But whatever they were, good or bad, she wouldn't be able to hide from them. She needed help right now, but the only thing she had was a drink and a dress.

"Go on. Just see what it looks like. If you don't like it, we'll find something else." Sarah's voice was kind and it struck a chord in Lani. For some reason, Lani felt herself beginning to trust Sarah, and even though it was only a tiny feeling inside, it was enough to give Lani the courage to step out of her shell and try on the dress.

Chapter 15

Friday came and like clockwork, Lani went into work and tried to avoid the Beastie Girls the best she could, however, Calli and Mandy didn't make the task an easy one. Anytime Lani was in earshot, they would over-extend their voices about some wonderful guy they just couldn't get enough of. And even though his name was never mentioned, they all knew who he was.

"I just can't get over how good looking he is, Calli. I'm so jealous. You're such a lucky girl." Mandy would then glance at Lani and give her a quick snide smile.

"I know. I have to fight tons, and I do mean tons, of other girls off him all the time. They all think he's sexy as hell and one of them offered to give me her Porsche for a month if I'd let her date him. Can you believe that?" Calli said, making sure Lani could hear every word, and she did, over and over and over again for at least two hours. And with every comment, Lani tried to tell herself it didn't hurt, but the ball of needles swelling in her throat called her a liar. Not able to take another second of how great this guy treated Calli, Lani took it upon herself to take her own break and walked out the door to the alley.

She pulled the door closed behind her hoping to block out the two of them, but it wasn't fast enough. Before the door shut, Lani got an ear full of laughing.

The kind of laughing where evil and pure meanness live, which only added to her feeling of worthlessness. Lani fought not to let it get the best of her. Her days with Mandy and Calli had never been good, but lately they had escalated to a new level of unbearable. There was unfriendly, which Lani was used to, and then there was just downright mean for the pleasure of hurting someone, which is where Mandy and Callie had recently taken up residency.

"Maybe I just miss Grace." Lani fell against the stone wall and slid to the ground.

Grace was supposed to be back today, but so far, she hadn't shown. She would have asked Ted about it, but he was gone too, which wasn't highly unusual but not very common either. Ted would disappear from time to time during the day. Either to pick up something that they had ran out of, or to run an errand or two, but he was never gone longer than an hour or so, and Lani hadn't seen him all day. She thought something was up, although she had no idea what it could be.

To get her mind off things, she thought of this evening. Other than her visit to see her grandfather, it was the start of *Operation Kick-Ass* at the bar and she was supposed to wear *The Dress.* She laughed quietly to herself. "Operation Kick-Ass." The very sound of it made her smile and that surprised her. She couldn't remember ever having something to look forward to like she was for tonight. "Operation Kick-Ass," she repeated. It was so ridiculous. She felt like a character in a Nancy Drew story or even Stephanie Plum out on a mission to bring in the bad guy. She liked the way that thought made her feel. It was exciting. Dressing up with a mission at hand and she was the key player, almost too good to be true. The one who was handpicked to investigate. The very thought of what she was going to do left her full of anticipation about what would happen tonight. Not to mention the sea of nerves tossing about in her stomach over wearing *The Dress.*

The restless energy blocked out thoughts of Calli and Mandy and even Carr and she welcomed that. She didn't care about any of them at the moment. They all seemed to disappear into the backdrop of a nervous smile. A smile that made her lose track of time and before she knew it, the back door opened and Mandy's snake-like head slid out and starting hissing at her.

"Hey, you're break was over like ten minutes ago. It's kind of rude of you not to get back in here."

Lani let out a deep sigh, slowly got to her feet and went back in. She finished her shift with no sign of Grace or Ted.

I hope no one's sick, she thought as she left the restaurant and headed to the nursing home. Lani kept her mind on Grace the entire way there. She didn't know what she'd ever do if something was wrong with Grace. She was the main person who made her job tolerable, and she couldn't stand the thought of her not being there anymore.

However, the thought vanished as she walked in those glass doors and her eyes fell on the gentle, warm smile that always melted away the coldness of her day.

"Good evening, sunshine. There's my girl. Right on time." Al smiled, holding his mop as his back leaned against the wall in the hallway.

"Hi, Al. How was your day?"

"Doesn't matter how it was, it matters how it is, and right now, it is perfect."

Lani smiled. "Mine too." She gave a nod and the two of them walked down the hall shoulder to shoulder as if they were each holding up the other from all the heaviness of their lives. Everything that had weighed them down before that very moment when the two of them came together seemed to no longer matter. Both feeling stronger in the gentle presence of the other. When they got to the door, Lani slipped inside and Al left to get his chair, a feeling of pure happiness inside him.

"Hi, grandfather. Did you have a good day?" Lani approached the bed right as he turned to her.

"Who are you? I don't remember seeing you before?" His eyes were hard and icy as if a demon had slipped inside and forced out his identity. "Go away and let me rot in the hell I deserve." He turned his head back to the drawn curtains. "I don't need anyone's pity."

Lani set her stuff down and eased over beside him. She took his hand in hers and held it tightly. "It's okay. It's okay that you don't remember me," she whispered as if giving him permission to forget.

He tugged his hand away. "I'm a horrible man. You don't need to see me. Why are you here? Why do you keep coming back?" he growled at her, but all Lani heard was the hurt he tried to hide in his anger. "I know you hate me just like everyone else. Just leave. Leave now so I can finally come to peace with it." His voice was full of bitterness laced with regret and it broke Lani's heart to hear him speak as he did. He did it from time to time as if he had forgotten everything but at the same time remembered more than he ever wanted to. They were hard memories. Memories full of sharp edges that sliced a person's heart with each passing second they were called back. Memories that tore through all that was left of an old man and his crumbled heart. Memories that refused to stop cutting until there was nothing left of its host except a pile of shards that once resembled someone beautiful. "There are so many that hate me. You don't know the monster I really am." His voice was low and hard.

Lani took his hand again, firmer this time, wrapping her fingers around his palm. "No. No, you're not. You're my grandfather and I love you. I love everything about you. You're kind and gentle and warm and I love you."

"You don't know me, child. If you did you would never come see me again. I'm a bad man, a very bad person and I don't deserve your kindness. I don't deserve anything except to waste away into this tormented darkness alone."

Lani didn't respond, but she refused to let him go. She stood there over his bed in silence, her hand cemented to his as her heart ached for this man she loved. She stood there until his anger passed and he finally squeezed her hand in return and she knew he loved her. He needed her. He needed forgiveness for things he'd never tell her, but it didn't matter to Lani. She would give him the acceptance he craved. She'd love him through whatever demons and razored memories he carried around in his lost past. She would love him beyond all the cuts and bruises and darkness he came from.

"I love you, and no matter what you say, that will never change," she spoke over him.

His body shook with pain and Lani saw tears fall from his eyes. He refused to look at her, but the touch of his hand was enough. The way it embraced hers, almost swallowing it whole as his grip welded back into hers.

And then there was Al, who sat in the doorway, quietly listening while lifting his hand to wipe away his own falling tears for his friend inside.

By the time her evening was over, she made a quick dash home to get ready, knowing how important the night was to Nikki and Sarah. Lani didn't know why exactly, but she didn't want to let them down and was going to make her best attempt to dress the part they had asked her to. She knew the whole idea behind what she was doing was truly absurd. She didn't smoke pot and had no intention to, but some small part of her had begun to like Nikki and Sarah and for that, she was willing to help them. She knew their desire to hang out with her would be short-lived once they got what they wanted, but for now, Lani just didn't care. After all, it was helping her get away from the madness in her head over a stupid guy who obviously was playing her for a fool.

When Lani walked into the bar, Nikki almost fell over onto the table she was waiting on. And judging from the other faces, so were they. Jaws dropped, beers froze in mid-motion, and eyes doubled in size. The place grew silent and the only noise was Def Leopard pulsating into the air from the speakers in the corners.

No one expected Lani to be a walking show stopper from a simple dress, but it was more than that. She hadn't stopped at a mere change of clothes. She had her hair down, flowing in big loose curls over her shoulders, her makeup was more pronounced, her eyes sparkled with a line of soft glitter, and her lips shined with a deep shade of lipstick.

She thought she was just playing the part, just like Nikki and Sarah had expected, but now she suddenly thought she had gone too far. A bit overboard and she felt herself begin to sweat from nerves.

Sarah walked over, stared at Lani for a second, then quickly set her tray down, and made a beeline for her.

"Oh my god, Lani. You're breathtaking. This is great." Sarah's voice rose with excitement. "There's no way in hell Jake will be able to resist you now."

Sarah took Lani's arm and led her to the back. As they passed Nikki, Lani looked at her and Nikki could tell she was nervous. "You look good, Happy Days." Nikki nodded with genuine encouragement and gave Lani a smile.

"She sure would make my day happy," a voice from a table mumbled and Lani tried to hide the small bubble of joy she felt sliding across her lips.

Seconds later, the three girls were standing in a huddle in the back, their voices low, going over some minor details of their plan. When they were done, Sarah reached over and touched Lani's hair.

"You look beautiful, Lani. Thanks for doing this. You didn't have to help us." The soft tone of Sarah's voice calmed Lani. Her nerves finally settled like the waves from a storm breaking on the beach before gently rolling away.

"Sure. It's no big deal." Lani shrugged, already having one of the best nights of her life. She couldn't have been more pleased with her decision to do this for them.

"Yeah. You're a lot cooler than I thought. Thanks for pitching in. I'll share my loot with you once it's recovered." Nikki gave a firm nod. "Yep, with the way you look, Jake will be spilling his rotten guts in no time, and the three of us will be out celebrating at closing time."

Lani gave a deep sigh and crossed her fingers. "Here's to hoping." She made her way over to the bar and waited for Jake to make her drink and slide it to her as usual. She saw him pick up a glass, fill it with ice, and begin to spay it full of coke when he glanced over to her. His jaw fell and he froze, even his thumb pressed on the coke button didn't move. Lani gave a sexy look in return, trying not to feel awkward at his reaction, but this was new to her. Having so many eyes watch her in a way that were not smirking made her face flush with embarrassment, but she fought to hold her stare. She didn't want to let Nikki and Sarah down even if it was over something as stupid as weed. So she held Jake's stare until the sound of spilling liquid broke his trance and forced his gaze off Lani and onto the wet floor.

Lani couldn't help herself. She walked over, grabbed the rag that was resting over his shoulder and bent over to clean up the mess. Jake instantly knelt down beside her, his head close to hers, but still didn't speak. Lani could feel his eyes on her face, then to her body, and she knew it was a great time to start her interrogation.

"So," she began softly. "Know of anyone who could hook me up with a good time?"

"Uh...," he hesitated, clearly still trying to form a cohesive thought. "Um....what, what, um, what kind of good time are you looking for?" he stammered, still watching her.

Lani took her time cleaning the mess, playfully swirling the rag around on the floor as she talked. "Oh, I don't know." She looked at him, burning her eyes into his and suddenly feeling a bit more confident. "What do you suggest?" Her voice was soft and smooth and she could tell she was having an effect on him.

"Well, if you're looking for a date for the evening, I may know of someone."

"Oh, really?" Lani slowly stood and Jake followed. "Who would that be?"

"Well, I mean, I'm free. We could go hang out if you're interested."

"And what would we do exactly?"

"Whatever you want." Jake nodded as if hypnotized and was slowly waiting for his next command. "Whatever you want," he repeated.

Lani leaned against the bar, her back facing the crowd, and smiled at Jake. Something was coming over her. She felt a slow-rising power inside. She'd never felt so in control before. Not at work, not over herself, and certainly not over another person. By the look on Jake's face, Lani knew she could ask him anything right now and he would spill his guts all over the place, and if she wasn't careful, she might be wiping them off the floor next.

"I've been kind of stressed lately. Know of anything that might help with that?"

Jake rested his body on the bar next to hers, both of their backs facing the front now. Nikki and Sarah watched curiously as they moved about from table to table, both grinning with the delight of victory. By the look of what they saw, Lani would have Jake not only confessing to what he'd done, but offering to make it up to them as well, which to Nikki only meant a bag of free weed. Something that made her almost squeal with joy as she set down a round of beers.

Jake gently took the rag from Lani hands, ready to suggest the perfect spot for a night of relaxation after the bar closed: his place, but was interrupted before he could get the words out.

"Excuse me?"

Lani and Jake turned at the sound of a voice coming from the other side of the bar.

"What do you think you're doing?" Carr stood there, an angry look on his face as he bore his eyes into Lani.

"Sorry," Jake instantly said, snapping out of his trance. He stiffened and reached for a beer. "You're usual?" he offered soberly.

"Are you talking to me?" Lani said with more bravo than she expected, suddenly feeling like Dirty Harry in a Clint Eastwood movie.

"I'm looking at you, aren't I?" Carr didn't take his eyes off her, and she could tell he was not moved by her new look, in fact, he looked rather pissed off by it.

"I'm working." Lani's voice filled with defensive overtones, which only seemed to add fuel to Carr's fire. A fire she had no idea why it was burning to begin with.

"Doesn't look like work from where I'm standing."

"Then stand someplace else. No one told you to come over here."

Jake whipped his head toward Lani, a look of horror on his face. He was clearly shocked by her actions. Lani knew she had always been the quiet one, but honestly, she felt like Jake and Carr were completely overreacting at the moment.

Jake looked back at Carr. "We were working, just discussing some new drinks for the bar. Which," Jake shook his finger rapidly in the air, "I'm getting yours right now. Lani," Jake said forcefully. "We'll finish our talk at break. Here's your tray." Jake tried to hand the plastic black tray to Lani for her to start her rounds, but she ignored him, her eyes burning right back at Carr with as much fire as he was blasting toward her.

"You have a problem with my job?"

"Uhhh..., Lani? I don't think that's a good idea." Jake's voice trailed in the background, but neither she nor Carr was interested in what he was saying.

"As a matter of fact, I do." Carr turned and walked full force around the bar back to where she was standing. He grabbed her by the arm and began to drag her out toward the front door.

"What do you think you're doing? Get your hands off me!" Lani demanded, but Carr only became more determined to get her out of there. He went behind her and wrapped both his arms around her, locking her arms down by her sides, then picked her off the ground and carried her through the crowd and out the front door with everyone watching.

"Oh, shit," Nikki said as she saw what Carr was doing. "This could be bad," she looked at Sarah, who was standing shoulder to shoulder with Nikki.

"I hope we didn't get her fired."

"After I have my say, she will be," a voice sounded from a table nearby and the two girls looked over. Calli was sitting there with Mandy. The two of them must have just arrived because they weren't there a moment ago. "Who the hell does that little hand-me-down think she is anyway?" Calli smirked and Nikki felt herself lunge for her.

Sarah quickly stepped in front of her friend, grabbing her fist and forcing it down. "Nope, not here. Not now." Sarah waited until she felt Nikki's body relax then stepped back. "Let's just finish our shift, then we'll go find Lani. We both know Carr won't hurt her."

Nikki glared at Calli, who only smiled and titled her head as she spat out, "Bye, Bye, now." She waved and smirked at the two girls. "Back to work you go."

Mandy laughed, which only fueled Nikki's rage. "I'm going to get them. Both of them."

"And I'll be right by your side, but for now, just ignore it." Sarah gave Nikki a light push in the opposite direction of Calli and Mandy, who eventually left with some guys leaving Nikki and Sarah to work in peace, except for thoughts of Lani.

"Put me down." Lani kicked her feet as Carr carried her out of the bar and into the night air. "You can't just force me out of a place, you know?"

Carr huffed and tightening his grip around her. "Looks like I can, now doesn't it?"

"Put me down!" Lani kicked harder, but Carr only ignored it as he carried her further down the sidewalk.

"Not until you settle down."

"Settle down?" Her loud voice carried down the block, and although many people were staring, no one gave the commotion a second thought. "How can I settle down when I'm being dragged down the street by a psycho?"

"Well, technically, I'm not dragging you. I'm carrying you."

"Shut up and put me down."

Carr smiled into Lani's hair, knowing he just won that conversation and her brute commands only made him enjoy having his arms wrapped around her even that much more. He wondered how long he could keep this up until she was beyond furious.

"Nope. Not until you calm down."

He was tall enough that he could still see over her head, which was tucked up close to his. He was careful not to run her into anyone, but people naturally moved out of the way when they heard Lani making a fuss behind them.

"How calm do you expect me to be when I'm being dragged away against my will?"

"Well, I can't think of anyone who would be dragged away *with* their will."

"Shut up and put me down," she said again, full of force. "And stop laughing. I can feel you shake behind me so don't deny it."

"Say please," he insisted and Lani kicked him hard in the shin. "Now that wasn't nice at all, was it? I think we'll go for another block or two after that little stunt."

Lani threw her head back in frustration. "Please put me down."

Carr stopped, his arms still wrapped around her as he talked quietly into her ear. If she wasn't so mad, his breath on her skin would have flooded her with goosebumps, but for the moment, she was immune to his charm, mostly anyway. However, she still felt a tiny bit of disturbing pleasure at having him so close to her. "If you try to take off, I'll just pick you up again, so don't test me. I think we both know I'm much stronger than you."

"FINE." Lani waited to be released then instantly turned and faced him. "What are you doing?"

Carr grabbed her arm and began walking again, forcing her to stay by his side. "Walking," he said calmly as if he'd done absolutely nothing out of the ordinary.

"What are you doing with me?" Lani tried again, wondering what it was going to take to get a straight answer out of him.

"Walking," he repeated as if she didn't get it the first time.

"Fine. Where are we going?" Lani shook her head in defeat, knowing this conversation was going nowhere.

"You'll see."

Lani spat out a puff of air and shook her head again. "There's just no winning with you, is there?"

He tugged her arm, forcing her to look at him. "Now that remains to be seen, doesn't it?"

Lani turned around. "I don't know what you're up to, but I don't I'll like it."

"Again," Carr said. "That remains to be seen." He kept his grip on her arm, keeping her close to his side as they disappeared down the sidewalk and into the night air.

Chapter 16

Carr led Lani down an alley and although it was dark, the surroundings were still familiar. It was the alley to the bar where the bike was at. Lani walked along by his side, his hand still holding her arm as if she were a lost child or one who had just tried to run away and was now being hauled back to her room by an angry parent.

"Ouch." She wavered, trying to catch her balance from a hole in the dirt her foot slipped in to. She felt Carr instantly grab for her, catching her by the waist and stopping her from hitting the ground.

He pulled her up, his face close to hers, and looked down into her eyes through the yellow light of the alley lamp. For a second, he said nothing and let his eyes roam her face. Her makeup was darker than usual and although it accentuated her eyes, the red on her lips was all wrong. "That's not your color." He didn't give her a chance to respond; instead, he lifted his hand and wiped them clean with his thumb.

"Like you know my color," Lani retorted, trying to hide the way her body quivered under his touch. She felt herself shake and wondered if he could feel her skin pulsate with the rush of energy he just caused.

He leaned into her slightly and cocked his head, his nose almost touching hers. "I'd say I'm a pretty good guesser." He wanted to let his body go the rest of the way into hers, landing his lips gently on hers but feared her reaction. She was already pretty mad at him for carrying her out of the bar and halfway down the sidewalk and now down an alley that he didn't want to make matters worse with an unwelcomed kiss.

And besides that, he didn't know if he would be able to stop with just a kiss. Being this close to her was already playing with fire the way she caused his blood to boil. He knew for a fact he wouldn't be able to simply just taste her then pull away. There would be no stopping him once he started. He wanted more than a kiss from her. He wanted all of her. He wanted to consume her whole and savor every tiny taste. No. He couldn't kiss her. Not yet. Not in an alley and not when she seemed to have forgotten who she was. He pulled back. "You really should watch where you're going. I'm not always going to be around to save you all the time."

"You didn't save me." Lani tried to pull her arm free as he pulled away but his grip had not loosened. She started to shake her arm as if she just spotted a giant spider on it and was about to lose all signs of sanity to get him to let go of her. "And I don't need you to guide me down the damn road. I'm a big girl. I can walk by myself."

"Now, that remains to be seen, doesn't it?" He released her arm, knowing they were almost there anyway. "Come on." He began to take off but then stopped and turned back. Lani was still standing there, arms folded across her chest in a gesture of defiance.

He took a step toward her and lowered his voice. "Oh, I see." Lani watched him slip a challenging smile across his lips. "You want me to carry you again, don't you? Okay," He lifted his hands. "You don't have to play hard to get, you know. All you have to do is say so. You could say, 'Carr, I want you to carry me. I really like the way I feel in your big, strong arms. Please do it again'. He raised his eyebrows in playful mockery. "Go ahead, now you try it."

Lani's arms shot down like lead weights to her sides and she let out a loud sound of frustration. "Don't you touch me. I can walk on my own." She took off and Carr quickly caught up to her side. "You're so unbelievable," she spat out.

"You have no idea."

Seconds later, Carr opened the back door to the garage and motioned for Lani to go in first. He flipped on the lights then shut the door. Music and loud voices were muffled from the walls to the bar upfront. It filled the space with noise, although conversation was still audible between the two of them. However, Lani didn't feel like talking at the moment. She had no idea why Carr had taken her away and brought her here, and he wasn't offering any help on the matter, so what was the point on asking further. She decided to just wait and see what he did.

He walked over to a large, baby blue old fashioned refrigerator and pulled the metal lever to open the door. He retrieved two beers, opened them and walked over to her. "Here." He extended his arm, but she only turned around and faced her back to him.

"Suit yourself."

Lani let her eyes scan the place for the bike but she didn't see it. She wanted to ask, but that would mean talking, and she wasn't giving in so fast. She would just have to find out later where the bike was, it's not like he was going to keep it. She slowly walked around the shop, looking at the old pieces of furniture that were there. There were a few end tables, a dresser, an old bookcase that was partially sanded, and an antique record player sitting on a counter next to a jukebox.

She went closer to get a better look at the jukebox. It was covered in a thick film of dust and grease, but she could still make out a few songs through the yellow stained window. *I Love Rock n' Roll, Manic Monday*...... She reached up and wiped the glass, but the film was equally as thick on the inside of the glass doing little to clear her view of the other song titles. She turned and her eyes fell upon a beautiful coffee table in the corner. It looked as if it was made from old barn wood as chips of red paint were still stuck on the planks that formed the top. Something drew her in, transfixing her gaze longer than she wanted until she forced herself away. When she turned, she found Carr looking at her like she had been looking at the table. She wanted to tell him to stop it, but that would mean speaking to him, and she still wasn't ready to do that.

Instead, she just looked back at him and raised her eyebrows as if saying, ‘now what’.

Without a word, he left and went through the door leading out to the bar. He didn’t shut the door behind him and Lani wondered if she was supposed to follow him. She looked around and tapped her foot while thinking over her options. She could follow him, stand there and wait for him to return, or leave. “Sounds like a no-brainer to me.” She turned to head out the alley door, but as she did, Carr returned. This time he shut the door muffling the noise once again and walked straight to her, carrying something in his hand.

“And where do you think you’re going?”

Lani faced him, her patients now wearing thin with these games and spoke. “What am I doing here, Carr? I’m supposed to be at work. You took me away from my job and other important things. I was in the middle of something right before you showed up and pulled your little Neanderthal act.”

“Don’t worry about your job. It’ll be fine.”

“What makes you so sure? Do you have a magic wand you wave to fix everything you mess up, or am I just supposed to take your word?”

“I know the owner. You’ll be fine. Trust me.”

“I don’t even know the owner and I work there. How do you know him?”

Carr shrugged. “I know a lot of people, and he’s one of them, so again trust me. You’re absolutely fine.”

Lani took a deep breath. His tone was solid, reassuring and she felt like maybe he was telling the truth. Her shoulders fell from the release of tension and she looked at him, her eyes soft but her voice serious. "What am I doing here, Carr?"

He lifted his hand. "You forgot this. I had it in the bike basket but brought it in here, hoping you'd come by."

"What? What is that?" She took the item from his hand and unfolded it. "The T-shirt from the bar? You brought me all the way over here in the middle of my shift for this?" Her eyes widened and he knew a battle was coming. She was prime for eruption and he felt as if he just turned up the pressure a bit too far. "Are. You. Kidding. Me?"

Lani took a step closer to him with each word. Her steps as firm as her tone.

Carr only smiled. "It looked like you needed help dressing tonight, being's how you forgot half your clothes and all. See, here I am again saving the day. Seriously, Lani, how have you made it through life this far without me? It's a wonder you haven't been run over or arrested for indecent exposure already."

She cocked her head to the side. "Well, I have been ran over, remember? You're the one who almost killed me in the middle of the street. I'm starting to think you did hit your head. If you had been paying attention to where you were going, I wouldn't have been knocked viciously off my bike and splattered onto the pavement. And speaking of the bike, where is it?"

"I'll tell you when you put the shirt on."

"I'm not putting this shirt on."

"Lani?" His voice was determined.

"What?"

"You're boobs are falling out. Put the shirt on."

She darted her eyes to her chest, then back up to him. "No, they're not." And that was true; they weren't falling out, at least not by much. But if she were honest, she knew a mere sneeze would have those babies right out and into full view.

Carr only looked at her as if knowing at any second she was going to give in, but she wasn't going to, at least she wasn't planning on it but then the words that followed rendered her all but defenseless. "You're way too beautiful for that dress. It's not you. Put the shirt on." He closed the gap between them, reached for the shirt, then slipped it over her head, helping her arms through the sleeves. He then tugged it down over her waist and looked at her. "When you're refinishing something rare and priceless, you have to be careful not to strip it down too much or you run the risk of losing all the character that made it so beautiful in the first place."

Lani swallowed, feeling something inside melt, causing her to want to defend her actions. "I was trying to help out some friends."

"Nothing wrong with that. Just don't lose sight of who you are in the process." He didn't give her a chance to respond. Instead, he reached down and grabbed her hand and the next thing she knew, he was leading her through the door to the bar.

Just as Lani had expected from the noise she had heard in the garage, the place was packed with people and roaring with music. Carr led her to a seat behind the bar and leaned in to talk close to her ear. His hot breath almost tickling her as he spoke. “If you don’t drink beer, what can I get you?”

Lani shook her head. She really had no idea. It wasn’t that she didn’t drink beer, but she didn’t drink any alcohol other than the other night with Nikki and Sarah. Her life up to this point had never called for a celebration or a night out or even a night in. She simply was an alcoholic virgin, not to mention a virgin of another kind as well, but that was beside point at the moment, although spending time with Carr made that more of the point than she ever realized. The way he carried her, the way he touched her, even the way he said her name told her she had to be careful around him. He made her weak and she wasn’t sure where that weakness might lead, especially if he was seeing someone else right now.

“Um,” she began but stopped mid-sentence when she caught a glimpse of Calli in the crowd. *Holy hell, there’s no escaping her, is there.* “On second thought, I’m really not in the mood to be at a bar. Do you mind if we go?”

“Not at all.” Carr took Lani by the hand and they slipped through the crowd unnoticed by Calli, or so

Lani thought. But when she was at the door, Lani turned to find Calli glaring at her with daggers in her eyes. Lani looked away, subconsciously tightening her hand around Carr's as they went out into the night. Lani didn't know what was going on between herself and Carr, or him and Calli for that matter, but at this very second, she didn't care. She never expected to be the girl with the guy and didn't know what to do with that exactly, except enjoy it. She didn't know why if Carr was seeing Calli, he seemed to have an interest in her. All she knew was the feeling she had every time he touched her, and with his hand wrapped tightly over hers, she felt as if she had just won one small battle. Although, she knew the war to follow might be a very different story.

Chapter 17

As soon as they were out on the street, Lani slipped her hand free of Carr's. As she did, he looked sideways at her to gauge her expression, but before he could look long enough, she glanced over at him.

"What?" Her tone was harsh. "Why are you staring at me?"

"Why are you so defensive? I'm not going to hurt you, Lani?"

She swallowed and looked away. Although he had just dragged her out of work and down several blocks with his arms locked tightly around her, she knew he was right. A person could usually tell if someone meant them harm. A deep, disturbing knot in their gut or a warning bell that won't stop ringing, but not with Carr. Even when he wouldn't let her go, Lani knew she wasn't in any danger.

"So, why did you? Take me out of work, that is? I actually do have a lot of bills and tips are pretty good on the weekends. I can't make that up." She spoke while looking into the night crowd on the streets. Austin was a busy city 24 hours a day and she loved that about this place. It was warm and the air pulsed with energy and life and freedom. Nothing like the icy cave she grew up in.

"You needed me. Why else would I do it? You just didn't know it at the time," he said as if she just asked the most obvious question ever. "And I told you not to worry about work. I can fix that."

"Who are you, Superman?" Lani's voice tinged with sarcasm as she stepped sideways to let a large group pass between them.

"Whoa," a voice from the crowd said and a rather large built guy made his way over to Lani. "Well, hello, beautiful." He came closer and it took Lani a second before she realized he was talking to her. She watched his eyes slowly sculpt her body.

"Excuse me? I don't believe I know you." She eyed him right back.

"Maybe we could spend the evening changing that."

When the thickness of the crowd passed, Carr could see Lani or rather the guy standing inches in front of her with a stance of a predator and something inside of him went off.

Carr was by her side within seconds and his body seemed to grow as he looked at the guy lingering in close to her. Carr's shoulders came back, his chest swelled, his neck stiffened and his arms bowed out from his sides, but even with all of that, Carr was still half a foot shorter and two feet more narrow than the man flirting with Lani. Nevertheless, Carr's eyes became hard. "She's with me." His tone sounded as a warning shot right before an attack. If the guy didn't back down, Carr wouldn't hesitate to strike.

Carr couldn't blame the guy for stopping, though. Even with the shirt pulled down over Lani's dress, she was still sexy. The dress was so short that one could see most of her slender legs and the heels she wore only accentuated the toned muscles of her cafes. The muscles one gets from walking miles upon miles a day from waiting tables. And the soft, full curls of her long dark hair were mesmerizing against the blue of the shirt. She looked like an angel straight off the staircase from heaven. One that made men weak and vulnerable and even act like fools.

The guy pulled back from Lani and looked over to Carr. For a second, neither of them spoke, sizing the other up, mentally playing out their next move when a voice sounded from out from the distance. "Gates, let's go. You're holding us up."

The guy kept his glare on Carr for a long second before glancing back to Lani. "I'll see you around." His voice was soft but Lani didn't respond.

"I wouldn't bet on it," Carr said then reached for Lani. His hand slipped into hers while his eyes stayed on the guy's face.

"Whatever." He stepped back and turned away to go join the group that was slowly growing impatient.

Carr tugged on Lani and she moved in step beside him, her hand still in his. This time she didn't pull away. If she were to ask him why he did that, she was already sure of the answer: *Because you needed me. Wasn't it obvious?* Did she need him? Would that guy have done something? *Who's knows*, she thought and instead of thinking on it further, focused of the way her hand felt wrapped inside his. She was an average size girl, more on the petit side really, something that was only amplified in Carr's presence. He was a good half-foot taller than she was, with a lean but broad build and enough muscle to carry her effortlessly down the street for what had felt like forever. His arms had swallowed her whole, just the way his hand was doing to hers right now. Her grip all but disappeared in his and she couldn't help but glance down and look. Her fingertips were barely visible around his palm, just poking out on the edge of his hand. She liked the way it looked. The way it made her feel.

Her heart smiled as if someone had reached in and tickled her from the inside.

She didn't know the protocol for someone who had just grabbed your hand while attempting to save you from the advances of a stranger, and whether the act was innocent or not, what do you do with it now? She wondered if she should just let it happen, see where it took her. See how far they would walk before he released her. But then that thought filled her with a terrifying feeling and she instantly pulled away.

She had to, before he did.

Lani slipped her hand free and in its absence, an awkward void slipped in and stalled in the space between them. She couldn't bring herself to look at him, so she kept her eyes on the crowd ahead. Carr did the exact opposite. He couldn't think of anything or anyone he wanted to look at more than Lani, especially when she kept pulling away from him. He tilted his head ever so slightly and watched her watching the night. He didn't know why she wouldn't let him hold her, but for now he would let it pass. For now.

"I guess I'll just head home," Lani said, her tone flat.

"I guess you'll do no such thing." Carr wasn't about to let her go. The night was still young and the only thing on his mind was trying to figure out the mysteries Lani tried to hide away from the rest of the world so well. She may not want to tell him, but that wouldn't stop him from trying to find out for himself.

"Well, then, it's back to work I go."

"Wrong again."

Lani stopped and whirled around. "Who made you the dictator of my night all of a sudden? I'm a big girl with a mind of my own, and I don't need a chaperone."

"Okay. Good point. How about a date then?"

"You mean with you?"

"No. I mean with steroid junkie back there. I was just about to go track him down and drag him back so the two of you could hit it off."

Lani shook her head as a large dose of hesitation swept in and camped right next to the large helping of restless nerves stomping around in the pit of her stomach and she couldn't wrap her head around what to do with it all.

She was no good with people, she was no good with friends, and she certainly was no good with guys. Thoughts she had lived by for a long time now and they had served her well. For that creed had kept her from ever hearing those ugly words from her childhood again and she wanted to keep it that way.

She bit her lip for a second, gathering her words. "Carr, I'm not really the dating type. I've got a lot on my plate right now, and there's just not a lot of room for extras."

"Okay, I'll take it," he said without hesitation and eased in to her, his eyes full of softness. He wasn't about to let her go yet. Not without spending more time with her. He didn't care how long or short it was.

"You'll take what? I just said I don't have room in my life for anything right now."

"No, you didn't. You said there's not A LOT of room and to that, I responded: I'll take it. Whatever tiny, little spot you have, I'll take."

"That's not exactly what I meant."

"Too late. That's what you said and there are no take-backs."

Lani let her eyes soak into his face and focus on the warmth in his eyes. A warmth that beckoned her to join him. To let herself open up just a crack and see what it could melt away inside her.

"Okay," she whispered, feeling as if the answer was coming from someone other than her. Feeling like someone else had slipped inside her and was taking over, making her decisions for her and all she wanted to do was let it happen. She pushed the fear of regret from her thoughts. "Okay," she repeated louder this time. "What are we going to do?"

"First," Carr began as he inched in closer. "I am going to take your hand and you're not going to pull away." Their eyes locked for a second before he slowly reached for her and let his fingers slide between hers. Lani felt a beautiful sensation rise over her as if someone had just blasted her with hot air full of dreams, if there was such a thing. She bit her bottom lip from nerves but didn't avert her eyes from his.

Carr liked the way she looked at him. He could tell his touch affected her and wondered if she could tell hers did the same for him. The way her small hand made him feel stronger as he held it safely in his own, not wanting anything or anyone to harm her. He could tell she had been hurt. The way she constantly responded with such defensiveness, the way she always refused to be held, even as something as small as a hand. He had dated enough girls to tell when one had been wounded. Most of them were not just confident but downright conceited, which he hated. He enjoyed a strong personality, which he saw overtly in Lani, but something was holding her back. Something had her in a cage and he was bound and determined to set her free.

"Now," he let a smile slip across his face as he saw her eyes light up. "I know the perfect place. You'll going to love it."

"We'll see about that," Lani said out of the corner of her mouth.

Carr fought the urge to reach up and gently touch her lips. He imagined his thumb softly gliding over them as he watched the reaction on her face. *Oh, the many ways I could make you smile, Lani.* The very thought of what he would do made his pulse quicken and blood rush to parts of him that if he didn't stop, were about to cause a whole lot of trouble.

He took a deep breath then turned away, pulling her to his side. They walked down the sidewalk in the night air, her body close to his, exactly where she belonged. Moments later, they were walking through a door to see a cover band sing Coldplay songs. The place was dim with a soft blue glow coming from lights lining the walls. The center of the room was filled with tables packed with people drinking and laughing and socializing. Something Lani wasn't a pro at. Most of time, she wasn't even comfortable around people, let alone relaxed as they seemed to be. Women were sitting on guys' laps, drinking and laughing and kissing. Others were parked up next to each other, obviously enjoying what looked like a girls' night out.

Lani felt a tiny pang of hurt somewhere deep inside at the emptiness of never having those memories that she was witnessing now. Nowhere in her life had she sat around a table and laughed with such freedom and such friends.

She felt Carr tug her and she obliged. He led them up to the bar, then let go of her hand and instantly slipped his hands around her waist. He lifted her off the ground, gently setting her up on a barstool.

"You didn't have to do that. I can sit by myself."

"I wanted to," he whispered then looked at her, keeping the distance close between them. "What do you want to drink?"

Lani shook her head, trying to stay calm as her face rushed with heat. She loved having him next to her. His gentle yet firm touch. The way she always imagined a guy's touch would be. His soft breath on her cheek sent tingles down her neck and she fought not to react. "I'm not too experienced with drinking." She stared back at him, letting her eyes lock into his.

"Do you trust me?" He gave her a half-smile, the kind that fills you full of suspicion coupled with anticipation of what may follow.

"That sounds like a loaded question." She bit her bottom lip again, a horrible habit she knew she would have to quit before she chewed it right off, but for now, it helped her focused and not think about the way his cologne smelled like an invitation to a dangerous world. A world she just might jump into if she didn't keep her wits about her. She put her fingers on his chest and gently pushed him back.

He stood upright and looked down at her, a glint of amusement in his eyes. He turned and ordered two drinks which the bartender made in front of them then pushed them over to Carr, who paid then handed one to Lani.

"And here you go."

Lani took the glass and looked at it carefully, suddenly feeling like one of the drunken girls she waits on at work. Images of girls too drunk to stand and being carried out by guys they just met dashed through her mind and she hesitated.

"What?" Carr looked at her. "You don't want it?"

One drink isn't going to make you suddenly strip down to your panties and go crazy on the bar, she told herself. *It's just one drink.* She then lifted the glass to her lips and took a sip. "Wow. This is good. What is it? I've never seen it?"

"For someone who delivers drinks all night, I can't believe you don't know what this is."

"Hey, just because I bring people alcohol doesn't mean I know all about the stuff. I just repeat what they order to the bartender. I don't sample it all."

"Glad to hear it. I would hate to think of you as an alcoholic at such a young age."

"Look who's talking." Lani gave a playful smirk, which only made Carr huff with amusement.

He then ordered them another round and Lani tried to hear the name, but the noise around her blocked his voice. When the drink came, he set it into the palm of her hand and tapped his glass to hers. "I promise to take good care of you, Lani. I won't let you get plastered or take advantage of you. So enjoy." And he meant it. There was no denying that he wanted to get close to her, but only with her full and sober permission. Preying on drunken women was never something he had or would ever do. Carr considered hunting helpless girls repulsive. Not a trait on his character list. "However," he raised an eyebrow, "I'm fully opened if you would like to take advantage of me. I know it can be hard to keep your hands to yourself, so I'm available for squeezing at any time."

"Oh, really?" Lani swallowed down the restless feeling his invitation spurred in her. "I can promise you there will be no squeezing tonight."

"Well, that's a shame," he whispered close to her, then downed the second drink. Lani did the same as thoughts of him camped out in her head. She wanted to be with him. She knew that the tingling in her stomach was pure attraction to him. There was no denying that. There was something about him that made her want to forget the rest of the world and lose herself somewhere in the night with him, maybe slip through a portal to a place where she was a different girl, someone worthy of him. Someone good enough to belong on his arm in front of the world. Someone he could be proud of. But until such a portal opened, she'd have to settle on the mystery drinks. They were doing a pretty good job of making her feel as if she were already slipping down a rabbit hole all by themselves.

She grinned at him, and it reminded Carr of a little girl who just finished playing in the rain. A look of pure bliss lost in an innocence only nature could bring. Unlike the greed of his past girlfriends who would rather fight their way through a stampede over a sale of Jimmy Choo shoes or a Gucci handbag. But not this girl. Not Lani. She seemed so perfectly and fully content just standing by his side in clothes he wouldn't be able to name for the life of him, and he liked it that way. She was beautiful. She was genuine and he felt himself being pulled further into her.

Lani watched him watching her as songs of Coldplay drifted through the air. She couldn't help but smile, maybe it was because he was so close, maybe it was those damn nerves or even the alcohol already causing the heavy air to spin around her, or maybe it was simply him. His eyes on her made her feel as if he was leading her through that portal that very instant, and all she wanted to do was fall with him.

He reached up and took a long strand of her hair between his fingers. "It's hard for me to keep my hands off you. Where have you been all this time?"

"Working." Lani focused on keeping her chest steady as not to give away her rapid pulse from his touch. Having him so near made her feel as if all her insides were turning to water and he was the moon that controlled her currents. His touch was powerful and she found that all she was thinking about was his hand roaming her body.

She swallowed hard, forcing herself to calm the storm and act as normal as possible. Not that she was ever considered a normal girl, so she just aimed for keeping herself together under the influence of his touch, not to mention the drinks that were quickly taking their toll. *Didn't know I was such a lightweight.*

Note to self, never drink with strangers. Good to know, she mentally nodded to herself.

"So close, yet I never knew." Carr took the end of her hair and lightly tickled her face with it.

Lani laughed then reached up, placing her hand on his to stop him. "What does that mean? So close. So close to what?"

"Not what, but who?" He pulled back a tad, not wanting to linger too long. The smell of sweetness rising from her skin was making her unbearable to resist. And he did promise after all.

"Okay." Lani shook her head. "Then *who*?"

"You, of course. Who else would I be talking about?"

She gave him a puzzled look, but he offered no further details. Instead, he grabbed her hand and pulled her away. "Dance with me?" He felt her shudder then pull back. "Um, no. We don't have to dance. We can just sit and talk and listen like we were doing."

Lani had never been to a dance before. Ever. And the thought of Carr seeing that she was clueless on the dance floor made her quiver with dread. She looked up at him, knowing that the best thing to do right now was probably to just leave before he found out that she was a dud, but that was the last thing she wanted to do. She tried to think of the perfect thing to say, but before she had the chance, someone caught her eye. She looked over Carr's shoulder and found Calli and Mandy standing shortly behind him in the distance. Both girls had their arms crossed, tapping a foot and staring at Lani as if she had just been caught after escaping captivity where she was to be served up as a human sacrifice to save the world.

What? Are you following me?! Lani thought, but before she had a chance to see what was going on, Carr turned and followed her gaze. "What the hell?" His voice was loud but Lani couldn't make out his tone. Was he happy, mad, what exactly? Before Lani knew what was happening, Carr was making his way over to them, and by the look of triumphant on Calli and Mandy's faces, that's exactly what they had wanted.

Lani felt an instant pain burn inside her chest. What had she been thinking? What kind of guy was Carr? He seemed so wonderful to her but what if he was just playing her? It was obvious there was something between him and Calli and Lani suddenly felt very betrayed. She forced down the razors emerging in her throat and scolded herself. *What am I even doing with him? Who Am I kidding? Why is he with me when he obviously would rather be with Calli? And who can blame him? She's worlds different than I am. I should have known better. I'll never be the kind of girl someone like Carr wants. My father was right.* And that was the blade she just couldn't swallow. That was the blade that hung in her throat, slicing her deeper the longer she watched Carr push his way through the crowd toward another girl.

Lani couldn't take it. The image of him wrapping Calli in his arms made her feel as if someone had just swung a sledgehammer into her chest, crushing her ability to ever breathe again.

She quickly turned and pushed her way through the crowd in the opposite direction Carr was going. Lani went out the door and didn't stop until she was home, fighting back tears the whole way. She didn't want anyone to see her and she would have made it had it not been for the two intruders standing in her hall.

Chapter 18

Sarah was standing with her back against Lani's door while Nikki sat in front of it, gently rapping the back of her head against it.

As Lani approached, the two girls came to attention as if their captain had just walked into the barracks hall. They all but saluted her as she came closer.

"So...?" Sarah said as Lani stopped to fumble for her keys, hoping to dry her eyes before they noticed.

"What?" Lani pushed past them to get to the door. "What are you both doing here?"

"Getting the details, what do you think?" Nikki said as she and Sarah followed her inside.

"What details?" Lani hung her pocket purse on the first of three doorknobs attached to the wall in a frame that severed as coat hangers. An idea she picked up while visiting the thrift store.

"Oh, please. We saw you get dragged out of work tonight and we came to get the scoop. It looks like someone's been holding out on us." Nikki plopped down on the couch and Sarah followed.

Lani looked at them and they both stared back as if they were children gathered for storytime. "Fine." Lani caved and joined them on the couch. "But I'll tell you upfront, you're fixing to be highly disappointed. *Just like I was*, Lani thought then continued, hoping that she could get through this with her emotions intact. “And just a forewarning, there is no happy ending. But here it goes. I was at the bar sweet-talking Jake as we had planned to see if he'd tell me anything about your missing hash stash-”

“Ha!” Nikki laughed. “That's great. We should change the name to Operation *Hash Stash*.”

“Shut up, Nikki. That's stupid and you're ruining the story.” Sarah slapped her on the thigh. “Continue, Lani. You were saying...”

Nikki rubbed her leg and shot her friend a look of angst.

“Oh, really?” Sarah interjected before Lani started up again. “That hurt? That tiny, little slap actually hurt you?” Sarah teased her friend.

“Maybe it did,” Nikki responded matter of factly.

“With as much pot as you smoke, I'm surprised you can still feel your own tongue half the time.”

“Now, you can shut up. You're ruining Lani's story,” Nikki mimicked then motioned for Lani to continue while still rubbing her thigh in protest.

“As I was saying, I was talking to Jake when that guy showed up and for some reason got mad and carried me out of work. That's it. The end.” Lani tossed her hands in the air as if signally the grand finale of a fireworks show.

“Oh, shut up, Lani. You're lying,” Nikki said playfully.

“Told you you'd be disappointed.” Lani got up and made her way to the kitchen.

"So..." Sarah began with a look of suspicion. "Who's the guy?"

Nikki's eyes glanced to Sarah with a puzzled look. "What are you doing? We know who he is." Her voice was low enough that Lani couldn't hear her.

"I want to see something," Sarah whispered back.

"I don't know, really. His name is Carr and I practically just met him." Lani filled a glass with water and offered it to the girls. They both shook their heads and exchanged a quick look of amusement between them.

Sarah got up and walked closer to the kitchen. "Well, do you know his last name or what he does for a living?" Her eyes darted to a plate of chocolate cupcakes sitting on the bar. "Yum, those look good." Sarah made her way over to the plate, but Lani jumped in front of her.

"No! Those....," Lani panicked, searching for something to say. "They're not ready yet." Lani grabbed the plate and franticly began to empty them into the trash.

"Whoa." Nikki came over to see what was going on. "You said they weren't ready, but you're acting like they were made from a poisonous apple. What the hell, Lani? What's wrong?"

"Uh," Lani fought to regain her composure. She knew she had acted irrationally, or at least to them, but not as far as she was concerned. She was only saving herself from their reaction once they found out she sucked at baking, and she wasn't in the mood for another disappointment tonight. "I think the milk I used was old. I just don't want you to get sick," she lied.

"Sure. No problem. Thanks, I guess." Sarah shrugged then resumed back to the previous topic. "So, *do you* know anything about him?"

"Nope." Lani shook her head, glad that the cupcake incident was over and felt her pulse return to normal. "Although," she hesitated for a moment, her eyes rolling up as if recalling something. "I asked if he was a doctor, but for some reason, he seemed angry with that question. He didn't say much beyond that. I don't know." Lani turned around, opened the fridge, and pulled out a yogurt.

Sarah glanced back to Nikki, who was now standing right behind her.

"Oh my god. She has no idea who he is," Nikki whispered.

"I know," Sarah mouthed back. Both girls shocked at the revelation.

"Should we tell her?"

Sarah shook her head. "No. Let's just see what happens."

Nikki nodded in agreement as Lani turned around. "Yogurt?" she offered.

"Pass," both of them said and walked further into the kitchen. Nikki jumped up and sat on the counter while Sarah leaned against the other side.

"So, are you going to see him again?" Sarah crossed her arms, trying to act as relaxed as possible.

Lani shrugged. "I don't know. I guess I have to. He still has something of mine but, after I get it back, never again." The image of him and Calli flashed back to her, burning the retina of her mind's eye. It was like an image the sun scorches into your eyes, and no matter how tightly you try to shut out the glowing silhouette, it only burns brighter the tighter you squeeze. Lani blinked a few times, trying to get the image to fade. She had to get the topic off of Carr. "Oh," she suddenly said. "I almost forgot. Did you have any luck with Jake after I left?"

"Hell no. Not even a peep." Nikki's shoulders deflated as if finally admitting defeat. "We tried but he's not talking. At least not to us."

"We're going to have to approach this differently." Sarah pushed herself off the counter, ready to dive into a new plan when a knock at the door caused everyone to freeze, including Lani.

"Come on." Nikki bounced off the counter. "Let's go see who it is." Nikki filled with excitement as she went to the door, Sarah quickly on her heels. They were both hoping the same thing, that it was the very guy they were just whispering about.

They stopped at the door to let Lani pass. She peek through the hole to see who it was then shot the girls a quick look. "Speak of the devil." Lani pulled the door opened to find Carr standing on the other side with his hands pushed down deep into his pockets. Nikki and Sarah stood hidden behind the door.

"Hey." His voice was soft and Lani had to force herself not to melt under its warmth, despite how hurt she was. "What happened to you? I went back to get you but you were gone."

"What do you want?" Her tone was hard and he knew she was angry at him.

"I just wanted to invite you to a get together I'm having tomorrow down at the lake around noon. I want you to come."

Just as she was about to open her mouth with a harsh refusal, Nikki and Sarah popped out from behind the door. Carr's face washed over in surprise, but before he could say anything, Sarah accepted his invitation. "She'll be there. We'll make sure of it."

"And so will we," Nikki threw in, then quickly shut the door and with it, shutting out Carr's chance to say anything else.

"What?" Lani twirled around and stared wide-eyed at both of them. "What did you just do? I don't want to go anywhere with him. He has a girlfriend, and I am not getting in the middle of that!" Lani delved past them, feeling the hurt burn the inside of her skin like she had just swallowed flames in a circus act.

"What do you mean he has a girlfriend? Who?" Sarah was on Lani's heels, ready to begin an interrogation. She wanted details and was ready to get Lani to spill what she knew.

Lani walked over to the fridge again and opened it once more out of frustration. She wasn't used to having people around, especially ones asking her questions and accepting invitations on her behalf. She stood there and let the cool air soothe her burning face, trying to avoid letting Sarah or Nikki know just how much she really liked Carr. She couldn't help it and she only hated herself more that he still affected her even after what she saw tonight.

"Someone I wait tables with at *TED's*." Lani called over her shoulder. "Her name is Calli."

"Oh, my, god. That poor girl," Nikki whispered with a mixture of something between sadness and amusement.

"We've got to help her," Sarah whispered through the small gaps of her fingers covering her mouth, trying to block out her reaction. It was an innocent laugh. They liked Lani but knew she was clueless. "We've *got* to help her," Sarah repeated and looked at Nikki sternly.

Nikki nodded. "We will."

The girls dropped their hands as Lani shut the fridge and turned toward them. "I really don't want to go tomorrow. I don't want to see him again." Her voice was now the one that sounded like defeat and Sarah instantly moved to her. She wrapped her arm over Lani's shoulder as a mother hen protecting her chick and gave her a light squeeze.

"Trust me on this, Lani. You'll be glad you went."

"Yep." Nikki nodded. "It's what's best and don't worry. We'll be there with you. If Calli shows up, I'll drown her in the lake and do the world a favor."

"You act like you know her." Lani exhaled.

Nikki and Sarah exchanged a quick glance then Sarah took Lani by both shoulders. “I hate to say this, but I think you may need our help with your wardrobe for tomorrow.

“Not this time.” Lani’s eyes darted between Nikki and Sarah as she thought of the way Carr had put that shirt on her. The words he had said still hung with her, and despite his relationship with her archenemy, those words were like diamonds to a kid on welfare, ones she wanted to keep forever and never sell. She’d starve before she let go of that treasure. “I think I’ll just go as myself. No offense, but it’s just who I am.”

Something inside Sarah and Nikki suddenly felt very small and ashamed. They both looked at Lani as if seeing her in a whole new light. A light that made them regret ever having said anything snide about her at all. They were already starting to genuinely like her, but now it was something more.

Something like friendship.

Chapter 19

Around noon the next day, there was a knock at Lani's door. She knew it was Sarah and Nikki to pick her up as promised, although she still didn't know why they were so quick to insist that she attend something that Carr had set up.

She dressed in a poofy layered white cotton skirt, a navy tank, and flip flops. The skirt reminded her of something Cindy Lauper would wear in an MTV video and had a fun feel to it, although she feared that today would be anything but fun. She wore her swimming suit underneath, just in case. She wasn't intending on getting wet, but she was going to the lake and wanted to be prepared just the same. Her long dark hair was pulled back in a looped ponytail as usual and already had a few strands breaking away and resting along the curves of her face. She tucked them behind her ears and went to the door.

"Oh, Ms. Belsky."

"You were expecting someone else, dear?" The woman tilted her head with intrigue. "Just who might that be? Unless..." She narrowed her eyes and glanced over Lani, "that fine-looking boy from the other day is on his way. If that's the case, I need to go change into something a bit more fitting, say one of my sundresses with a beautiful hat. And speaking of dresses, you look like a lovely flash from the 80's today. Just lovely, Lani."

Lani knew Ms. Belsky meant her comments, both: the one about changing into something sexier and how Lani looked and this alone reaffirmed her decision to stick to what she was comfortable with and not what Sarah and Nikki had wanted.

"Thank you, and no, that young man is not coming over. I am going to a cookout at the lake."

"Oh, I see. Well, that does sound promising. You've never been one for going out, so what changed?"

"Lani," a voice called from down the hall. "We're here," Nikki said as she and Sarah walked toward them carrying a few heavy trash bags.

"Hello, girls." Ms. Belsky gave a warm smile as Lani introduced everyone. "Well then, I'll leave you at it. Lani, I would love to have you over for tea when you have time."

"Yes, Ms. Belsky. I'll stop by soon."

"Hello, Mrs. Robinson," Sarah said as soon as Lani shut the door.

"She's a very sweet lady." Lani walked over to where the bags were being emptied onto the living room floor.

"It's not an insult. I hope I look that good when I'm her age. But for now, we need your help on looking good now."

"What's all this?" Lani scanned over the piles of clothes strewn about as Sarah and Nikki stood up, hands resting on their hips.

"This," Sarah began, "Is all of my mother's old clothes that she no longer wears. She's a packrat from hell and never throws anything out. So as you can see, if we include all the hand-me-downs she has, we have clothes spanning at least six decades here."

"Yeah, no kidding. But what are you doing with it all?" Lani wondered.

"Nikki and I started talking on the way home last night. If you are going to the party, or whatever it is, dressed in vintage, then so are we."

"We don't want you to feel out of place, and besides, there's power in numbers and all that shit from *Braveheart* or whatever movie it is." Nikki shrugged then began to lift up shirts and hold them to her chest.

Lani watched in silence and blinked rapidly to dry the moisture she felt pooling in her lids. No one had ever done anything like this before. Usually, girls were against her, not with her. Especially girls like Nikki and Sarah, who were attractive and confident and outgoing. Girls like them were never the outcast, yet here they were becoming one for Lani. The very thought of it all grabbed at her chest.

"I like this one." Sarah held up a pink jacket with large shoulder pads and big gold buttons. Nikki looked up and both girls glanced at Lani, then diverted their eyes down into the pile and began strumming through more tops, but not before Lani was able to catch the glistening of tears in their eyes before they had looked away.

Something inside Lani moved. If felt like warm water ran over her as if she just stepped into a hot shower. Without dragging out an awkward moment further, Lani dropped down to the floor and joined in the shuffling. "Let's start with the bottoms then find a top to match."

"What about these?" Nikki held up a pair of hot pink knitted leg warmers.

"Oh, my god!" Sarah lunged through the clothes and grabbed them out of Nikki's hands. "I have to try those on. I remember pictures where my mom was wearing these, she looked hilarious. I made so much fun of her, and now here I am about to do the same!"

"Circle of life, it's the damnedest thing." Lani looked at Sarah and they all started laughing.

Sarah pulled on the leg warmers, then jumped up and began dancing around the room as if in a scene from *Flashdance.* She began to flail her arms about in no particular rhythm and looked more like a girl in the middle of a bee attack than one trying to dance. However, it wasn't until she dragged a chair over and attempted to lie across the front only to have it fold and crash her to the floor that Lani and Nikki lost it. They laughed so hard, they cried. All of them, losing themselves into a pile of memories while forming even better ones of their own. And for the first time ever, Lani was a part of something magical between friends.

****

The three girls showed up to the lake an hour later. Nikki had settled on a short mini skirt with an oversized shirt that hung loosely off her shoulder and wore large loop earrings. Sarah was wearing a pair of parachute pants and one of Lani's tank tops. They parked the car and made their way down to the crowd by the water.

There was a grill already burning and filling the air with a scent of charcoal. A nice companion to the muggy scent of the lake. The girls looked about but didn't spot Carr and now Lani was having second thoughts as they approached. Besides Sarah and Nikki, she didn't know anyone except Carr, and he was nowhere to be seen.

"Hey," Nikki called out as they joined the crowd.

"Yo," a shirtless guy replied, sitting on top of a cooler. "Have a drink." He stood and opened the lid to the ice chest to reveal a treasure of old fashioned bottled Cokes, Root beers, and Orange Crush. "Or," the shirtless guy began as he opened the lid to a second cooler packed with bottled water and Gatorades. "Have one of these."

Lani was surprised. She half expected ice buckets of beer about the place, but neither Nikki nor Sarah seemed to be surprised with what they saw. Nikki walked over and pulled out an Orange Crush then turned back to Sarah and Lani.

"Same," Sarah said as she walked over to Nikki.

Not knowing what else to do, Lani followed. "Sure. I'll take one too."

"Yo," shirtless guy said as he resumed his seat back on the cooler. "You girls up for some tubing? I'm assuming you have swimsuits under those very interesting threads."

"Ha!" Nikki retorted. "Very funny. You have a problem with something?" She was standing close to him and as she asked the question, she leaned over to get right in his face, unintentionally giving him a nice view down her shirt.

"Oh, god no. I love what you're wearing. In fact, I could stare at your, um, clothes all day."

It didn't take Nikki long to see what he was referring to and straightened back up. "Pervert," she said and took a drink.

The guy raised his eyebrows up and down and grinned at Nikki. "When Carr gets backs, we'll take a turn on the tube."

"Where is Carr?" Sarah asked, saving Lani the trouble.

"Out on the boat with Calli and a few others. They'll be back in a few."

Nikki and Sarah instantly looked at Lani and could tell that was the last thing she wanted to hear. Out of instinct, Sarah grabbed Lani's arm. "Don't react. It'll be fine. Just trust us. We're here."

"I know, but so is she." Lani's face looked betrayed and they knew she was getting ready to bolt.

The girls pulled Lani over to the side out of earshot of the others.

"It'll be fine, Lani. Please just trust us." Nikki kept her voice low because judging by the way shirtless guy was about to fall off the ice chest from leaning toward them, he just might be close enough to pick up on their conversation.

"I told you he was seeing her. I don't want to be here. I'm not good at this sort of thing. She already hates me, and I still have to work with her."

"You work with Calli?" Nikki said in surprise.

Sarah, who would have normally elbowed Nikki for such a reaction, was too stunned herself to do anything. "Calli has a job?"

"What's with you two? I told you that last night. How'd you miss it? And you two act like you know something. What am I missing here?" Lani squinted her eyes and looked back and forth between them. "What's going on?"

"Uh...," Sarah started but thankfully was interrupted from someone a few feet over.

"Oh, my god, it's the Breakfast Club."

The three of them turned to find Calli standing there with a group of girls by her side; one of them, of course, was Mandy. "Who the hell invited you?"

"Yo!" Shirtless guy popped up and yelled down to the water to Carr, who was still abroad the boat. The guy cupped his hands to his mouth and shouted, "We're next!"

Carr didn't respond other than a wave of his arm, gesturing him over.

Shirtless guy whipped around to face Nikki. "Ready?"

"Oh, yeah." Nikki nodded with pleasure, knowing that they were taking Lani over to Carr and there wasn't a damn thing Calli could do about it.

"Ready for what?" Calli's hand snapped to her waist, "Hammer Time."

"I'm going to hammer your face," Nikki lunged toward Calli but Sarah pulled her back.

The group circling Calli started laughing, which made Lani want to hammer Calli herself. Perhaps just wrap her hands around Calli's snooty little neck just a tiny bit. Lani knew it was more than just the laughing that was making her so angry. It was more than Call's act of entitlement and demeaning attitude toward everyone who wasn't latched at her waist. Is was that she was here and Carr was here. Why did he show up at her place last night and insist that she come today when he was planning to be with Calli all along?

"Nice and easy," Sarah said to Nikki. "Remember, we have Lani."

Nikki relaxed and she and Sarah both took a step toward Calli. "Oh, please." Calli made a sound of exasperation. "What are you two going to do? Stand around and wait for M.C. Hammer to call for his pants back." Calli gave a look of disgust at Sarah then turned to Nikki. "And who the hell are you supposed to be? The Material Girl. Jesus, you all look like idiots. I guess bad taste is contagious, isn't it, Lani?" She gave Lani a snide smile. Nikki and Sarah could see Lani's jaw tightened.

Sarah eased her way over to Lani and gently took her arm. "We've totally got your back, but whatever you're thinking about doing right this second, just wait," she whispered. "Trust me," Sarah repeated and locked her eyes onto Lani's. She kept them there until Lani gave a slight nod of agreement.

And besides, Lani didn't really know what she was going to do. She knew what she wanted to do, she wanted to reach over and nail Calli's lips together then drag her behind the boat for the pure fun of it. She was sure that would make her feel better, but for now, she decided to do exactly what Sarah had said and just trust her.

Sarah kept hold of Lani's arm and began walking away, Nikki bringing up the rear. When they passed Calli, Sarah gave a huge, fake grin, Lani kept her jaws clenched and Nikki paused right in front of Calli and quietly said, "Guess where we're going?" She didn't wait for an answer before resuming her way right toward the boat where Carr was waiting for them.

Nikki didn't turn around to see Calli's face, but by the angry growl she made, Nikki knew Calli was pissed, something that made dressing like Material Girl totally worth it.

By the time they got to the boat, shirtless guy was already there and yelling up to Carr about taking them on a ride around the lake. However, Carr wasn't listening. His eyes had fallen to Lani as soon as she had gotten close enough for him to recognize that it was her.

His heart melted a little when he saw what she was wearing. Most girls showed up today half-naked. Nothing like a day at the lake to give a girl an excuse to let it all hang out. But Lani showed up in a knee-length skirt and a modest yet perfect tank. "Classy," he said to himself as he watched her look at him. She looked angry and he wondered if she was mad that it was taking a while to finish up the bike or at least give it back to her. He had finished it already but couldn't bring himself to part with it just yet. He liked having an excuse to see her and that bike bought him a free pass.

"Yo? You ready for us?" blond, shirtless guy called out again to Carr.

Carr kept the boat steady to the dock so everyone could climb on. "Yep, all aboard." He stood behind the wheel, wearing a striped muscle shirt and swim trunks. On top of his head sat a tired looking sombrero and there where white stripes of sunblock under his eyes and nose.

He watched Lani carefully step on the deck as if she were half expecting it to slip out from under like it was on a sheet of ice. She then waited for Nikki and Sarah and the shirtless guy along with a handful of others to climb on as well. All wanting to take a turn to be chauffeured in a tube out on the water.

As the group congregated toward the back, Carr kept his eye on Lani, who was doing a particularly good job at pretending she hadn't seen him yet. *I wondered if Nikki and Sarah had anything to do with that,* he thought. Carr knew the girls from work and, therefore, wouldn't put it past either of them to give Lani girl advice on topics she was doing just fine on by herself.

"Glad you made it." Carr winked at Lani as she passed him on her way to the back. Sarah and Nikki watched carefully for her response.

Lani let her eyes rest on his face just long enough to see his wink then darted her stare toward the water, completely ignoring him.

He chuckled then pulled the boat out, turned around and headed out to the center of the lake.

"Yo, Material Girl. You gonna swim in that mini skirt?"

"I didn't plan on it." Nikki, while sitting on the bench that lined the edge of the boat, slipped off her skirt and top, revealing a neon green two piece, which looked amazing against her deep brown skin.

"Whoa...." shirtless guy stared and after a few seconds, Sarah slapped his jaw shut, causing him to chomp down on his tongue. "Ow." He jerked his head around to Sarah. "That really hurt," he said as if talking with a mouth full of cotton.

"Didn't you momma teach you it's not nice to stare."

"I was just enjoying the scenery the way God intended. He's the one that created it after all," he looked back over to Nikki, "maybe you should slam his jaw shut."

"Wow, a man of deep thought." Sarah rolled her eyes. "But then again, you two sound perfect for each other. What's your name?"

"Yo, I'm Ty."

"Great." Sarah grabbed his arm and drug him over to Nikki. "Ty, Nikki, Nikki, Ty." Sarah then left and went back to sit with Lani.

"What are you doing?" Lani said as she watched Nikki begin to blush as soon as Ty sat close to her.

"They're a match made in heaven. Nikki's in the process of frying her brain cells with weed and it's obvious that our boy here already has."

Lani laughed and watched as Ty leaned in close to Nikki and said something that made her smile. "How'd you know she would like him?"

"Nikki and I have been friends since third grade. I can pick out who she'll end up with at a party before she's even stepped a foot in the door."

Lani nodded then looked away and let her eyes scan the blue water. She'd missed out on so much growing up. How nice it would have been to have someone that close to you. Someone who knew what color of lipstick you should wear or what hairstyle looked best on you. Someone you could call when your heart was broken and would let you cry with them over ice cream and old movies, not even caring what it would do to their figure. Someone who would call just to check on you after a bad day or come over when you're still sleeping and jump on your bed to get you up because they couldn't wait to start the day just hanging out with you.

"Hey." Sarah nudged her. "Do you want to go down below and change into your swimsuit? I know you have it on already, but I'm not sure if you're comfortable changing in front of all these strangers."

Lani hesitated but then shook her head. "No. If Nikki can do it then so can I."

"That a girl." Sarah smiled. "Come on, we'll do it together."

The two of them eased off their clothes and within seconds, Lani was standing carefully by the bench folding her skirt and tank top when all of a sudden, the boat swerved sharply sending everyone stumbling to the other side.

"What the hell are you doing, Carr? That sombrero blocking your view?" a guy yelled out as he pulled himself back up to his feet.

"Sorry. There was something in the water," Carr yelled, gland no one knew he was lying. He had glanced back to check on Lani and saw her standing there in a two-piece bikini. He was somewhat stunned by what he'd seen. He had her pegged for a one-piece type of girl and seeing her standing there in a black top and black and white polka dot bottoms threw him for a loop. Everything was completely covered, not that she had much to hide. Her breast were on the smaller side, especially compared to Nikki's or even Sarah's. Her waist was tiny and her skin was pale, yet everything about her was absolutely stunning. And the longer Carr had stared at her, the more perfect she looked. But then the whole steering the boat thing had abruptly interrupted his view.

He slowed down once they reached the center of the lake and turned around, still keeping one hand on the wheel. "Who's first?"

There were two inner tubes tied to the back of the boat with rope and one oversized raft in the center of the tubes.

"We'll go." Ty shot up and grabbed two life jackets from the pile in the center. He tossed one to Nikki then slipped his on. When the jackets were secured, they both jumped overboard and swam out to the inner tubes.

"I'm going," another guy said as he followed suit with the jacket and was quickly joined with the two girls he had been talking to.

Three others stayed on the boat with Lani and Sarah.

Carr waited for everyone to give the signal before taking off again, slowly picking up speed as they skimmed over the water. He kept the boat straight while still stealing glimpses back at Lani.

Lani sat on the bench on her knees as she watched Nikki being thrown about behind the boat. The wake bounced the tubes, throwing them high in the air then slamming them back down again. But no matter how hard the water treated Nikki, all she did was laugh and fight to hold on until finally, she flew off after one too many hits.

"Man down," Sarah called and Carr slowed the boat.

Everyone watched as Ty let go of his tube and swam back to where Nikki was.

As the boat rocked gently on the waves, Carr turned, hoping to talk to Lani, but as he watched her sitting and laughing at Nikki all he wanted to do was stare at her. It was the first time he had seen her having such a good time that it felt wrong to disturb her, so he just observed. No one saw him; everyone was turned around giving him the perfect opportunity to soak in her beauty undetected.

Her skin was the color of vanilla ice cream, her hair like a soft, warm dream, her laughter the sound of his favorite song, and her smile...her smile was a bullet straight to his heart.

He stood there and stared at her for so long that he hadn't even noticed when Sarah had turned and was now watching him. When he finally felt eyes on him, he looked at her and neither said a word. They both knew. A look like that was unmistakable. They knew he had fallen for the quiet, odd, and somewhat reserved fair maiden.

Sarah gave a half-smile at Carr and he wondered what she was up to. Would she be friend or foe? His thought was interrupted with the yelling from the water, letting him know they were set for round two. He waved back then slowly took off again and just the same as before, within a few minutes, someone else had flown off and the process repeated. This went on for about five more rounds until the first group was abused enough and ready for a break. When they all climbed back up, Sarah, Lani and the few of the others strapped on and dove in.

With Lani in the water, Carr found steering to be even more of a chore. All he wanted to do was watch her, but since that was out of the question, he focused on driving as gently as possible, but the water was rough and before long, Lani went flying off, slamming back down into the hard surface. Carr watched for her to come back up but she was taking too long, something that made Carr very anxious.

"Ty, take the wheel," he commanded and before anyone knew what was going on, Carr dove overboard and headed straight to where Lani had gone under.

Chapter 20

Within minutes, she finally resurfaced and Carr felt an indescribable feeling in his chest, the thought of her getting hurt had consumed him like a fire burning through a haystack and seeing her face quickly extinguished that burning fear. "Are you okay?" Carr spat as soon as she popped out of the water. He swam up close to her, stopping only inches away.

"Yeah, I'm fine." She pushed her wet hair out of her face. "Just hit. a little. hard is all. Knocked the air. out of me for a second." Her words were chopping as she tried to get air back into her lungs.

Without thinking, Carr placed his hands on her arms and lifted her further out of the water. He had to see for himself that she wasn't hurt.

"What. Are you doing? I said. I'm fine. I don't need to be carried back."

"I wasn't going to carry you. I was just double-checking."

For some reason, that comment set her off. "Oh, really. I'm the one that has a problem with telling the truth, am I?"

"No, that's not what I meant. I just know how girls are. You know, they say they're fine but any guy in his right mind knows better. I didn't mean to make you mad. I was just checking on you, Lani." Carr had eased her down but still remained close, treading water while watching her carefully.

"I'm fine, thank you very much, so why don't you just go check on your little girlfriend."

Sarah was not far away and could hear their conversation. So at that comment, she dived off the raft and swam over but not before Lani had taken off toward the boat.

"What the hell does that mean? Lani!" He called. "Lani!" But as he started after her, Sarah swam in front of him and cut him off.

"Whoa, there, big boy. Not so fast."

"Out of my way. There's something wrong with her and I'm damn sure going to find out what."

Sarah grabbed his arm, preventing him from leaving. "Not if you want a shot with her, you won't."

Carr stopped and eyed Sarah. "What are you talking about? What's going on?" Sarah waited to answer, trying to give Lani a head start, but Carr continued. "And while we're at it, you want to tell me what you two were doing at her place last night? Lani has nothing in common with either of you."

"Stop being so defensive and just listen." Sarah released his arm to keep herself afloat. Treading water wasn't easy and she was already getting tired, even with the life jacket.

"What?" Carr shook his head, trying to wrap his mind around Lani being friends with Sarah and Nikki. Lani was as opposite to them as sugar to acid. Lani was sweet and innocent and Sarah and Nikki were aggressive and experienced. Carr couldn't imagine the three of them ever becoming friends. "Get on with it," he said with a bit more superiority than he intended.

"You know what?" Sarah said, her voice turning into a shield from his arrogance. "Never mind, you figure it out. Good luck with that." She turned and began to swim away, but this time, he grabbed her to keep her from leaving.

"I'm sorry. I have no right. We're not at work and I apologize. Please, if you know something tell me."

"First, *you* need to get something straight. Don't you ever judge me again? If Nikki was out here, she'd kick your ass up and down this damn lake. I happen to like Lani and so does Nikki, so next time, keep your damn condescending tone to yourself."

"Okay," Carr nodded in agreement. "I was obviously wrong. Again, I apologize. I was out of line. When we get back on the boat, I'll let Nikki slap the hell out of me." And he meant it. By Sarah's reaction, he had misjudged them and now he felt like shit for doing so.

"Don't think she won't."

"I welcome it."

"Hey, are we doing another round, or are you two just going to stay out there all day and talk?" a guy from the boat called out to them.

"Yeah, yeah." Carr waved him off. "Just give us a second." He looked back at Sarah. "What's going on with Lani? Why's she upset and making ridiculous comments about other girls?"

"Because she thinks you are seeing someone."

"I never told her that. Why would she think that?" His face turned hard. "Did you or Nikki say that? Did you two fill her head full of lies?"

"Hey! Let's go already!" a second person called out to them.

"No." Sarah ignored the calls from the boat and pointed her finger in Carr's face. "We didn't say a word. It's someone else. I'll tell you later, just don't say anything to Lani right now." Sarah didn't want to tell him it was Calli until she could be there to help Lani stand up for herself. So she left it at that and swam back to the raft, pulling herself up for another round.

Carr hesitated but finally swam to the boat. He climbed on, glanced at Lani, who was intentionally not looking at him, and regained control of the wheel.

They did a few more turns of tubing, Lani staying on the boat each time thereafter. She didn't want to give Carr another reason to come rescue her. She felt betrayed by him, so she sat there, watching and laughing on the outside while silently regretting her decision to come on the inside.

When Carr docked the boat, there was already another group waiting to go out on the water. And although Carr wanted to decline and stay onshore, he didn't. He was the one who had planned today and felt obliged to see it through.

As Lani walked by him, all he could think of was reaching out and grabbing her and telling her there was no one else. He wasn't seeing another girl. Hell, truth be told, he wasn't really even seeing Lani although he wanted to.

But in all honesty, he still wasn't sure she wanted to be with him. Maybe he was misreading her signals. *Bullshit*, he told himself. *Girls don't get mad if they're not interested and Lani is definitely mad right now.* He tried to comfort himself with that as one of his friends came on the boat and gave him a cold Coke.

"Thought you might want one." Zeke handed him the drink then watched as Carr's gaze stuck to Lani until she was in the sand and heading back toward the others. "She's different than your normal M.O. What's up?" Zeke eyed Carr in a look that begged for details.

"Yeah," his other friend Neil said as he came up on Carr's other side. "Stop holding out. We've seen the way you look at her at work. We know something's up."

"Not right now, it's not. She thinks I'm seeing someone." Carr pulled the boat out and slowly picked up speed.

"*Are* you seeing someone?" Zeke asked with suspicion. "I mean, you are a man of secrets and all, but I'd like to think your closest friends would know if you were hooked up already."

Neil threw his arm over Zeke's shoulder. "I don't know, bro. You remember Tina? He dated her for like five days before we even saw her face. I mean, that's like almost a full week."

"True," Zeke nodded, playing along with the exaggerated accusations. "Hell, at that rate, they could have been halfway down the aisle before we even got an invite." He punched Carr on the arm. "I mean, how dare you. No consideration for your friends. I'm so taking my wedding gift back."

Carr laughed and shook his head. "You two really know how to play it up. And all this time I thought girls were the drama junkies. Man, did I get that wrong."

"Ha, ha," Neil said dryly.

"Seriously, bro." Zeke eyed Carr. "You're not seeing someone, are you? I mean, we *would* know about it, right?"

"You'd know sooner or later." Carr kept his eyes on the water as he took the boat further out. "You always do."

"So then what's up with the little hottie who put fish hooks in your eyes and yanked them out as she walked by?" Neil eyed Carr, waiting for a response.

"Someone who's been misinformed, and I'm racking my brains trying to figure out who did it."

"So, a girl you like thinks you like someone else." Neil summarized.

"I think so." Carr glanced at him. "Any idea who would have done it?"

"You mean excluding the hundreds of girls who are already seething at the bit and making murder plans for any girl that hooks up with you other than themselves?"

"Yeah, other than them. Other than all those other fabricated girls." He gave a huff and all but rolled his eyes.

"You know it's true. You're a sexy beast. But down to business. My guess is on Mandy," Zeke said. "That girl's as conniving as they come."

"Not true." Neil glanced at them rather quickly. "We all know there's only one evil queen in this realm." His eyebrows arched and Carr and Zeke slowly nodded in agreement. They knew exactly who Neil was referring to. But Carr, best of all, knew just how malicious Calli could be. Without another word between them, Carr slowed the boat, turned it around, and headed back to shore.

When Calli saw the three girls walking back from the boat, she instantly became enraged. Not just at the fact that they had been riding about having a good time with Carr, but to add salt to injury, Lani looked surprisingly good in a swimsuit.

"That damn, bitch. I so hate her." Calli glared at them as they drew closer.

Nikki and Sarah couldn't help but smile when they saw the twisted look on Calli's face. A look any girl could identify from a mile away: pure jealously.

"That sight alone made today worth it," Sarah said under her breath to Nikki.

"God yes. And with any luck, it's only going to get better from here."

Both the girls smirked, which made Calli fume more. Both she and Mandy watched the way Lani drifted closer, looking better than any other girl there and they knew it.

"We've got to do something before Carr gets with her." Mandy stood beside Calli with both her hands on her waist in a prissy stance.

"What do you think we've been doing, might I remind you? And by the way, none of your damn, stupid ideas have worked. We have followed her all over this damn city, and it hasn't done a thing to stop her getting with Carr."

"Don't get bitchy with me. It's not my fault she suddenly picked up a posse of pot-heads. And might I remind you that they weren't all my ideas. You had some bombers thrown in there as well, remember?"

"Shut up. We've got to do something." Calli turned and forcefully grabbed Mandy's arm. "Come on. I have an idea."

"Fine, but let go of me." Mandy tore her arm free. "I'm not your rag doll."

"Don't challenge me." Calli glared at her. "Now shut up and come on. We don't have much time."

"I wonder what they're up to?" Sarah said as she saw Calli and Mandy bickering under a tree.

"Looks like they're arguing." Lani watched as the girls stomped off.

"Or planning." Nikki glanced at Sarah.

"Oh, no." Lani stopped then quickly turned back. "We forgot our clothes on the boat.

"Don't worry. We'll get them later." Sarah pulled her along. "Come on. Let's go see what those two are up to."

Lani started walking but then stopped again. "Do you really think that's a good idea?"

"Of course it is," Nikki agreed then took Lani by the other arm. Sarah was on the far side and they put Lani in between them as they marched right over to Calli and Mandy.

Mandy spotted them coming and stopped talking. Calli kept on rambling on about how she could make an anonymous tip on weed and get them arrested at work until Mandy reached up and covered Calli's mouth then whirled her around before she could bite her hand off.

"What the hell do you want?" Calli said as she eyed the three girls.

"Well, let's see." Nikki sauntered closer. She put her finger up to her lips and gave a mischievous smile. "What indeed?"

"Ahh, I know." Sarah cocked her head. "Why don't you tell Lani here about you and Carr? Seems like you have her believing you two are...oh, I don't know, dating."

"What? NO!" Lani looked at Sarah in horror. "I don't want to hear about that."

Calli tightened her jaw, making her face look as if it were being sucked through a vacuum. “Because it’s none of her business, that’s why. Or yours.”

“Oh, I disagree.” Nikki took a step closer to Calli. “I think it’s more Lani’s business than anyone else’s here.”

“Shut up, tramp. I could have you fired in a heartbeat.”

“And I can kick your ass twenty ways to Sunday. So why don’t we get started and see who finishes first.” Nikki’s words were low and firm as she spoke, giving them time to sink in.

“Hey,” Lani said calmly, quickly assessing that things were about to get seriously out of hand, and if there was one thing Lani knew for sure was that she was not comfortable in a fight. If fighting was a team sport, she’d be the girl picked last. Lani knew she would be the first knocked out and she doubted that she’d get back up any time soon thereafter. She had to stop this. “It’s okay. I really don’t care what’s going on between the two of them. She’s right. It’s none of my business.”

Sarah turned to Lani and looked her firmly in the eyes. “It *is* your business, Lani. You are not going to let her or anyone else play you for a fool, do you hear me? I’m not going to let her treat you like this and neither are you.”

“Look, I appreciate this, I really do, but I’m not good at this sort of thing.”

Sarah pulled Lani off to the side where they were out of earshot from the others. "No one is good at this sort of thing, Lani. But you have been letting people treat you like crap for far too long. Myself and Nikki included. And I am really sorry about that." Sarah took her hand. "I really am. But now we're going to help you. I know this is hard, but it's time you start using that mouth of yours for the weapon it can be. You are so much more than you give yourself credit for. Honestly. And you're in good hands, so trust me on this. Nikki and I are right here and we won't leave you." Sarah squeezed Lani's hand then released it. "You can do this. No get over there and stand up to that no good, conniving bitch. You are better than she is and it's time you believe that."

Lani took a deep breath, still not sure about any of this. One thing Sarah was right about, though, it was time for Lani to stand up for herself. She had spent her whole life just complying, obeying, and doing exactly what she was told because to do anything else only caused a vicious outburst from her father. But she wasn't in that life anymore. She had left that life back in the cold snow of Michigan and was now in the hot and humid city of Austin, Texas, where it was time to finally feel the warmth.

Lani felt herself shake as she slowly turned around to face Calli. Luckily, Nikki had been doing a good job at keeping Calli engaged with banter so no one was focused on Sarah's little pep talk, but that changed when Lani reappeared.

Calli glared, put her hands to her hips, and began her death stare on Lani. "What? You have something to say to me? Not that it matters. No one cares what comes out of your mouth. But you need to understand one thing. Stay the hell away from Carr. He's not your type, or more accurately, you're not his." Calli scanned over Lani, starting at her feet and stopping on her face. "I mean, just look at you. You're one of the most pathetic looking creatures I've ever seen. Maybe if I slapped you a few times, I'd improve that thing you call a face."

Nikki's hands curled and she knew if Lani didn't say something soon, that she would be all over Calli and it wouldn't be slaps that hit her in the face. Sarah instantly shook her head at Nikki, warning her to stay back and let Lani run with this just like they had talked about. Lani needed more self-confidence and standing up to Calli was the best confidence booster for any girl this side of the Rio Grande.

The small quake inside Lani was escalating and she felt herself going numb. Turn to ice, just like she had always done. It was the one thing that had preserved her for so long. Her father's berating comments, her mother's silence, her lack of friends, her fear of acceptance all turned to ice. So cold it shut out all feelings and allowed her to carry on, but now she felt trapped beneath the ice. All she wanted to do was keep her mouth shut, just like always, and walk away. That same lifelong routine that had always kept her safe. Not happy, but safe, at least that's what she had wanted to believe, although others may disagree.

Without a word, Nikki and Sarah came and stood beside her, putting Lani back in the middle of them again. They stepped in close to her where she could feel their presence and they both felt the shaking inside her calm.

Nikki and Sarah's warmth gave Lani a silent power and she felt herself steady. She looked straight at Calli, blocking out the small group that had circled around the commotion.

"You don't know anything about me. You don't get to tell me who I can see or what type of guy I like. I'll do whatever I want. This is my life and it doesn't need your stamp of approval. And if Carr is more interested in me than-"

"Hey," Carr's voice broke in from a few feet away as he quickly approached the crowd. "What's going on here?" He glanced at Lani then glared at Calli. "What the hell are you up to now?" He didn't give Calli a chance to answer. The color draining from her face was all the answer he needed. "Wait. Before you say anything, I think some introductions are in order." Carr bore his eyes into Calli with a look of authority. "Calli, this is Lani." He then broke his stare and gently looked at Lani. "And, Lani, this is Calli, the most conniving, underhanded, deceitful, and vain girl I know. Otherwise known as my sister."

Calli's face turned the color of fresh blood, and as she opened her mouth, Carr spoke before she had a chance for a rebuttal. "I haven't talked to dad lately. Maybe I should give him a quick call and catch him up on how well you're doing working at that diner. I'm sure he'd be pleased to know that you haven't learnt a single thing yet."

"Carr," Calli pleaded. "She's doesn't even know who we are. She's not like us. Just look at her." Calli realized that right now, Lani looked like a movie star and quickly tried to cover up her mistake. "I mean, not the way she looks now, but just think of the way she normally dresses. It's like she shops in the garbage or something. You and me, we're better than her. We're better than the rest of them." Calli lifted her head to include Nikki and Sarah. "I'm only trying to make sure you end up with someone like us. That's what you deserve."

"Stop it, Calli. No one designated you my keeper and if I know you, which we all can say I do, then I know the only thing you're really trying to do is make someone else feel like shit. So knock it off. You're no better than anyone here and you're definitely not better than Lani."

Carr turned and stared at Lani. He then reached over and took her hand. "I'm sorry. I should have known she was behind this." He shook his head. "I'm so sorry."

Lani didn't say anything. She took in the sincere look in his eyes and the way it made her feel like someone just cleared out a world of dark clouds and she was finally seeing the beauty of a clear, blue sky.

It was beautiful. He was beautiful and she loved the way he was looking at her that very second.

Calli stormed off stomping her feet with her small group of fans on her heels. The rest of the crowd left to resume their activities of playing frisbee, laying out, and wading around in the water.

Sarah looked at Nikki. They both smiled then walked away at the sound of Ty calling for them to go back out on the boat with Neil taking over as captain.

Carr reached up, letting his hand cup Lani's face. He felt so relieved that all this was just his sister up to her usual tricks. Something he hated but was sadly used to. As he looked at Lani, he had a strong urge to lean down and kiss her, but considering what Calli had put her through, didn't think it was the right time. Not here. Not with an audience.

He let his thumb fall gently over her cheek and locked his eyes onto hers. "Come with me. I have a place I want you to see."

She wanted to say, *I'd go anywhere with you.* But instead, only smiled softly and let him lead her to a new, warm spot in the sun.

Chapter 21

Carr held Lani's hand as he took her some twenty minutes away until finally stopping. He looked at her to catch her reaction to the spot in front of them. It was a small cove completely isolated on a tiny stretch of beach with soft rolling waves easing in. It reminded Lani of the tip of a hook. It was too small for a boat, except maybe a rowboat or canoe, but it was cozy and definitely worth the hike.

"What do you think?" Carr almost held his breath waiting for her response. He wanted her to like it. He wanted her to love it as much as he did. He was no stranger to this place. His family had come to this lake many times during his youth, and he had found this spot on one of those trips. He never told anyone else about it, and as far as he knew, no one else came here, at least not that he ever saw. It was a place that he would visit after one of his arguments with his dad on the days his family came to the lake together. Arguments that were inevitable and always seemed to happen when all Carr wanted to do was to have a good time.

"It's small." Lani looked at him, her eyes twinkling with approval. "And wonderful. How did you find it?"

He grabbed her hand and walked down to the farthest point on the sand where the water reached. It was as if one tiny finger of the lake stretched out, tried to touch something out of reach before pulling back only to return and try again.

"I've been here a lot over the years. Used to come here with my family. Not just my parents and Calli but also my aunts, uncles, grandparents, and cousins. One time, when I was around ten or so, I just needed to get away from all the noise - my dad mostly, and I just started walking and this is where I ended up." He sat by the edge of the water and gently pulled her down beside him.

"Really, only ten years old? Didn't anyone know you were gone?"

"No. Not with my sister around demanding all the attention. She's been exhausting everyone ever since she busted out of the womb."

Lani stretched her legs out in front of her and leaned back on her palms. "I've got to tell you that I didn't know you two were related. I'm still pretty surprised over it."

"That's because she didn't want you to know. She's very deceitful, in case you didn't know that either," he teased.

"No, I got that. That one's not hard to miss. Don't know how you two are brother and sister, though? You don't seem anything like her. At least not yet." She eyed him curiously.

"I'm going to let that one slid since I can understand where you're coming from. It's not easy being her brother. I catch all kinds of hell over what she does."

"How'd you two end up so different anyway?"

"I don't know. My guess is that's what happens when you give a kid everything."

"But didn't your parents give you the same as her?"

"Not exactly. My father has always been hard on me. I mean, I know he loves me, and I know a lot of other people had it a lot worse than I did, so I don't mean to complain, but we weren't exactly the best of buds growing up. My father expected me to earn my keep. He kept telling me it was how men are supposed to be. You work for what you want, which I respect and agree with, but even when I was young, I knew I didn't want to earn my living the way he wanted me to, which caused a lot of friction between us. But when Calli was born, it was different. She was his little princess and could do no wrong. At least until recently." Carr leaned back on his hands the same as Lani and placed his fingers gently over hers, causing a swarm of butteries to flutter in her stomach.

"What happened? Did she forget to do the dishes, wreck the car, burn the house down?"

"More like spent eleven thousand dollars furnishing her dorm last semester. And that was *after* maxing out three other credit cards, so now my dad is actually making her pay some of it off. Shocked the hell out of all of us, especially Calli."

"Whoa." Lani shot up. "What do your parents do for a living?"

"My dad is ranked as one of the top cardiologists in the country. He makes a pretty impressive salary. However, he doesn't even need to work because my mother is a high profiled socialite that comes from a very wealthy family. Old money as they say. One that donates millions to charities and museums and such. One that believes women are something to be admired and pampered but never made to work. That's the man's job. And so, ever since I was old enough to talk, my dialogue with my father has always been one of a medical vocabulary. Even on holidays when I should have been cutting free and playing with my cousins. But my dad disagreed. He would call me over with all my uncles standing around, all of which are some sort of top-rated doctor in his field, and they would ambush me with topics I was clearly too young for."

"I'm taking it that you don't want to be a doctor?"

"You'd be correct. At the age of six I could tell you what tools are used to cut open a man's chest for heart surgery or how long recovery time would be for a torn ACL or the best way to re-route a clogged artery. Things no six-year-old should ever know. At least not one who didn't want to know. It'd been different if I had been interested in those things, but I wasn't. Instead, I would sit in a stiff, cold, leather chair in my dad's study and listened to a group of stuffy men talk to me about stories of blood and joints and tubes while I watched my sister through the window sit at the table eating strawberry cake and playing with a tea set made from real china."

"Wow. Maybe she can't help it. I guess we all carry some sort of childhood demons around still trying to control what we do. Somehow managing to latch on and imprison us to a life we never wanted to begin with."

Carr looked at Lani, his eyes soft on her face. "I knew you'd get it. You seemed like someone with some substance, not just fluff between your beautiful and..., he paused, reached over and eased her hair behind her ears. "Absolutely stunning eyes."

Lani looked down, thinking about what she just said, referring to her own demons more than anyone else's. Carr eased his hand back, sensing her hesitation, but instead of keeping his distance, he scooted over closer. He placed his arm around her, bringing her into his chest and letting her head rest on his shoulder. He didn't say a word but just held her in his arms and she let him. The feeling of his body wrapped around her was the most physical affection she had ever received and was surprised how something so small made her feel so valid. Like she really did matter. Like someone truly wanted her. The only other man who has ever come close to making her feel like that was her grandfather, but it was different with Carr. He reached that deep cold spot in her heart that she felt would always stay frozen like a small chunk of ice buried in the darkest place on Earth under miles of stone and ice.

She could feel his hands move up her back and into her hair and all she could do was shut her eyes and soak in every stroke of his touch. His touch, full of strength and softness, just the way she imagined a guy's touch would be. The way love and safety were supposed to feel like.

When she pulled back, Carr reached down and took her hand again, pulling it over and resting it in his lap. "Tell me about you. I want to know everything."

"No, you don't. Trust me. It's not a feel-good story by any means." As wonderful as she felt next to Carr, she still didn't trust him to know her secrets. "Oh," she said full of energy, hoping to change the subject. "How's the bike? I would think it should be ready about now." Lani gave a playful face.

"I'll tell you what. If you will let me pick you up tomorrow and take you on a date, I will show you what I've done with the bike."

"I can't. I have to work."

"Call in. People do it all the time, Lani. Come on. Go out with me. I promise you won't regret it."

"But you don't understand. I need that money. I really need every cent of it. I can't afford to lose any more hours."

There was something in her voice that made Carr back down. Maybe the sound of desperation or pain, but whatever it was, he stopped. "Okay. Not a problem. I'll think of something else." He smiled and Lani felt the tension in her shoulders ease.

She turned back and looked out at the openness before them, her hand wrapped tightly in his, and they talked until the orange glow of the sun faded off the glass surface of the water and dissolve into the starry sky.

Chapter 22

When Lani got back to work the next day, Calli and Mandy avoided her altogether, which was strange enough behavior for Grace to notice within a few minutes after coming in to work. She sat in the kitchen and watched the front through the opened window in the wall. Lani hadn't noticed she was there until Grace waved at her.

"Hey." Lani walked up. "Where've you been? I was starting to think you ditched me."

"Hey, yourself," Ted called from the grill. "You act like being left alone here would be a bad thing."

"Not bad," Lani consoled, "Just better with a friendly face around." Lani gave Grace a puzzled look. "What are you doing in the kitchen? Did you get a promotion?"

"Nobody gets promoted around here," a voice hollered.

"I need to talk to you," Grace said, waving off Ted's comment.

"Let me clean this mess, then I'll meet you out back." Lani finished clearing the dishes from her last table then slipped out to the alley after telling Ted she was going on break.

"Yeah, yeah. I know. I can hear too." He motioned her off then called out to Calli and Mandy to take care of Lani's station.

"As soon as my dad gets off this punishment phase of his, I'm walking out of here and breaking every damn dish as I go." Calli heaved a breath of hatred before calling back. "Sure. No problem."

"And I'll be right behind you." Mandy bobbed her head slightly as she spoke as if that gesture gave her words more meaning, then went and waited on a table that just sat down.

When Lani got out back, she walked up to Grace and noticed she wasn't wearing her apron. "Okay, what's up? This," Lani waved her hand over Grace. "Is not normal. Spill."

Grace took a deep breath, then turned and let her weight fall against the brick wall, a small smile forming on her lips and a distant look in her eyes. "Oh, Lani."

Lani watched Grace for a second, a glow about her radiated pure happiness, making Lani even more anxious about what Grace had to say. "You're killing me. Tell me already."

Grace looked at Lani through the corner of her eye and held up her hand. She fluttered her fingers about then stopped and waited for Lani's reaction.

"Oh, my god, Grace," Lani's voice was almost a whisper. "You got married. I didn't even know you were seeing someone." Lani took Grace's hand, bringing it closer to see the diamond on her finger. "It's so beautiful. And perfect. And I just don't know what else to say." Lani dropped Grace's hand and the two embraced.

"I know. I wanted to tell you but Ted wanted to keep it a secret."

"No!" Lani pulled away. "You married Ted? Our Ted? Ted who owns *TED*'s Ted? Oh my god, how could I have missed that? How could you not tell me?"

"I tried, but it didn't work, and then I had to leave town for a few days and let my family know, and now I'm back and just readjusting to everything and this is my first chance to tell you. Please don't hate me for not telling you sooner, Lani. I really wanted to."

Lani reached out and hugged Grace with all her might again. "Never. I'm just so surprised. I don't know what to say except that I'm really, really happy for you."

They turned at the sound of the screen door to the alley slamming shut and found Ted walking over to them. "I guess you know now, kiddo." He looked at Lani then wrapped an arm around his new wife. "She wanted to tell you. It was me that wanted things kept quiet and simple. It's just the kind of man I am."

Lani watched them, still trying to adjust to the news as Ted kissed Grace on the cheek.

"Congratulations. I can't believe it but it's great."

Ted grinned. "Thanks. We just went down to the JP then Grace left town afterwards. No one really knew about it, but now that it's done, we want to have a reception next week. Grace will fill you in." Ted kissed his wife on the cheek again then disappeared back inside.

"You two already look like you belong together."

"Oh, my gosh. I never thought I'd be so in love again but it happened right under my nose. I've always liked him, but never knew he felt the same until one night when I came back after closing because I left my wallet in my locker. He was here alone going over the books and he started talking to me and one thing led to another and now..." Grace held up her hand and gazed at the ring. "But," she dropped her hand, "back to business for now."

"Right. The reception."

"Oh, no. I'm talking about Calli and Mandy. You know I'm part boss now?" Grace looked at Lani with a twinkle in her eye. "And I'm thinking we have a score to settle." She looped her arm inside of Lani's and they both leaned back against the wall.

"What did you have in mind?"

"For starters, I'm thinking the kitchen will need an extra cleaning, the floor will need a good scrubbing and a good coat of wax, the toilets are looking a little dingy and all the silverware has spots that will need to be buffed out by hand."

Lani smiled. "I can't wait to see their faces."

"Well, sorry to say, but you, my dear, won't be here."

"What?" Lani kicked off the wall.

"Nope. You..." Grace reached behind Lani and untied her apron. "Are taking the next two days off."

"Uh, no. You know I can't do that."

"Oh, did I forget to mention it will count as your paid vacation. Something I now oversee here at the diner."

"Really?" Lani looked off in the distance. "Wow, I don't even know what I will do with time off."

"Well, whatever it is, enjoy. And don't even think about coming to check on things. Got it?"

"Already so bossy," Lani said with a warm tone. "I got it."

When Lani walked back through the front, she passed Calli and gave her a large smile.

"What the hell are you so happy about? You're life sucks."

"My life might, but my day sure won't. I'm off to find Carr, you're brother," Lani lied, at least partially. She was off but had no intention of going to find Carr. It just sounded good and felt even better to see the angry look on Calli's face afterwards. Lani had never been the person to speak so directly back to others, but after this weekend, she felt a little braver. And she had Sarah and Nikki to thank for that.

Calli scrunched her eyes down as if she were trying to crack nuts in between her lids, then quickly shrugged. "Whatever. He'll just use you like he does every other girl and then you're life will suck even more, if that's possible."

"We'll see about that," a voice sounded in front of Lani.

Lani turned just in time to stop herself from colliding into Carr.

Carr didn't hesitate and instantly grabbed her arms. "Still trying to run me over, I see." He then leaned in close to her ear. "Maybe I should just let you so I could feel you close to me again."

Lani pulled back, her faced flushed. Partially because she did almost run him flat over but more from the feel of his breath on her ear. It was like a hot blanket that caused tiny heat waves of pleasure and she was thankful no one else could see. She bit her lip then quickly replied before Calli could respond. "I was just coming to see you."

Carr felt his heartbeat give a few hard thrusts in his chest. He wasn't expecting this. He'd come here to see her, but he only imagined it would be from a booth in the corner while she worked. This was so much better. He gently squeezed her arms. "Don't tease me. I'm warning you. I can't be held responsible for my actions." He gave a soft smile and Lani could feel her knees weaken beneath her.

"Let's go." She nodded toward the door.

"You're the boss." Carr swerved in behind her, blocking Lani's view of Calli but not before she caught a glimpse of a very pissed off glare. Something that had a wonderful feel to it.

"I'm the boss," Lani repeated with a teasing smile, then led Carr out the door, her hand clenching his, never wanting to let go.

Chapter 23

“**So, where we** heading?” Carr wrapped his fingers tighter around hers, loving the way she fit perfectly inside his. The sun beat down on their faces causing a glistening strip of sweat to sparkle across Carr’s forehead.

Lani stopped and looked up at him. “I really don’t know. I was out of my zone there for a moment and just said the first thing that popped into my head. Your sister gets to me sometimes.”

“My sister can get to everyone sometimes, but let’s not talk about that.” He turned his body into hers and pulled her to him. He could see Lani’s breathing shallow, and he wanted to wrap her in his arms and kiss her until she was too weak to stand.

Lani locked eyes with him, not wanting to turn away and not caring that they were completely frozen in the middle of the sidewalk in the burning sun where everyone could see. She just didn’t care and she liked that. She gently bit her lip out of nerves from standing so close to him and all she wanted was for him to pull her in closer until his body meshed with hers. “What then? What do you want to do?”

“You shouldn’t ask me that.” His voice was but a whisper and she could almost taste his lips on hers. He touched her hair and let his fingers run through the back, causing her to hold her breath.

She slowly drew in a deep pocket of air, feeling the way her chest inflated before gently releasing it. This was not the place to lose herself, so she started talking in hopes of regaining her strength. "The bike." Her voice was low. "Let's go take a look. It should be finished now, right?"

Carr gave an easy smile, loving the way she both pulled him in and pushed him away within seconds of each other. He let his thumb trace her lips, staring over every inch of her face, wanting to lean down and taste her for the first time, but knowing he would not be able to stop once he did. "Yeah, it's ready." He dropped his hand. "Come on. I'll take you there."

They walked to the garage in silence. A comfortable, strengthening silence that both of them welcomed. They felt at ease and concentrated on the way their palms felt rubbing against the other's as they held hands.

The walk felt shorter than Lani remembered but she figured that was because she didn't want it to end. She knew then that she'd walk to hell and back if he came with her. She felt wanted by someone. Someone she wanted just as much in return and that was a beautiful, new feeling. She could understand now what she missed out on all the years of never having someone to love her. Something no one should ever be denied.

Carr opened the door to the garage and they both stepped inside. The only light was coming from the windows on the door. It was dim but light enough to see around. Lani glanced from wall to wall then to Carr. "I don't see it. I see an old car, dressers, motorcycles, but no bike. Where is it?"

Carr walked over to her and his body stopped inches from hers. Without a word, he reached up and cradled her face in his hands. Lani could hear her own breath leaving her lungs then return quickly only to rapidly escape again. He brought his face down to hers, his scent of sweat and cologne circling around her. She knew she wouldn't be able to stop if he kissed her. She didn't want to stop. She wanted to feel his lips on hers, his chest against hers, and his body tangled up with her own. "I need you." His words were soft and Lani felt a chunk of herself melt as he finally brought his lips down upon hers.

At first, his touch was gentle, his tongue softly tasting her lips as it rolled over the top then the bottom but then her mouth opened, accepting his touch, inviting him in and he could no longer hold himself back from her. His hands slid through her hair, gently wrapping her head and pulling her further into him. His tongue found hers in the dark as their bodies fell back against the rusted frame of a 1967 Chevy Malibu, the doors were missing but the original vinyl seats were still intact.

Lani put her arms all the way around him, tightly pulling him into her, feeling the broadness of his frame swallow her whole. Her breathing heavy with his as she tasted every bit of his lips, tongue, mouth. Her hands slid into his hair and he lifted her against the car, his mouth moving down to her neck. She shut her eyes, wrapped her legs around his waist and let her head fall back, giving him access to whatever he wanted.

He kissed her neck at first then gently sucked at her nape, causing her to moan as heat and chills consumed her. He grazed his hands up to her chest, cupping her breast as his thumbs gently played with her nipples from the outside of her shirt. He lifted her further onto the car as he eased down to her stomach. He lifted her shirt and let his lips taste her skin. He kissed her, gently moving further down to the edge of her pants and let his tongue ease down inside the brim. He could feel her entire body pulsate under his touch, causing him to only burn for her more. He wanted to consume her. Wanted to cover every inch of her with his mouth, his hands, his body.

Lani tightened her legs, feeling as if she were crushing him between them but he only kissed her harder, causing her to moan more as her head pressed into the metal hood. Carr picked her up, her body falling forward into his arms, her weight sliding down to where their lips met again, kissing the other's with full force.

With her in his arms, he moved to the back of the car and eased her down flat into the back seat, his weight coming to rest on hers. Their hands moved wildly over each other, not able to get to the naked skin fast enough. Lani pulled Carr's shirt over his head and threw it somewhere out the opening from the missing door. Carr scooped his hands under her shirt and removed it along with her bra. He then moved down to one of her breast, taking it all into his mouth as his hand consumed the other one. When her moans became louder, he moved down to her pants, unbuttoned them and slipped them off along with her panties. As he dropped them to the floor, he stopped and looked at her through the shadows of the backseat. Her fair skin a brilliant contrast against the dark vinyl. All he could do was stare at her, totally consumed by her naked body. Every inch of her glowing before him. "You're so beautiful," he whispered, then brought his lips down and began kissing her legs, making his way up. His tongue stopping to taste her inner thighs, the scent of her pushing him over the edge. As he kissed her lower body, he slipped off his pants then brought his full naked weight upon hers.

Her head was back, her eyes closed and she moaned with pleasure, the softness of her voice a song to his ears. He reached up and slipped his hand under the back of her head, lifting it slightly, forcing her to look at him. Their eyes silently rested on the others in the dark. After a few seconds of silence, Lani spoke. "What?" she whispered. "What is it?"

Carr came closer to her face, his voice deep and intense. "You're absolutely the most beautiful woman I've ever seen. You're like a star against the night sky, so memorizing I could watch you forever."

Lani reached up and forced his lips to hers and he returned her kiss. As their mouths devoured the other's, Carr eased himself inside her and her legs wrapped around him.

"Oh my god." Lani shut her eyes, her head falling back again as Carr kissed her neck, his body now moving with the rhythm of hers as they danced in the dark to the beat of their own love song.

Chapter 24

Carr held Lani in his arms, both still naked in the back seat, their legs tangled together. Carr moved Lani's hair from her face and kissed her. "You were amazing."

"I don't know if I am supposed to say thank you to that or what exactly."

Carr could see her smile through the shadows. He playfully touched the tip of her nose. "I'm sure I'm not the first guy to tell you that." He could see the whites of her eyes shift down and he propped himself up. He touched her face and lifted her gaze back to his. "Lani?" He paused, watching her look nervously over his face. "Lani,...am I your first?" She looked away and he slipped his fingers to the back of her head, picking up its weight and pulling her up to him. "Look at me, Lani." His voice commanded and she slowly obeyed. "Am. I. Your. First?"

She watched as his eyes bore into hers feeling herself become hypnotized by their power and she slowly nodded. "Yes."

Carr grabbed her, pulling her so far into him that their bodies all but morphed together. He then began kissing her neck softly, moving up to her mouth. He kissed her then pulled her back, allowing her full sight of his face. "You are a dream. My dream. No wonder you didn't know what to say."

She bit her lip and glanced down but he shook her gently. "No, Lani. Don't you dare be ashamed of who you are. You hold your head up and be proud. Not every girl can shine. But you, you can and you do. You are perfect. Every inch of you."

A ball of light burst into the dark like a fireball causing them to freeze with fright. Lani looked at Carr, her eyes as petrified coal. He quietly slipped a finger to her lips then covered her with his own body as the sound of footsteps came closer to the car.

"Boss, you out here?" a voice sounded from the back. Lani almost stopped breathing as the fear of being caught naked in the back seat of a car all but paralyzed her. After a few seconds, the footsteps retreated then disappeared behind the sound of a shutting door.

Carr eased off of Lani and looked at her. Within seconds, they both burst out laughing, the fear releasing as they did.

"Oh, my, god. I don't think I've ever been so scared in my life." Lani placed her hand on her chest to calm her heart rate.

"Allow me." Carr eased his hand under hers, letting it come to rest against her skin. "I love the way you feel."

"What? My heart ninja kicking your hand right now feels good?"

"Lani." He waited for her to look at him. "You know I would never let anyone see you like this. I would keep you covered. This body is not for anyone to see but me."

Lani could feel her heartbeat subside at the sound of his words, feeling like he really would protect her from being embarrassed or humiliated. Something she did not expect or ever experience before and she liked the way it made her feel.

"Thanks." Her voice was soft and she let her gaze melt into his and for a few seconds, they stayed like that. Lani wrapped in his arms, their naked bodies pressed tightly together and no words, just a look of complete contentment. "Hey," Lani broke the silence. "Who was that guy looking for?"

"Um," Carr hesitated. "I guess that would be me."

"Why did he call you boss?"

"Well, I guess that would be because I own this bar."

"Really?" Lani sounded shocked. "You own this whole place? The bar in the front and the garage?"

Carr nodded. "Yeah, I do. Why do you sound so surprised?"

"I don't know. I guess I just thought you did something else."

"Like what? What did you think I did for a living?"

"Well, guess I didn't know? So, if you own this place, why doesn't Calli work for you as a punishment for her transgressions? Why is she at *TED*'s making my life hell?"

"First, she's not going to mess with you anymore. Now that I know, I put a stop to it. As long as I'm around, no one will ever mess with you." He stared at her making sure she understood. Lani didn't know what to say, so she nodded lightly to let him know she believed him. Then he continued. "And secondly, because I said no. She wanted to but having her work here would be like having and hole in a rowboat. She'd sink the whole damn place. I could already picture her sitting up on the bar, barking out orders while giving away a slew of free drinks. Not my idea of her learning her lesson."

"Good point. So, what made you want to buy a bar of all things?"

"I didn't want to have anything to do with the medical field for starters." He reached down and looped his fingers around hers, letting her arm come to rest on her stomach. "Beyond that, I found that I'm pretty good at investing. Especially when it comes to real estate. So far, I haven't made a bad purchase yet."

"So far? What else have you bought?"

"A couple of places here and there. I like to fix up old things. Furniture, buildings, bikes." He smiled then continued. "I like to find old, run-down shops, rebuild them and sell them for a profit. Once I had a good flow of money, I moved into buying small businesses. Nothing major. So far, just a couple of bars."

"Like how many bars?"

"Seven."

Lani propped herself up, her elbow pressing into the seat. "I didn't see that coming."

"What does that mean?"

"You seem too young to own seven bars."

He pulled her over and kissed her. "I'll take that as a compliment. But in all fairness, I did start young. Cashed in my college fund and bought my first shop. Sold it for two and a half times what I put into it. Of course, my father was beyond pissed, but I did pay back the fund. It still didn't matter though, at least not to him. He had his sights set on me becoming a heart surgeon and he hasn't forgiven me since. We talk but it's not usually a warm conversation." He kissed her again. "I like what I do, a lot actually. However, I do spend a chunk of time tracking down more investment opportunities that I'm not around the places I own a lot. And when I'm not doing that, I'm usually tucked away in this garage refinishing something, at least until here recently. Things have just started to settle down, but that's pretty much how my life's been." He leaned down to her and softly kissed her cheek several times. Lani just closed her eyes and took in the feel of his lips on her face, bathing in the warmth his touch brought her. "But enough about me. Tell me about you. I want to know your hopes and dreams and all the fights you had with your parents," he teased as he ran his fingers up through her long hair.

"Not much to say, really. Which reminds me, I have to be getting home," she lied, suddenly feeling the air around her too stuffy to breathe. "A friend of my just got married and is having a reception. I have to make cupcakes." She shot up and slid herself out of the seat, looking for her clothes.

"Did I say something wrong, Lani?" Carr slid out behind her, watching her dress as if someone just pulled the fire alarm.

"No. It just takes a long time to make what I need to, and I want to get started. I have to work the rest of the week so today is the only time for me to get it done," she lied but didn't really care at the moment as he stared at her, questioning her every move and she knew if she didn't get out of there fast, he would be able to see right through her, see her every flaw, every weakness, every insufficient part of her that was lacking of ever being good enough for someone as wonderful as him. Her father's face loomed in front of her, his voice drowning in her ears. *"You're no good, Lani. You'll never be good enough. You're weak and boys don't like weak."*

She suddenly felt hands on her, lightly shaking her back into focus. "Lani? Are you listening?" She glanced up, a blank look on her face as she threw the rest of her clothes on. Carr stood in front of her, his clothes still scattered about the floor as he pulled her into his chest. "Please, stop. Tell me what's going on. I can help. You're acting like you hate me all of a sudden. What is it?"

"Carr," Lani freed herself from his grasp. "It's nothing. I just really need to get started, you know, time is of the essence and all that." She pulled away and darted to the back door.

"Please don't leave like this," he softly pleaded, dashing after her. "Hey, I can go with you. I'm pretty good in the kitchen, maybe I can help."

"No!" Lani shut her eyes in pain, realizing she just yelled at him. She hated the way her voice sounded. It was harsh and impatient and she knew he was only trying to help, but that's not what she needed right now. She needed to get away from him before he pushed her away first. It's was so much easier to leave on her own terms before he began scrutinizing every little bad thing about her. Running was so, so much easier.

She swung the door opened and flew out of the garage before Carr had a chance to say another word.

He stood there, still naked in the doorway. He wanted to run after her but feared she'd only push him away further. He wondered if she regretted what just happened in the car. Not the most romantic place for a girl to lose her virginity. Did she hate him now?

"God, Lani. What's wrong?" He thrust his fingers through his hair and thought of her. If she only knew what she did for him. She was the one who made everything in his life have meaning. She made him feel like everything was exactly the way it was meant to be. She didn't judge him. She had no expectations of him, so unlike his family. "When you come from money, you should act like it," his father would say. "Stop messing around with these damn bars full of drunks and get some respect for yourself. Go to medical school. You owe me that." But not Lani. She didn't even know how rich his family was, and she sure didn't want to date him for the status that brought. For the first time, Carr felt like he was with a girl who only wanted one thing from him. Himself.

He stood and watched her run down the alley, then shut the door. He gathered up his clothes, pushing away the ache in his chest and went back to the car. He sat in the front seat and let his hands rest on the large, thin steering wheel. He closed his eyes as his head fell back, his heart bleeding emptiness in her absences.

He didn't expect her to have hit him like this. So hard, so fast. He knew he had liked her from the second he saw her in the bar. Before they had even spoken a single word between them. He had wanted her before she had even seen his face; he just didn't know how much until now.

Chapter 25

When Lani got home, she was too angry to cook or bake or do anything else that required patience. Instead, she went straight to an old chest, flung back the heavy lid and started digging frantically inside. When her hand hit her high school tennis racket, she whipped it out along with a few balls and stuffed them in a bag. She then ran back down the stairs, full of restless energy digging a hole in the pit of her stomach and hit the sidewalk. Her feet pushed off the cement faster and faster until she broke out into a full sprint.

She ran for the next few blocks until coming to a park. She made her way over to the empty tennis courts, took out her racket and began hitting balls against the backboard.

The first one hit with a solid strike, returning the ball quickly back to her only to be hit again, harder than before. As she swung, her father's voice made an unwanted return.

"You call that good, Lani? Hell, I know men without any arms that could hit a ball harder than you can. Hit the damn ball, girl. Your scrawny little body should ache with pain after you hit that thing. If it doesn't hurt, then you aren't doing it right!"

That was the day that he had flung one of her rackets across the court at her. The one that had grazed her forehead, leaving it dripping with blood and a scar.

She pushed that day from her mind and struck the ball again, slamming it so hard against the wall that when it hit, a loud boom filled the air. She hit it again. Faster this time, sweat forming in her hair and pooling on her temples. She hit it again, harder. Her father's voice pounding in her ears. "Hit that goddamn ball. If you really wanted to be good, you would be. There's no excuse for losing. There are no excuses for being scored on. Either you're the best or you don't deserve to live under my roof. You're pathetic. Everybody's going to laugh at me. Hit that goddamn ball like you mean it or so help me!"

She swung the racket with all her might, hitting the ball so hard that she was sure she'd snap the strings, but they stayed intact and she swung again. She hit it over and over, his face still in front of her. "I am good," she whispered under her breath, then hit the ball again. "I am good," she said louder.

Her shirt clung to her chest, wet with anger and hurt from yearning to be loved. "I am good." Her words became louder as she wrapped both hands tightly around the leather grip. "I am good." The ball flew back at her and she once again sent it sailing through the air, forcing it to go where she wanted before it returned. "Shut up. Shut up. Just shut up!" she yelled into the space around her. "I am good. I am good. I *am* good. You have *no* right!"

Her father's image tried to speak. "You're no goo-"

"SHUT UP! I AM GOOD! I AM!" She hit it again and again and again, each time her own words pushing out those of pain. Those of hurt. She hit the ball with all her might, causing her wrists to sting with pain. She hit it again, feeling everything inside her yell for help. She struck the ball harder and harder until her arms throbbed, her heart broke, and her soul cried out. The last swing finally sent the ball as far away as she could. She missed the wall on purpose, sending the ball whirling threw the tree line, where it finally fell to rest in a wide-open space in the grass. She crashed to the ground, tears pouring, getting lost in the sweat streaming down her face. "I am good," she whispered, bringing her legs up to her chest. She rocked herself gently back and forth in the middle of the empty court, not caring if others could see. Her head fell to her knees as her feet hinged to and fro, rocking her back and forth. "I am good. I am. I am. I am." Her chest shook with pain. "I am good. Just leave me alone. Don't ever come back."

She sat there for a long time, forcing her father's voice into total silence. Convincing herself that she did have some tiny bit of worth. Slowly breaking his wall of control that had kept her locked away from the rest of the world even long after she'd left it. Forcing his face out of her mind, his words out of her heart, purging them from her life and killing them both. When she finally felt peace, she stood and went home, leaving her racket in the middle of the court for good.

She walked up the stairs slowly this time, exhaustion consuming her. She dragged each leg up behind her until finally reaching the top step. She then made her way down the hall to her door. As she reached for her key, Ms. Belsky opened her door and stood in the threshold.

"Hello, dear."

Lani turned and found her neighbor wearing a large hat and a warm smile.

"Hi." Lani gave a light wave, feeling too tired for conversation.

"Now, now." Ms. Belsky came further into the hall, instantly putting her arm around Lani. "If I know anything, it's a face that's in need of a nice cup of tea."

"Oh, Ms. Belsky, I don't know if this is a good time." Lani tried to protest.

"No, dear." Ms. Belsky guided her into the apartment and shut the door behind them. "It's the perfect time." The older woman kept her arms wrapped around Lani, bringing her to a seat in her small kitchen. "And I know just the one. A nice, raspberry chamomile with a touch of honey. You just sit here and relax, dear. I won't be but a second."

Lani accepted the invitation to silence. She leaned back and watched Ms. Belsky fill a bright red teapot with water and place it on the stove. She then retrieved two floral tea cups from the cabinet and filled them with a few drops of honey.

Lani let her eyes leave the motion of the kitchen and float around the apartment. It was bigger than her own, almost twice the size for the one Ms. Belsky lived in was not a studio but a full-sized one bedroom apartment.

It was decorated with elaborate yet comfortable furnishings, somewhere between Queen Victorian meets Lazy Boy. Her couch had large red and pink roses with a heavy ornate frame and big swirly legs that met a Persian rug on top of a worn wood floor. In the corner were two high back formal chairs with a small table tucked nicely in between and - what a minute. Lani perked up as her eyes fell to something behind the chairs.

"Is that?" She stood and walked over behind the chairs. "Oh, my, god. When did this get here?" Lani pointed to the bike resting quietly along the chair rail on the wall. She carefully eased the bike out and brought it to the middle of the room, where she could view it free from obstruction.

Ms. Belsky hollered from the kitchen, "Is that the bike you're talking about, dear?"

"Yes," Lani answered, her fingers gliding along the yellow frame painted with a hint of orange.

"That young man brought it by half an hour ago. Right to my door." She came around the corner. "Well, I naturally invited him in, where he told me the story that he'd seen you riding it and couldn't help himself but walk right up to you and offer to repaint the old thing."

Lani twirled around, both appreciating and ignoring the small white lie Carr had told because something more pressing grabbed her attention. “Oh, Ms. Belsky,” her voice reflected a tinge of panic. “I’m so sorry. I hope the color is all right. I didn’t mean to-”

“Nonsense. I love that color. He told me he was going to paint it a nice fire engine red, but something changed his mind. Said if I didn’t like it, he’d repaint it any color I wanted. I told him he’d do no such thing. Never in all my years have I seen that bike look so beautiful, not even when it was brand new. And just look at that basket. It’s perfect. I could get two bags of groceries in there. And the color.” She walked over to the bike, cupping her hands together and letting them fall to her waist. “It reminds me of the sunset. The ones Harold and I used to watch after our rides in the country. It makes me feel like he’s standing right beside me every time I look at it.” She brought her hand up and lightly touched her heart. “He said he’d take it back downstairs and lock it up, but I just can’t part with it.” She was silent as her eyes danced over the bike as if it were a door to another world where she and Harold were riding off into their very own sunset at that very second. She jumped slightly when the whistle of the kettle blew. “Tea time,” she said, then disappeared again, returning shortly with two cups of hot liquid.

“Thank you.” Lani left the bike in the middle of the room and sat on one of the chairs, scooting back on the cushion until her feet came off the ground and dangled in front of her.

Ms. Belsky took the other one. "Some people think it's too hot for tea, but truth is, it's never too hot. Tea is full of magic, and magic is good any time of the year.

They both took a sip and Lani instantly felt calm, almost as if the honey itself was full of magic. A powerful magic that swept through her, healing small cuts of life along the way. She closed her eyes and took another sip. "This is good."

Ms. Belsky smiled and looked Lani straight in the eye. "Now, let's talk about that handsome young man who really came by about a girl, not a bike, and I don't mean me, dear."

"He's just a guy I ran into on the street." Lani brushed back her hair, still damp with sweat, and exhaled. She had to face it, she and Carr came from two entirely different worlds and hers wasn't one that produced quality people, no matter how much she pushed her father out of it, the damage was still done and could never be changed. "Nothing more."

Chapter 26

The rest of the week passed in silence. Lani did make the cupcakes, four dozen frosted balls with mixed fillings and topped with creamy white and yellow clouds of pure sweetness. And although she had no intention of taking them to the reception, she let them sit on her counter, saturating her tiny place with the scent of heaven just because she liked the way they looked.

At *TED's*, Calli and Mandy went out of their way to avoid her. Neither said as much as one word to her even when Mandy accidentally bumped right into Lani as she was wiping down a table. Lani looked up just in time to see Mandy scurry off out of sight, trying to avoid any type of confrontation. Calli wouldn't even make eye contact, which seemed a bit extreme in Lani's opinion. It was if the two of them had been threatened by an angry mob boss to an inch of their lives not to mess with her anymore. She knew Carr had had something to do with it but wondered if Grace did too, for Lani would find her keeping watch on her from the kitchen.

Grace still bussed tables and such but not as much now. She spent most of her time in the back helping her new husband run what was now, their business and in Lani's opinion, the food only got better.

At her second job, Lani tried to lose herself in work hoping it would pass the time, trying to keep Carr out of her head, although he stayed closer to her than she ever knew. He knew the perfect place between two wooden columns off in a corner where he could to sit and remain undetected by the crowd. And that's where he would be every night that she worked. He would sit there willing her to notice him. Wanting her more than he ever wanted anyone in his life. She was the part of him that made him feel like he finally had someone to care for. Someone to take by his side and hold forever.

As he sat, he welded together another plan on how to approach her again. He figured, or at least hoped, that she only needed time. Time to calm and gather her own thoughts before coming back to him, and time was something he was willing to give, especially since he was able to watch her. But he wouldn't give her forever. If she didn't come to him soon, he would go after her and wouldn't let her walk away this time. She was going to tell him what was wrong even if he had to kidnapped her and tie her up to get her to do so. Although he'd like to tie her up for other reasons entirely.

As he watched her, he smiled softly when he saw Sarah high-five her after seeing the forty dollar tip a table had just left her.

"You deserve so much more than tips, Lani. Please let me take care of you. I promise I'll never hurt you," he whispered as his eyes bore over her.

By the time Thursday rolled around, Carr had found it overwhelmingly difficult to stay back. She was more beautiful with each passing day and by the time the end of the night came, he felt himself losing the battle to stay away. He wanted to carry her to a place where he could relish every inch of her. He pictured running his fingers through her long soft hair, watching it as it fell over her face as he rolled her on top of him, her bare chest pressing against his.

With that thought, he went and snagged himself another beer to calm the restlessness storming inside him then went back to his seat. Seconds later, his friend Neil found him and took a chair.

"Haven't seen you in a while. What gives?" He downed a drink as he followed Carr's stare then set his beer down. "Oh, yes. Her again. I'm telling you there's something about that girl, I'll give you that."

Carr gave a light nod, more to himself than anyone. "That there is."

Another guy joined the table. "Long time no see, buddy. Thought you left town to go hunt down some big real estate tip or something." Zeke eyed his friend.

"Hell, I've got more than I need for now. I'm not looking for anything else at the moment."

"Are you sure about that?" Zeke said, watching Carr watch Lani with a fire of pure obsession burning in his eyes. "Never seen you hunt so hard before."

"I'm not hunting." Carr's voice was solid with a hint of don't-mess-with-me and the guys left it at that. Carr was not one to be teased when it came to certain issues, and the way he was shielding this girl from further probing meant back the hell off, and they all knew what would happen if they didn't.

Neil and Zeke exchanged a look and instantly knew what the other was thinking, the past coming back to them rather quickly. Two years ago, Carr was dating a girl named Sabrina, the love of his life until one night changed everything. Carr and Sabrina were walking hand and hand down 6th street on their way to see a band at a night club when a guy stopped Sabrina. He instantly grabbed her hand and asked her when she'd be back by to see him. He smiled at her then made a comment about paying her double if she would work him in early.

Neil and Zeke were with Carr that night, both had a date of their own. When they heard the guy's comment to Sabrina, they stepped close behind Carr with a bad feeling in their gut. Carr was crazy over Sabrina, they would watch him sit and stare at her for hours on end, the same stare he was now watching Lani with.

Carr was a pretty rational guy. Calm and collective most of the time until someone pushed the wrong button. And his girlfriend was definitely the wrong button.

Carr leaned in and ripped the guy's hand off Sabrina then shoved him into a parked car along the curb. The guy rebounded toward Carr, yelling, "What the hell? I'm a paying customer just like you, so get the fuck off me, dude."

Carr grabbed the guy's shirt, slamming him back into the car. "Watch your mouth, *dude*. You're talking about my girl, someone you clearly have confused with someone else."

The guy smirked and Carr punched him in the face, causing the guy to tumble off the car. "Hey." The guy stood up, lifting his hands in the air as a sign of surrendering. "Perhaps," he spit out a pocket of blood. "Your girl is not just yours. I've been emptying my wallet out on her for months now, and let me tell you she was worth every cent."

Before Neil or Zeke could get to him, Carr was already on top of the guy bloodying his fists against the guy's face as if it were a balloon that just wouldn't pop. They eventually pulled him off, but not before Carr had broken the guy's nose and possibly his jaw.

"Come on, Carr. He's not worth it. Let's go." Zeke tugged him back further.

Carr felt his body surge with rage as he watched the guy stumble away. Others who had stopped to watch the show were now moving on as well with nothing more to see. Carr heaved with anger and tried to contain his thoughts as the guy's words lingered in his head. After a few seconds, he turned to Sabrina. "You've been awfully quiet." Carr's stare was cold and distant, fearing the worst was actually true. "Do you know that guy?"

Sabrina looked at Carr, her mouth slightly opened but no words came.

Carr took a step closer to her. "I said, do you know that guy?"

"No," she quickly spat out.

"You're lying. You always pause right before you lie or try to hide something. So which is it?" He took another step, his voice low and unnervingly calm. "Or is it both?"

"Let's just go," one of the other girls said, hoping to avoid another bad scene.

Carr ignored her as his eyes bore into Sabrina. "It's true, isn't it? You've been sleeping around for money while waiting for me to propose. You don't care who you end up with as long as the guy has a nice, fat bank account, is that it?"

Sabrina tilted her head and eased into Carr, slipping her fingers through his hair. "Don't be angry. I'm just trying to survive. Once you marry me, I'll be all yours. Forever. That's what you want, isn't it? To have me all to yourself."

He reached up and pulled her hand from his body. "No." He shook his head then released her hand. "What I want is for you to get the hell away from me and make no mistake, Sabrina, *that* is what I want....permanently."

He turned and walked away, never mentioning her name after that and never letting himself fall so hard for another girl again. Until now.

Zeke and Neil looked back at Carr, who was still watching Lani and tried to engage him in conversation.

"Well, what are your plans for the weekend? Are we going out on the boat again?" Zeke asked.

"Don't know yet. I think Calli has talked my father into letting her use it, although I don't know why, it's not like she'll drive the damn thing. She'll just have someone else do it."

"Oh, the privileged life." Neil lifted his beer. "One thing's for sure. At least it hasn't ruined you, my friend."

"Well, not yet," Zeke teased, causing Carr to take his eyes off Lani.

"What the hell does that mean?" Carr knew his friend was only ragging on him, but he couldn't help but take the bait.

"You keep sitting on your ass all day and you'll find out. I'm sure that gets addicting fast. Sit back, kick your feet up, drink in hand while you pass the days away, just staring at a pretty girl. I'm telling you, if you were poor like your brothers here, that would never happen."

"Fine." Carr put his hands up, caving. "What the hell do you broke ass brothers want to do?"

"Now we're talking." They all three stood, Carr giving Lani one last glance. "Come on, my brother," Neil ebbed him forward. "Tonight's on me. You're going to see just how un-broke your brothers really are. There's an abandoned place I want you to look at and I just happen to have the keys."

"Lead the way." Carr followed his friends out the door, shaking his head. He should have known they were up to something, and getting Carr's input before buying real estate was something his friends did often, but tonight would be different, just how different, he didn't know.

Thirty minutes later, the three of them walked into a dark, empty building.

"What is this place?" Carr tried to adjust his eyes while Neil searched for a light switch.

"You'll see. Just be patient. You're going to love it."

"Yeah, and stop moving around before you bump into something," Zeke threw in.

"Ah, here we go. Are you ready?" Neil said with a mysterious tone, causing Carr to laugh.

"What the hell? Of course, I'm ready. Oh no!" Carr instantly said as if suddenly remembering something. "You didn't."

"Oh, yes, we did." The light came on and out sprang a room full of people.

"Surprise!" was yelled out a couple dozen times and Carr could feel his face burn with embarrassment. If there was one thing he didn't like, it was being the center of attention, which was exactly what he was at the moment. He'd totally forgotten that today was his birthday and now fully regretted leaving the bar.

He turned to his buddies, shaking his head, a smile across a red face. "You guys suck."

The room burst out laughing which only got louder from there. The music came on, the drinks came out, and people got crazy. As the crowd went wild, Carr sat back, no longer the focus of the party, and looked around the place. It was abandoned that part was true. It was an old restaurant that had been forgotten about by the looks of it. The kitchen still had some of its appliances, sporting nice mellow, yellow wallpaper from the sixties, peeling and bubbling as if it were giving its last effort to cling to something. The floor had worn linoleum tiles covered with grease and grim, and who knows what else. The drywall was exposed in parts and was crumbling onto the floor. And a rather large section of the ceiling was falling down but no one seemed to care. They were all lost in the music, and dancing, and drinking, and eating.

Carr, however, stood back in the shadows out of the way, yearning for Lani. Wishing she were with him. He knew it was bad this time. He was not only falling for her but already felt like she belonged with him, today, tomorrow and as long as she'd have him. But he couldn't get the image of her running away from him down the alley out of his head. Did she want him the way he wanted her?

By her actions, he would have to say no.

But he just wasn't ready to accept that.

Chapter 27

Friday morning came and all Lani could think about was going to see her grandfather. Although she went every Friday, for some reason, it had felt like months since she'd last seen him. She hated to be away from him. Even the days when he tried to push her away she didn't want to leave. Those days where he felt as if he was the most evil of men. Saying he was a monster and she needed to turn and run and never return. He acted as if when she touched him, she'd become tainted herself and all he wanted to do was protect her from evil. From him. But Lani never saw the monster he warned her about. She blamed the sickness for his irrational outbursts, a man lost in a world of regret sealed with a disease that toyed with pain.

She loved him, no matter what, and in return he had given her no less than the same, if not more. He made her feel normal and to her that was a feeling she'd return to him a thousand times over for. He was pure love to her and she'd do anything for him. He was the only one who ever gave her full acceptance of herself and all her falling parts. The parts that no matter how hard she had tried to hold up for her father's approval, were always beat back down and with a return label stamped *damaged goods*, *return to sender.*

If she could take her grandfather's sickness and trade places with him, she would.

Her shift at *TED's* went by in a daze. She smiled and served and swept and repeated in one big cycle, watching the legs of the clock dance its circle wishing every song wasn't so slow. Calli and Mandy seemed to all but fade in the background as Lani's mind saw nothing but her grandfather. She had splurged on a new book she was going to start tonight: *The Unlikely Pilgrimage of Harold Fry.* The girl at the counter had recommended it and she hoped he'd like it. Him and Al both.

The clocked finally finished its last song of her shift and she was out on the street and on her way in no time. The sun was still bright above her and she could hear the buzz of the city sing as she approached the nursing home. Several bikes were moving about, making her think of Carr and the work he'd done on Ms. Belsky's bike. It was a beautiful turnout.

The bike had stayed parked in the middle of the room while they had had tea, and all Lani had done that day was think of her time with Carr in his garage. Thoughts that made her feel hot beneath her skin. Thoughts that made her happy, so happy that all she had wanted to do was run down the stairs and all the way back to his arms where they would be together again in that old, beautiful car.

Then there were the dark thoughts. The ones that made her believe that no matter how hard she tried, that she would always come up short. She hated those the most because they had been rooted in experience. Those dark, hopeless thoughts. The stealers of light. The ones that filled her with lead and threw her in the ocean where she had to fight for each breath. And the harder she swam, the further she sank. All the air from her lungs, all the hope in her heart draining with each kick of her feet until she finally stopped fighting and let herself fall to the bottom. Right where her father had kept her.

"Dear," Ms. Belsky had said, then reached over and took her hand. "Are you okay?"

Lani had nodded then returned her listening back to Ms. Belsky's story of her and Harold's trip to Florida long ago. But moments later, Lani had excused herself, feeling like she needed away from the bike and left to make cupcakes.

But today, she felt hopeful again. A hope she knew sprung from the one man she loved most. As she drew closer to the nursing home, she wondered what he'd think of their new book, something she was just as excited over as he would be.

She pulled opened the glass doors as always, but instead of strolling in with a cheer in her step, she froze in place. A feeling of dread instantly smothered over her.

Al was not there, standing in his usual spot against the wall pretending to be mopping as he waited for her. He was nowhere to be seen. But it was more than that. Not only was he gone but there were lots of people standing around in small clusters. People she'd never seen before. The type of people that only showed when something was wrong.

Lani entered slowly, trying to scan the new faces and figure out what was going on. But as she eased her way closer to her grandfather's room, she noticed more and more eyes on her. People stopped talking and turned toward her as she passed, and although she did not know them, they all seemed to look at her with disgust in their eyes and bitterness in their glares.

With each step, her heart beat harder and she could feel a ball of sweat sticking to her armpits. The back of her neck became clammy. She bit down on her lower lip, unaware of it until the pain shot through her jaw. She uncurled her lip and cautiously kept on her path.

"Is that her?" she heard a man ask in a repulsive tone.

"Damn vultures," a heavy reply came. "They're everywhere. Can't turn your back for a second before they're trying to rob you blind."

Everything inside Lani told her to turn and run. Get out now. Don't stop, don't hesitate, just leave. But she forged forward against the warning screaming inside her.

When she came to the door to his room, she found it opened with people stacked two deep in the entry. As she approached, they all turned and stared at her with disapproving looks. They did not move, forcing Lani to push her way further inside.

When she was finally close enough to see her grandfather, she stopped in shock. Her heart sunk and she felt everything inside her all but empty out, leaving behind a mere shell of a scared girl.

He was paler than normal, his dark eyes were tunnels of dirt. He looked up at her and his dry lips cracked as he tried to smile.

"There's my girl." His voice broke her. She pushed past the strangers and went to him, falling by his side. She took his hand as her weight came to rest on the edge of the bed.

"What's wrong?" Her voice split as she spoke, tears pooled and fell on the white sheets. "Please be okay. I need you," she whispered, feeling her chest shake with fear.

He squeezed her hand with all his might. "Don't cry, Lani. I'll never leave you. You are the one I wanted to see today. You have always been the one. You are the star that brightens my miserable life ever since you found me and brought me here. You saved me that day and have been saving me ever since." He was fading but she refused to let him go.

"No!" Lani panic. "Please don't go. Please don't go. I need you so much." She barely got her words out through her pain, knowing he was on the edge of death, but she couldn't be without him. "I need you to stay. Please stay with me." She clutched his hand as she begged by his side, wiping the tears from her cheeks. "Please don't leave me."

"Now, now," his voice was a broken whisper, but he fought to continue. "No tears, Starlight. No tears. I'll forever love you, Lani." His grip then weakened, his hand went limp, and the weight of his head came to rest fully into the pillow.

"You shouldn't be here," a shrill voice sounded from the other side of the room.

"You're an impostor! Now get out!" a second woman sounded through the heavy air, thick with strangers and pain. "He's not your grandfather. Who do you think you are?" The woman pushed closer to Lani as others stepped back, offering Lani up for sacrifice. "Do you think you can just show up and scam some poor old man so you can get all his money?" The woman charged Lani. "That money's mine and you'll never get your greedy, little hands on it. I didn't put up with that old bag all these years just so some no good, little girl can come along and clean me out."

"Hey, that money is mine too," a man's voice hit the air causing others to follow.

"And mine! If you think you two are cutting me out, I'll sue you both until you're bone dry."

The room was soon full of yelling and screaming. This person saying the money belonged to her while another one arguing that he gets a cut, only to cause an uprising of voices all grabbing for the same thing: a dead man's fortune.

All Lani could do was look back down at the only man she had ever called grandfather, now laying perfectly calm in a room of rioting. She gently reached up and drew his eyelids closed then pulled the sheet up snugly around him, careful to tuck him in just the way he liked. It had always made him feel calm after a bout of tormented memories. Lani then took his hand, tears still running down her face from a broken dam deep inside, and kissed him before letting his hand come back to rest on the crisp linens.

Thank you for loving me. I'll never forget you.

She then gave him one last look and eased her way out of the war scene unnoticed. Once in the hall, her feet picked up speed, and before she knew it, she was running past the ugliness spilling out from the room like a cloud of black, toxic smoke captured on the blur of faces as she went by.

She hit the doors with full force, throwing them open with enough strength to shatter the glass, trying to escape both the war over money and the pain of losing the one man who had ever invited her into his heart.

As her tears fell, she felt her chest cave with pain. Her body ached and she knew she was hardly breathing.

She swung her arms faster as she ran, hoping it would give her enough strength to make it all the way home where she could finally collapse without the world to watch her die.

Lani darted around people and street signs and cars until finally coming to her apartment. She dragged herself up the stairs, wiping tears away to no avail as she climbed up the mountain of steps. She hit her floor, ready to close herself up behind her locked door with the threat of never resurfacing, but her plan of self-destruction was interrupted when she was met by a familiar yet very unexpected face.

Carr stood right outside her door, knocking then stopping to listen to see if she was home.

Lani stood there and watched him, hating the fact that he was there. Cursing that he would see her with a wet face and crushed life. Why of all the times in the world there are to come over unannounced did he have to do it now?

I don't have to say anything, she thought just as he turned and spotted her.

Her eyes fell to the ground and she picked up her feet, barreling straight for him as if she were a bull and he the matador.

"Hey," he said as she approached but then quickly changed his tone. "What's going on?" He sounded worried, not knowing what to make of her appearance.

Lani ignored him, reaching for her keys, hoping to unlock the door without incident. She really wasn't even close to feeling like talking about what had just happened. Not only did the man she called her grandfather just die, but he really wasn't even her grandfather and now his entire family and half the world think she's a big fraud because of it.

She unlocked the door, feeling like she just might have a shot of getting out of this without a word when

Carr firmly took her by the arm. "Hey, what is it?" his voice was soft, causing Lani to cave even further into herself, if she didn't get some distance, there would be nothing left of her except a rumpled blanket of skin.

Lani stopped and her head fell to the door as tears wet the floor by her feet. Carr instantly turned her around and pulled her into him. "I don't know what's wrong but please don't cry. It kills me," he whispered into her soft hair. "I'm here for you, Lani. Whatever it is, I'm right here."

For a second, Lani let her weight come to rest in his arms, the smell of his cologne, the scent of his skin. She inhaled deeper, her eyes closed as he cradled her head to his chest. His arms felt as shields around her body, keeping her far from the attack of others. The attack she felt in that room. The attack she had felt her entire life from her father and lack of protection from her mother. This was what she needed. This was what she wanted. This was what she craved. She felt her shoulders shudder as she tried to muffle the pain but the more she cried, the stronger he held her and the harder she shook. "I'm here, Lani. I'm right here. I'll never leave you."

She knew that was a lie. She knew he'd leave. Just as soon as he knew her. The real her. The failure she had been her entire life. There would be nothing he'd want after he saw who she really was: a broken, little girl who no one ever loved. No one except a complete stranger she had found on the street one day, and now even he was gone.

"No." She snapped her head up and pushed him away. "No. You're a liar." She turned and dashed inside. She reached for the door to slam it shut, but Carr quickly appeared in the threshold, preventing her from shutting it.

"I'm not leaving, Lani. I refuse to go when you're like this." He pushed his way inside, then shut the door behind him. He looked at her, staring at her swollen and wet face. "Tell me. Maybe I can help. For god's sake let me in, Lani. Let me in." He stepped closer to her, her eyes hard on his face.

"Get out," she demanded. "Just leave!" She turned, looking for a place to get away from him but the smallness of her studio made that impossible. She walked into the kitchen and acted like she was busy. She pulled out bowls and measuring cups and sugar and flour and butter and pepper and whatever else she could think of. She knew her brain wasn't functioning right at the moment, but it didn't' matter. The only thing that did matter right now was that Carr had to leave.

Carr followed her into the kitchen. He slipped his hands into his pockets and watched her pull everything out of the fridge and place them on the counter. She was racing about, but he knew she'd run out of steam, and he'd be right here when she did.

Moments passed before she spoke again.

"Why are you still here? I said, get out." She didn't look at him, but kept busy moving about the kitchen, feeling him watch every move she made, which was only making her more furious. *I know he thinks I'm crazy, but I don't care. It's better for him to find out now so I won't have to cry again when he leaves. It's better if my life just implodes all on one day so I can finally quit hurting.* She twirled around and stared at him, angry that he was seeing her like this. "I said leave!" Her hands shook as she yelled. "Why are you here?" Her voice filled with pain and all he wanted to do was pick her up into his arms and hold her until she stopped hurting. "Why! Why! Why!" she screamed louder and Carr lifted his weight off the counter, knowing she was breaking but knowing she wasn't ready for him. Not yet. She had to get it out. Whatever it was, she had to get it out so she could finally let it go.

"Get out! Get out! Get out!" she screamed at the top of her lungs. "I don't want you here." She brushed back the ocean of tears but more waves only followed. She slammed her hands on the counter over and over. "No! No! No!" she repeated, filling with rage at every wrong act done against her at the hands of her father. "Stop it. Stop it." She looked around the kitchen, frantically searching for something to release her anger on. Her eyes fell to the cupcakes and she reached for the first plate.

"Those look delicious." Carr kept his voice calm, trying to soothe her. "Did you make them?"

Lani dumped the first plate into the trash. "Yes, and they're trash just like everything else in my life. Just like me. They're trash!" She watched as the second plate emptied, each cupcake sliding their way off and hitting the bottom of the plastic bag.

Without a word, Carr walked over, reached in and lifted one out of the trash. He unwrapped it and brought it to his lips, but before he could take a bit, Lani slapped it away. "No! Don't eat that."

Carr quietly reached in and took another one out. He slowly unwrapped it, but Lani once again, knocked it away. He reached back in and took out a third one. He then turned and fully faced Lani. "Did you make this?"

"Yes!" She stared at him, feeling nothing but rage barreling through her.

He took a step closer, held the cupcake up in front of her then took a bite before she could knock it away. "Then they're fucking perfect. Just like you."

"I told you not to do that. I told you they weren't any good. Why did you do that?" Panic filled her voice as if she were expecting her father to appear and berate her on her baking failures. Pointing and yelling how she did everything wrong and how no one would ever want something she made. No matter how hard she fought to shut that voice out, it always comes back. She began to shake, her face beading with sweat and she knew what was coming.

She lashed out at him, hitting him in the chest. "Don't eat that. I told you not to eat that." Carr absorbed her strikes and took another bite. Lani then reached up and tried to hit the cupcake out of his hands but he was too tall. He took another bite, letting the frosting set on his lips. He then grabbed Lani's arms, forcing them behind her.

"Stop it, Lani." His voice was firm and solid. "I don't know who crushed you, but I'm here to fix it if you'll just let me." She stared at him, seeing the frosting on his lips and watched as he gently took a small taste with the tip of his tongue. "Delicious," he whispered and lowered his head to her. "Just like you." He then kissed her and for the very first time, she tasted her own cupcake. Something she had always been too afraid to do.

She let the fluffy cream sink into her tongue, her mouth filling with a burst of orange and vanilla and the perfect touch of chocolate. It was the best cupcake she'd ever tasted. Carr kissed her again, softly letting her taste the frosting from his lips before bringing his mouth fully over hers. He grabbed her into his arms and kissed her, loving the way she tasted as she tasted him. He ran his fingers up into her hair, pushing her back against the counter, his lips devouring hers.

"I'm a fraud, Carr." She broke free. "Stop. You don't want me. I'm a fraud. I told a complete stranger that I was his granddaughter and now his whole family knows and hates me. They want to burn me at the stake."

He pulled back, wiped away her tears, then lifted her in his arms and carried her to the bed. "Not as long as I'm around they won't. That's a promise." He laid her down, then eased beside her, gently pulling her close to his chest. Her hair fell over her face and he pushed it back with one hand, the other cradled her cheek. "I don't care what demons you have inside, Lani. I'll go to hell and fight every last one if it means you'll be okay. I don't care how many times you break; I'll always be here to put you back together. You're mine and I will never leave you, Lani. Never."

He gently touched her face. "And you're not a fraud. You just wanted someone to love and there's nothing wrong with that. We all want to be loved; I'm just sorry it had to be with a stranger."

Lani looked at him. She knew she had lied. She knew that what she had done was wrong, but Carr was right. She did want someone to love. Someone who would love her back and she thought of the stranger who had done that very thing. "I'm not sorry. He was the best thing that ever happened to me. Until now."

Carr pulled her up to him and kissed her until their clothes came off. He then kissed her naked body until her only words were that of pure pleasure. He lifted himself on top of her, gently letting his weight rest on her small frame and found her. He moved inside her. His hands consuming every inch of her beautify body until they were completely lost into each other.

Lani then lay beside him, resting her head on his chest.

She waited for his heartbeat to settle while feeling his fingers lightly trace her thigh. He had pulled her leg over his body, where he held it in his hands. She loved the way he felt. She loved the way he held her. She loved everything about him, but most of all, she loved the way he stayed.

Chapter 28

The morning sun stretched in through the window and gently shook Lani. When she woke, her eyes fell upon Carr, who was already awake and smiling down at her as she opened her eyes.

"Good morning." He sat on the edge of her bed, wearing his boxers. She almost couldn't believe he was sitting there, his bare chest and handsome face meeting her smile, a most beautiful sight for her eyes to see first thing in the morning, and she knew she could get used to this. He held a cup of coffee in one hand and a cupcake in the other. "Which one would you like first?" Carr offered them both up.

"Um," Lani pulled herself up, the sheet going with her to cover her chest. "I'll take the coffee."

Instead of handing her the cup, Carr set it down on the crate beside her bed. He lifted the cupcake and dragged his finger across the top, scooping up a mound of frosting. He then took the frosting and rubbed it on her lips. He cradled her head and leaned in close to her. "I think I'll have the cupcake." He licked the frosting from her lips and the sheet fell, bringing Lani's bare chest into full view. Carr let out a deep sigh, his breath on her neck causing a wave of chills to sweep over her. Carr looked down and cupped her breast in his hands. "You are heaven to me, Lani."

She didn't know how to respond but could feel her cheeks flush with heat. Carr grinned, knowing he made her blush, then picked her up and took her to the bathroom. He turned on the shower and pulled her inside with him, where he slowly and meticulously washed her from head to toe and she him.

They went to the kitchen after they were fully dressed. He lifted her to the counter and pulled out a pan to make breakfast. Lani watched but her mind drifted away. Something didn't feel right. Was she forgetting something? Was she supposed to be somewhere? And then it hit her: work. She didn't go in last night. She had forgotten all about it, but truth be told, she doubted she would have gone in anyway. She didn't want to. *Why*? she thought. The only reason she was working so hard at two jobs was to be able to pay for her grandfather or the man she called grandfather, to have a place for him to live. Now that he was gone, she didn't need both jobs.

Carr cracked some eggs for an omelet but then stopped and looked at her. He walked over and gently touched her face. "What's wrong? We can go out if you'd like?"

"No, that's not it." She looked down and he lifted her face back to him.

"Tell me," he softly demanded and kissed her nose. "Tell me."

"I was supposed to go into work last night. I've never missed a day since I've been there and last night not only was I a no show, but I didn't even call."

"I think you'll be all right."

"You always say that about my job. There's no way you know that. And the sad thing is that I don't think I even care if they fire me. I was only working there because I needed the extra money, but all that's changed."

"Well, in that case." Carr kissed her then pulled back. "You're fired."

"What?" Lani looked at him strangely. "How would you know if they fired me or not?"

"Yeah, I've been meaning to tell you that I own that bar too. I'm actually your boss."

"What." Lani jumped down off the counter. "What do you mean, you're my boss?" Her eyes suddenly doubled and her jaw fell. "Why didn't you ever tell me?"

"I started to, but then you ran out of my garage before I had the chance, remember?"

She grabbed his shirt and pulled him to her. "You could have told me before that, and you know it." Her eyes twinkled as she shook her head in disbelief. "You could have said something."

"Guilty, but what's the fun in that?" He leaned into her ear. "You're not really fired by the way," he whispered. "I think I might just have to promote you." He pulled back and gave a sneaky grin when a soft knock sounded on Lani's door. "Expecting company? I hope it's not another boyfriend. I'll have to escort him downstairs with one hard throw."

"No." She smiled, knowing he was teasing as she made her way to the door. "It's probably just my neighbor.

"Good morning, Sunshine," a man greeted her when she opened the door.

"Al?" Lani said, surprised to see him. He opened his arms and Lani fell into them. "I'm so sorry."

Her eyes instantly stung with tears when they pulled apart. She nodded and quickly wiped her face. "Come in," she offered.

Once inside, Carr made his way over to them. "Good morning."

"Good morning."

They shook hands as Lani introduced them. "Al, this is Carr. Carr, this is Al, the gentleman who was looking after my grandfa-, my friend in the nursing home."

Al turned to Lani. "That's why I'm here."

They all sat in her tiny living room and Lani fought to keep her eyes dry. Carr moved close to her, taking her hand tightly into his as he put his other one around on her back.

"I don't know where to begin, Al. I guess I should start with an apology." Lani's head fell and her eyes closed. "I'm so sorry. I lied about him being my grandfather and I know I shouldn't have done what I did." She looked up, her face wet again. "But Al, I was never after his money. I didn't even know he had any. I promise I would never do that."

"You stop that right now, Lani. I know you better than that, but more importantly, so did George and he told me everything right from the very beginning." Al looked at Carr. "Let me tell you a story about our precious girl here. One day, this lovely young lady was walking down the street all alone and on her way to who knows where when she spotted an old man sitting on a bench. This old man was shaking his head from side to side and talking to no one in particular. He was aged, alone, and upset and as this young lady drew near, she could hear him muttering to himself about not knowing where to go. Not knowing who would want him now that he was sick.

And although this man did have family, it was family who only wanted one thing from him, his money. George knew none of them would take him in if he was sick. You see, somewhere in this old man's life, his kids had turned on him. The harder he had worked for them and the more he had given, the more it was never enough. Their greed continued to grow over time until one day it became unstoppable. It consumed everything. If George refused them what they wanted, they would push him away, forcing him to offer up more money just so he could see them. But soon their demands grew too steep and George couldn't keep up.

He stopped the payments to them and shut them out of his life, hoping it would help them realize just how bad things had become. Oh, they begged and pleaded and apologized a hundred times, but George knew it was only for the money. They didn't love him, they never did. And how could they when he always gave them what they wanted and not who they needed.

His oldest son fell into heavy debt and with no way out, he took his own life. Something George blamed himself for. He started sending the checks again, but it was too late. They saw him as a failure and it broke him even more. He turned bitter after that. He blamed himself for his children's shortcomings and regretted never teaching them how to value the things that really mattered in life. People. But, by then, the damage was done and the door shut.

When Lani saw him on that bench that day, she saw a lost old man full of despair and crying like an old fool.

George had said that without a word, Lani took a seat next to him. She sat silently at first and looked straight ahead; no doubt her mind was full of thoughts only she could know. She sat there and softly hummed to herself, bringing the old man into silence from his tears. He then looked at the girl and she at him, and he instantly reached out to her and to his delight, this young girl took his hand, her own eyes melting into his. And on that bench, two strangers sat hand and hand without a word between them.

The old man stared at this kind-hearted girl, and all he wanted to know was what it was like for someone to love him for himself and not his money. Someone who didn't know all the pain and darkness he had brought to others. Someone who just might look at him like he was full of goodness. This young stranger had sat beside him and had taken his hand and if that was all that ever happened between them, it would have been enough.

But then she spoke and his heart all but burst with joy.

"Can I help you find your home?"

"No," he replied softly. "I have no such thing," the man lied. Knowing that was only true in part. For he did have a home, but not one where he was welcomed. Not one where anyone looked or spoke to him as kindly as the stranger on the bench.

"Are you sick?" the girl had asked.

"Yes. I have something wrong with my brain. Something that makes me forget," he said, but again, he only gave half of the story.

"Alzheimer's?" the girl had asked.

"Yes," the man lied further. "I can't remember where I belong. I can't remember my address. I don't have any money. All I can think of is the name George. I think that's me."

"I have a couch. You could stay there until you remember more. I'm sure it won't be long before your loved ones come looking for you. I could call the police for you. They'd know what to do."

"No." He squeezed her hand softly. "None of that will work." He released her. "I must go." He tried to stand but quickly lost his balance and fell back to the bench.

Lani slid over to him. “That’s it. I’m taking you to get help.” She eased him back to his feet and they began walking down the street. Lani questioned him as they walked, asking him things she hoped would jog his memory, but he only lied with each inquiry. He knew his name. He had his wallet and he had enough money to take him wherever he wanted but being with her was so much better. A few blocks later, they passed a nursing home and the man had had a thought.

“Here. I live here.”

Lani stopped and read the sign. “Okay. Let’s go in. I’m sure they’re worried about you.”

They both made their way inside and up to the counter. The woman doing paperwork looked up and greeted them. “May I help you?”

George thought Lani had looked a bit surprised, probably wondering why they didn’t instantly recognized the old man but before she could say anything, the man turned to Lani.

“Do you mind sitting down the hall. I fear I might be in trouble, and it would be embarrassing for you see that.”

“Sure,” Lani agreed and disappeared as asked.

What she didn’t see was George pull out his wallet and show his ID to the woman. She read the name and looked back, her eyes wide with shock. She knew who he was. Most people did. Except our girl here.” Al nodded to Lani then continued. “He then gave the woman a large lump of cash, telling her he would need a room and that she was to act as if he already lived there. He then told the woman that the girl he was with was his granddaughter, but before he could go over the rest of the plan, Lani showed back up to the counter worried over him.

"Is everything okay?" She looked at the woman. "Does he belong here?"

"Yes," the woman replied. "We were just going over his financials."

"Oh, here." Lani pulled out her bag, reached in and emptied all her money onto the counter. Everything she had with her, she freely gave so a stranger could have a bed. "I'm sure that's not enough, but I get paid again next week and can bring in more then. Is that okay? You're not going to kick him out, are you? I think he's sick."

The woman looked at the man for guidance, but the man could only stare at the angel before him. He knew right then and there that he wanted this girl to love him. He didn't want to reject her offer and make her feel awkward, so he nodded to the woman to accept the money. The woman then led them down the hall to an empty room and joined in the charade that it was this stranger's home.

The woman made him sit on the bed, slipped off his shoes and began scolding him for running off like that. When she stopped, she looked at the man and could see a sparkle in his eye as he watched Lani. As the woman headed out the door, the man stopped her once more.

"Sue," he called her by the name he'd read on her tag. "I don't think you've been properly introduced. He looked at Lani. "This is my granddaughter. She helped me find my way back today."

Lani looked at the man for a second, but he only smiled. She didn't know what to do, so she looked at the woman. "Hi. I'm Lani." She reached for Sue's hand.

"You no doubt have your hands full with this one," Sue had said, then left them alone where the two of them spent the next few hours talking and laughing and feeling like for the first time, they had someone to love.

When Lani left that day, George picked up the phone and called me. His oldest friend. His butler and his conservator over all his estate. And he paid me very well to work there in that nursing home and look after him. You see, Lani, that old man was sick, but not with Alzheimer's. He had brain cancer and was told there was nothing anyone could do for him. Doctors gave him four months at the very most. But you gave him two years. You were the only one who came to see him. You were the only one who cared for him. You were the only one who loved him. His family never cared that he went missing and when they were told where he was, well....they never showed until yesterday. They showed only to make sure he died because every person in that room stood to gain a great fortune.

One of the other patients had mentioned that George had a granddaughter. One that came to see him often and once they knew it was none of them, they feared the worst. They figured you were there for the one thing they were, and as you saw, they will stop at nothing to get that money.

Carr looked at Al. "You mean to tell me this man took all of Lani's money when he had plenty of his own?"

Al put his hand up and patted the air as to calm Carr, who obviously felt that Lani had been taken advantage of. "All of it was put into an account for her. In order for him to do what he wanted without the encroachment of his family to fight for what he left for Lani, he had to. He had to show that Lani was making deposits herself and that all the money really belonged to her. At least in part. Once funds were merged the way George merged them, you see, it's all but impossible to separate them."

"Al, what are you talking about? The money I paid for that nursing home is not something that any of his family would find enticing. They all looked very well off. I'm sure my little bit of money is mere pennies to them."

"Twelve million dollars is pennies to no one." Al's eyes twinkled as he spoke. "George used your money as the originations to a fund he set up for you: The Starlite Foundation. Named after you because that's what you were to him. The one bright light in his dying and dark world. That money is already deposited into your account and will never be touched by anyone from his family. George was a very rich man with a very poor life. Until you."

Chapter 29

Over the next week, Lani wandered about in a daze. She didn't bother going into either job. She called Grace and told her she'd see her Friday at the reception then told her the story of what had happened. Within the next hour, Grace was pounding on Lani's front door bursting at the seams with excitement. "Oh, my god. I can't believe it. I just can't believe it." She hugged Lani, held her at arm's length, then hugged her again. "I'm so happy for you. This is just the most wonderful news." Grace then insisted on taking Lani out, where they spent the day at the spa getting their hair done, followed by pedicures. It was a first for Lani, and she walked out of there looking like she just had a visit from her fairy godmother.

Next came the shopping. Two hours' worth, but Lani didn't buy one single item, at least not for herself. For some reason, she just didn't feel comfortable yet. She did, however, buy her friend something. Grace had found the perfect dress for the reception, and as she was changing back into her clothes in the dressing room, Lani went up to the counter and had purchased it as a wedding gift.

After the girls spent the day out, Lani returned home to find Carr standing with his back against the door and several paper bags at his feet. He smiled the second he saw her face, sending chills sweeping over her.

"Oh, my god," he managed to get out as it felt like Mike Tyson had just punched him in the gut as she walked down the hall toward him. He'd never seen a more beautiful girl in his entire life. It was like the world around him froze and the only moving part was this goddess of a girl heading right toward him. He took a deep breath and tried to remain calm, although all he could think about was devouring the vision before him. "There's my girl. Thought you might have flown to Paris for pizza or something," he managed to choke out.

The door across the hall opened and out stepped Ms. Belsky.

"Wow." Lani's eyes lit up. "You look beautiful. You always look beautiful, but today you're absolutely stunning."

"I could say the same for you, dear."

Carr looked at Lani. "She's right. You're pretty stunning yourself."

Lani smiled, loving the way his eyes sparkled when he looked at her but then turned back to her neighbor.

"You are a vision, Ms. Belsky." Carr pushed off the door. "You must have a date?" Carr gave a charming smile.

"As a matter of fact, she does." A voice sounded from the end of the hall. An older gentleman dressed in a Sunday suit approached. "Forgive me for intruding on your conversation. I just happened to catch it as I finished the last bit of my climb."

"Hello. I'm Carr." Carr offered his hand and the gentleman graciously accepted.

"Stan." The man nodded then turned. "And this must be Lani."

"I am." Lani smiled and he lifted her hand softly and grinned.

"Delighted." He released her then turned to his date. "And you," he stepped closer. "Are the woman I'm here to sweep away. Hello, beautiful."

"Hello, Stan." Ms. Belsky's face blushed as her eyes sparkled, and it was obvious to everyone that she liked him. More than just a little.

"And what are you two kids up to this evening?" Ms. Belsky eyed the bags on the floor while still taking in how beautiful Lani looked.

"We," Carr began. "Are going to be busy in the kitchen baking all night. I don't know if you know this about Lani, but she makes the world's finest cupcakes."

Lani instantly shook her head in defiance, her insecurities resurfacing and causing her to become uncomfortable. "No, no, no. That's not true at all. Not even a little bit." Her voice was weak as she spoke.

Carr threw his arm around Lani, pulling her close to him. "We'll bring you a plate tomorrow and you can see for yourself."

"Oh, I have no doubt you speak the truth. I know this girl to be gifted at many things. I should know, she has been a gift to me." Ms. Belsky walked over to Lani and took her hand gently into hers. She then whispered in her ear. "Stop hiding yourself away and enjoy the person God made you. You are pure perfection and I love you dearly." She kissed Lani on the cheek then looked at Carr. "Don't overheat the kitchen." She raised her eyebrows and Carr couldn't help but chuckle. He liked this lady's spunk.

"My, dear." Stan offered his arm and Ms. Belsky accepted.

As they walked off, she called over her shoulder. "I'll be expecting those cupcakes at noon, Lani. And you along with them, dear."

Lani looked at Carr as if she were just sentenced to face the firing squad. "What are you doing?" Her lips moved as she spoke, but her teeth remained shut. "You're making orders I can't fill. What is she going to think when she eats one of those and hates them?"

Carr put his hands on her shoulders and looked her squarely in the eyes. "Did you hate them, Lani? You tasted them....what did you think? Stop seeing yourself as a failure and listen to the truth for once." He lifted her chin and kissed her until he felt her shoulders relax. "That's better." He leaned his forehead against hers. "Now, we're going to go into that kitchen, and I'm going to try to keep my hands off you, but I can tell you now, we need to hurry because you're stealing my breath away and I may just pass out right here."

"So you like what you see, uh?"

He backed up against the door. "More than like. Now, let's get to cooking. Grace's reception is tomorrow and I promised her cupcakes."

Lani gasped. "You didn't."

"Oh, yes, I did." He grinned. "And I plan on staying here all night to make sure you deliver. I even bought you an apron, and there's only one requirement when wearing it."

"Really? Just one? And what is that?" Lani's asked with sarcasm, seeing a mischievous twinkle in his eyes.

"You have to be naked." He flashed a toothy grin and she couldn't help but laugh.

"Nobody wants cupcakes made by a naked girl."

"Oh, you're sorely mistaken there. Right now, I can't think of anything I would want more."

Carr unlocked her door, picked Lani up and carried her inside. He kicked the door shut, leaving the bags of groceries setting in the hall and took Lani to her bed.

"What are you doing? I thought we were going to bake." She watched him as he slowly unbuttoned her shirt.

"We are. I just thought we'd start with the naked part first."

"You're naughty." Lani grinned, sending a wave of energy through Carr.

"No," he said. "I'm way past naughty with you." *I'm well into forever,* he thought then devoured her in the bed.

****

Noon the next day, Lani stood outside Ms. Belsky's door with a plate of cupcakes and knocked lightly. Carr stood behind her, leaning on the frame under the threshold of her apartment.

Lani knocked again and waited. She looked over her shoulder to Carr. "She did say noon, right?"

"That she did."

Lani knocked again, louder this time but still no answer. "I hope she's all right."

"I'm sure she's fine. She probably had a late night and is still sleeping, or....perhaps she stayed with her new friend. They did look like a couple taken with each other, if you know what I mean."

"Stop it," Lani teased and walked back inside with the plate. "I guess I'll try again later."

"She's fine, Lani, don't worry. I'm going out for a bit, but I'll be back to pick you up for tonight."

Lani set down the cupcakes and walked over to the opened door where Carr was still standing. "Okay." He kissed her and she couldn't help but to reach over and hug him. "I really, really like you." Her voice was soft and he could tell she was holding back.

"And I really, really like you." He rubbed the tip of his nose to hers. "And I really, really, like the way you looked in that apron. You're sexy as hell, Lani, and I just can't get you out of my mind."

"I know the feeling." This time she kissed him and it was all he could do to pull away and leave. He had something very important do this afternoon; otherwise, he would have picked her back up and kept her wrapped in his arms all day.

"See you soon."

He left and Lani closed the door. She spent the rest of the day alone in her apartment, her heart both hurting and happy at the same time. When she thought of Carr, she felt hopeful. Carr made her life seem that it really could be a place where she could finally find her spot. A spot next to a boy who had seen the worst of her and had remained by her side. However, nothing in life was a guarantee and she didn't want to believe too much too fast, although it was hard not to.

But then she thought of her grandfather and her heart tore again. Even though she had Carr, she still missed the man she loved so dearly. Today was Friday, and at first, she had woken excited about the book they would read today, but then remembered there would be no more reading. There would be no more visits. There would be no more seeing his face and feeling like she had family as she sat beside him talking. He was gone and she hurt in his absence. She would gladly give back every cent of that money to have him back in her life. She would gladly work forever to take care of him. Despite the lack of blood between them, to her, he would always be the loving, gentle man every girl dreams her grandfather to be.

She thought of all that money. It was more than she could even imagine spending in a lifetime. She had absolutely no thought of what she'd do with it all. As far as she was concerned, she would simply find another job and live life as she always had. Shopping where she had always shopped and living where she had always lived. It was hard to picture her life any other way. It was just too much and the thought of having twelve million dollars was more than overwhelming. Maybe in time, she would adjust.

She pushed the money away, took a shower and spent the rest of the day rereading *For Whom The Bell Tolls*. She read it out loud in her empty studio, picturing her grandfather sitting close by with his warm smile and eager ears. Every once in awhile, she would close her eyes and could smell the scent of waxed floors and crisp sheets and she knew he was there.

She even heard him whisper, "I'll never leave you, Lani. I'll be here every time you pick up one of our books. I'll always be with you."

Chapter 30

Carr showed up later an right on time and when Lani opened the door, the first thing he did was pull her to him. “We're going to have a great time tonight.” He spun her out and she twirled under his arm then made her way to the kitchen. “You look beautiful as always. That's one of my favorite skirts. It's the one you were wearing when you tried to run me over.”

“Hey,” Lani yelled playfully, picking up containers of cupcakes.

Carr went over and took them from her hands, giving her a wink. “I do love that skirt, though.”

Lani fell quiet for a second, relishing the way he made her feel like she was the prettiest girl in the world. *A feeling every girl should feel*, she thought, then picked up the plate for Ms. Belsky. She went across the hall and knocked on the door again. When no one answered, she let out a sigh and looked at Carr. “You really think she's all right.”

“I really do. Just set the plate down in front of her door. She'll get it sooner or later.”

Lani did just that then helped Carr with the large plastic containers. They walked down the stairs where Carr had parked his bike. He attached the cupcakes to the back then climbed on and started it. Lani then eased on just the way Carr had taught her and held both her legs over the same side. She reached up and looped her arms around him, happy to be so close.

I could get used to this, she thought and away they went.

When the got to the diner, a sign hung in the window: CLOSED FOR CELEBRATION and Lani couldn't help but smile. Two people falling in love right under her nose and she hadn't had a clue.

They unloaded and Grace met them at the door. "Hey," she sang, instantly motioning for Ted to help with the food. She then hugged Lani tightly and tried not to cry. "I'm so glad you here."

"Stop that." Lani brushed a tear from Grace's cheek. "Of course, I'm here. And you look stunning by the way. Love the dress."

"I can't thank you enough. You didn't have to do that..." Her eyes darted over to Ted as he pulled out the cupcakes and arranged them neatly on a long table covered with food.

The place was already filled with friends of the bride and groom while David Bowie's *White Wedding Day* played over the speakers.

"Ooo. Those look inviting." Grace went to the table, dragging Lani behind her and took a bright frosted cupcake. Lani held her breath as she watched her friend peel back the wrapper and lift the cake to her lips. As Grace bit into it, her eyes rolled back and she moaned. "Oh, my god, these are soooo good, Lani." Grace took another bite then another and another and within seconds, she had finished the entire thing. She reached for a second one, a pale yellow one this time. "Is this pineapple?" She took two large bites. "My god, it is, I love pineapple." She could barely get the words out from all the food in her mouth. She took another bite. "Why didn't you tell me you could do this? These are the absolute best cupcakes I've ever eaten."

Lani looked away, finding Carr's eyes watching her. He nodded then mouthed the words, *told you.*

"Well, well, well." A shrill voice came from the side and Lani looked over to find Calli holding a serving tray of drinks. "Of course you'd be here," she said loud enough for only Lani to hear.

"And you'd be right." Lani looked her straight in the eyes, determined to stand up for herself.

"Hell, I'm going to need this." Calli downed a glass of champagne then set it back on the tray. She then, surprisingly, handed one to Lani. "Here. Perhaps it'll make you more tolerable."

Lani took the glass and eyed Calli suspiciously. "Did you sprinkle it with arsenic?"

"I'm sure I can find some in the kitchen if you'd like. It'd be my pleasure." Calli smirked then walked away.

"She was actually nicer than usual," Lani said as she felt Carr come up behind her.

"I'd say you two are soon to be best buds."

"I'll take that arsenic before that happens."

Carr laughed into his glass of champagne and splattered liquid everywhere.

Lani laughed so hard that she spilt her drink and they both had to get another one. This time from Mandy, who simply served them with a big, fat fake smile smeared across her face.

Lani shook it off. She didn't care if they liked her or not. She had Carr and for the first time ever, friends of her own and it felt wonderful. She danced and drank and ate and laughed and soon it was midnight. Ms. Belsky flashed into her mind. She once again hoped she was fine. And she was. Better than fine, actually. For after Lani and Carr had left, Ms. Belsky's door had opened and the plate of cupcakes was picked up by the hands of a gentleman. Stan lifted the plate, then went into the kitchen and made two glasses of Mimosa and took the drinks and dessert back to the bedroom where Ms. Belsky anxiously awaited for her lover to return.

"Room service," Stan announced as he entered the room. He carried the tray of goodies over and set it on the bed between them. He lifted the sweet dessert to her lips and watched as she took a bite, smiling at the frosting she'd left on her nose.

"I love room service," Ms. Belsky smiled at Stan.

"Martha, if you'll have me, I'll bring you room service for the rest of your life."

She then embraced this new man in her life and the two stayed tucked away in each other's arms drinking and eating, so glad to have found love again.

After the last song, Carr grabbed Lani by the hand and led her out of the diner.

"Where are we going?" Lani stumbled over a crack on the sidewalk.

"It's a surprise. Just come with me, you drunk, little girl."

"Indeed, I am." She nodded excessively in agreement as if her head didn't know one nod was enough. "And I'm not so sure I should go with you as a drunk, little girl. You might make me wear that special apron again."

Carr stopped her and cupped her face. "I'll never make you do anything. And if it makes you feel any better, *I'll* wear that special apron."

"As a matter of fac-"

He cut her off with a kiss then led her down the sidewalk, holding her hand and laughing at how many times he had to straighten her back up from almost wobbling over. "You're a silly girl, Lani. I love that about you."

"Umm, what else do you love about me?" She grinned.

"So many things." He took her by the hand and they continued walking a few more blocks until stopping outside a dark shop.

"What's this? Where are we?" Lani looked around, unfamiliar with her surroundings.

"Come on, I'll show you." Carr unlocked the door and led Lani inside. It was the same place that his friends had held his surprise party at. He flicked on the lights and looked at Lani. "What do you think?"

Lani had a puzzled look on her face. "What do you mean, *what do I think*? You mean, what do I think of the holes in the walls, the grimy linoleum floor, the broken light fixture in the corner, the crumbled counters or what exactly?" She took a few steps and pivoted around to get a panoramic view. "What am I looking at here?"

"This place belongs to a friend of mine. You met him the day at the lake. It's been in his family for a very long time. They are very picking about who they will sell it to."

"Are you going to buy it? If you're as good at fixing things as you were with the bike, then I'd say do it. This place does have potential." She twirled again, nodding her head. "I bet you could do wonders in here."

"As of this afternoon, I can. They have given me, or rather someone else, the opportunity to buy it. But it really depends on you."

"On me? What do I have to do with it?"

"Everything." Carr took her hand and led her to the kitchen. "Imagine a few industrial ovens here," he mapped out against the wall with his hands. "And a stove over there. In this place, you could have a refrigerator unit built, a big walk-in one. Here you could have a marble counter island for your prep space. I would also install all new floors and fix-"

"Whoa." Lani's head started to spin, suddenly feeling very sober. "What are you saying, Carr? You think *I* should buy this place."

He walked over to her, an intense look in his eyes. "Yes, I do, Lani. I know real estate. This is a dream location and as you said yourself, it does have potential. This is perfect for you. I know you haven't said as much, but Lani, you could really do something here. You could open your own bakery. I could fix it up and you could bake miracles in here. This is you all over the place. I promise it will look amazing once I'm done. I won't let you down."

Lani let her eyes roam the walls, the counter, the floors. She let Carr's words sink in as she slowly started imagining the place transforming before her. She turned in one full circle, then did it again and again. Each time her mind raced as her head spun with all the possibilities before her. She could have her own bakery shop. Her very own bakery where she could bake every kind of cupcake imaginable. She spun faster, her arms easing out beside her, her eyes shutting, her heart dreaming. "Yes. Yes. Yes! I want this. I want this."

She spun until her feet lifted off the ground feeling as if she were flying and when she opened her eyes, she was. Carr had picked her up and flown her to a brand new place in her life. A place she never wanted to leave.

Chapter 31

Nine months later....

"**Wake up, beautiful.** I brought coffee." Carr walked into the bedroom dressed in his cotton pajama bottoms, his bare feet and chest becoming colder than he expected when he got out of bed this morning to start the coffee pot.

He had stayed the night with Lani again, making that the fourth time this week, their typical number of visits ever since Lani had gotten her new place. She had been bound and determined to stay right where she had been, but Carr had insisted she move. He wanted her in a safer place. Ms. Belsky was no longer living across the hall thanks to Stan whisking her away in marriage and moving her to a beautiful home in a suburb close by, and although Lani still visited for tea on occasion, it wasn't the same as having her right across the way.

After that, Carr was more determined than ever to get Lani into a new place. They had spent over two weeks looking and finally settled on a small condo downtown with a doorman, something else Carr had insisted on. However, if he had his way, he'd moved her in with him but had to force himself to slow down. There was no rush and Lani was still healing from a life of painful memories, although she had made remarkable progress in the past months. So full of confidence and life now.

Lani quit both her jobs after she bought the old restaurant and spent her days with Carr working on the place. She had jumped right in and took charge. She knew exactly how she wanted everything, which surprised her because not once in a million years would she have guessed she would be living this life.

She poured every bit of her soul into that place. She designed the kitchen to have five wall ovens, long metal counters with shelves, marble islands as Carr had suggested, and a wide quartz counter where customers ordered. She had glass display cases installed where her cupcakes could be seen and had insisted on a coffee bar as well.

Hiding behind the crumbling drywall had been beautiful brick walls, which Lani had cleaned up and left exposed. The ceiling was finished with an industrial feel and had long lights hanging down from it. She designed the eating space with wooden tables and stools dressed in deep red cushions. The floor had wide wood planks with a rustic finish which had anchored everything together perfectly.

All she had had to do was tell Carr exactly what she wanted and he worked his magic and made it happen. He was a master at his craft and had had a few ideas of his own that added more charm to the place. He refinished the long dresser he had in his garage and set it up as the self-serve coffee bar that held flavored creamers and syrups, a variety of toppers and, of course, whipped cream for anyone who wanted it.

They worked well as a team. Not one time did either lose their patience with the other, a sure sign that they belonged together, as Carr had mentioned often.

Now, nine months later, the place was finally finished and ready for business. The grand opening was tomorrow, but today, Lani was holding a preview for her friends.

Lani pulled herself up and rested her head against the headboard of her bed. Her hands shook as she pulled at the sheet and Carr could tell she was nervous.

He took her hand and held tightly in his. "You'll be fine, Lani. Don't worry."

"I just can't believe this day is finally here. It seemed like we'd never get finished and now, poof, it's all done."

Carr handed her the coffee. "I thought we did pretty well. Nine months for what we did isn't bad."

"Umm." Lani took a drink, trying to stay calm as the warm liquid soothed her. "This is perfect."

Carr smiled and brushed her hair back. "You're perfect, Lani. Nothing in my life has ever been as wonderful as you. Thank you."

"You're the one that saved me." She titled her head and looked at him. "I wouldn't have done any of this if it hadn't been for you."

"Well, I guess we're even then. I would have never been this happy if it hadn't been for you." He leaned in close and tugged at the sheet. "Room in there for two?" Carr then tackled her back into the bed where they stayed until late afternoon.

Later, Lani finally sat back up. Carr kept one arm around her as she looked down at him. His head was resting fully on the pillow and he had a calm look on his face.

"Are you not worried about tonight?" Lani titled her head as she spoke.

He sat up. "Worried about what? These are your friends. They all love you. There's absolutely nothing to be worried about."

"You're right." She looked away, her eyes full of weight. "I just miss him. I hate that I won't be able to share tonight with him. I think he would have been proud."

"He would have, Lani. He wanted you to be happy. He loved you as his own, you know that right?"

Lani nodded but didn't say a word, instead tears slipped down her face and her heart broke as she felt his absence.

Carr got out of bed then pulled Lani to her feet. "Come on. Let's go see him. You haven't been since they buried him and you need him now. I'll drive."

The ride was silent between them as Carr drove his motorcycle through town and into the cemetery. He took the winding trail up to the spot where her grandfather was laid to rest and parked the bike. He then helped her off, making sure she still had the box she had brought with her, then let her go alone to see him.

As Lani drew closer, she noticed a new headstone over his grave. When they had buried him, there was only the traditional stone with his name and date, but by the looks of it, that had been replaced. The funeral had been prepaid, so Lani wasn't needed to take care of any of the details, but she would have gladly. Al had mentioned that a new headstone was going to be delivered when it was ready, but those words had fallen on deaf ears at the time, for she remembered very little from that day. His family didn't even come to the funeral. It was her, Al, and a few people from the nursing home. It broke her heart that no one loved him like he deserved. That he had to go through life, much like her, always yearning yet never receiving.

Once in front of the headstone, the inscription became visible.

George Theodore Wilson
A Man Saved By A Stranger

Lani knelt down beside his grave and wept. She knew the message referred to her. She was The Stranger. She was the one who saved him, but if he were here, she'd say it was the other way around. Who knows what would have become of her once she moved away from home. She was young and afraid and so very damaged. She never knew love until that day on the bench when she sat beside a kind, old man she didn't know. He had changed her life forever.

She was quiet at first, thinking of all the time she had spent with him over the last two years. How she sat beside his bed, held his hand and read one book after another. How he smiled when he saw her face. How she smiled when she saw his. How he loved her and how she loved him. After a long pause, she wiped her tears and spoke. "Lani Love. Hurt, broken, damaged, and loved by you. I think you have it wrong, grandfather. For I was the one who was saved." She then opened the box and slipped out the most perfect cupcake she'd ever made. "For you." She set it in front of the tombstone, her fingers lightly tracing his name. "I'm sorry it took so long for me to bring it to you. If I could do it over, I would have brought you cupcakes every day. For every day with you was a celebration. Forgive me for being so scared. It's something I will always regret, but I am doing better now."

She wiped her eyes. "I opened a bakery, thanks to you. And in honor of your memory, I deliver cupcakes every Friday to your old nursing home. So far, they have been a big hit. Al even shows up for them. I know it hurts him to come knowing you're not there, but I think the cupcakes help." She let out a light sigh. "Cupcakes help more than I could have ever imagined." She stood, staring down at his name, feeling his touch in her heart, then looked up into the sky and as she stood there, it was if the cupcake left the ground and floated toward the heavens above. "I hope it brings you joy." Lani smiled and walked back to Carr, who took her into his arms where he held her until she was ready to leave.

They got on the bike and drove to the bakery just as the night sky was saying hello. Once there, Lani stood outside the window, Carr by her side. Her eyes drifted up to the sign above the door: *Cup of Joy Bakery*. It had seemed like the perfect title and Lani hoped that her cupcakes did bring joy into all who entered. For experience had taught her that life was not meant merely to be survived but enjoyed as well.

Carr slipped his fingers into hers and Lani watched the scene inside the bakery.

Everyone had already arrived and it was more crowded than Lani had thought it would be. She didn't realize just how many people wanted to be a part of her life now. She could see Grace and Ted sitting side by side as he looped his arm in with hers. They were lost in a lover's gaze and Lani knew it was a gaze to last a lifetime.

There was Nikki, wearing an outfit from the 80's. Her new favorite attire lately, and by the way Ty had been stuck to her side like a lost puppy, knew it was working its own kind of magic.

Operation Kick-Ass was finally closed when Jake confessed to smoking the missing weed...with Nikki one night after work. When Nikki found out what had happened, she was convinced that maybe it was time to quit. She's been clean since.

Lani's eyes found Sarah next. Someone who over the past months had shown up at Lani's place at least once a week. She would drag Lani out for lunch or pedicures or shopping. Sometimes she would just sit with Lani and they would talk and laugh as old friends. And that is exactly what Lani hoped they would become one day...old friends.

Calli and Mandy were there as well. Mandy was always where ever Calli was. Always standing right by her side, ready to say anything Calli needed her to say. She never said much to Lani, although she did tone down the fake smiles to the point of tolerable.

Calli was another story. She still didn't like Lani much, mainly because she hated the way everyone began to love her even though she was so different. Although every once in a while, when Calli thought no one was looking, Lani would see a tiny reflection of something resembling regret in her eyes, and Lani hoped it was only a matter of time before she became actually likable. She was, after all, Carr's only sister.

Al was there, looking dashing as ever with a beautiful young lady on his arm who only made him look more endearing. Lani loved Al and had remained in contact with him over the past months, mainly through the nursing home.

Then there was Ms. Belsky, or rather the new Mr. and Mrs. Stanley McCall. She was breathtaking as always and glowed as a woman in love.

The rest of the shop filled with others she had met over the months. Others she had come to know and fill her life with friendship as she filled theirs.

"You ready?" Carr gave her hand a tight squeeze.

She turned to him and smiled. "Yes. I'm ready."

Carr opened the door and Lani walked in, knowing she was finally home.

****

***Thank you for reading *STARLITE*. I do hope you enjoyed it and if so, I would greatly appreciate your time in leaving a review. And please feel free to stop by my blog for updates on current work and new releases at maeeastbooks.com

Best to you!
Mae

www.ingramcontent.com/pod-product-compliance
Lightning Source LLC
LaVergne TN
LVHW091110080826
845145LV00008B/1857

* 9 7 8 0 6 9 2 3 4 1 5 3 7 *